# IF I HAD A NICKEL

# BEN REHDER

*In memory of our sweet girl Nellie.*

# IF I HAD A NICKEL

BEN REHDER

# ACKNOWLEDGMENTS

Much appreciation to Tommy Blackwell, August Harris, Cisco Hobbs, Becky Rehder, Helen Haught Fanick, Mary Summerall, Marsha Moyer, Stacia Hernstrom, Linda Biel, and Leo Bricker. Special thanks to Martin Grantham for getting the idea started. All errors are my own.

**1**

If life gives you lemons, you're supposed to make lemonade—but what if life gives you size 48NN breasts? One option is to turn them into moneymakers, as Serenity Sweet had done. She'd learned a few years ago that there was a small population of men who would pay handsomely to have their heads and faces squashed, smashed, slapped, or smothered by her enormous boobs.

She called it "adult massage," and the intent was to give her clients a type of experience they couldn't get elsewhere. There were, however, some strict ground rules. Her clothes, skimpy as they were, stayed on at all times. The client could not touch Serenity or use any body part to rub against her. There might have been sexual gratification—wasn't that the point?—but there was never any actual sex.

For Serenity Sweet—which was quite obviously a fictitious name—her creative new career was transformational, from a personal standpoint. One day she was a large woman who was somewhat self-conscious about her buxom physique, the next she became a successful businesswoman in great demand for her unique physical attributes. Her self-confidence skyrocketed, as did her bank balance. All of this was according to a colorful profile a local website had written about her, complete with photos of Serenity in a flimsy halter top—clickbait extraordinaire. The reader comments beneath the article were appalling.

Miss Sweet's line of work was illegal, of course, but the Austin cops had more or less left her alone—until a recent evening when one of her clients died. The cause of death was still unclear, but the time of death appeared to coincide with Serenity's visit. She'd responded by getting the hell out of Dodge and later making an anonymous 911 call, but she was caught on the home's front-door security camera, so it didn't take the detectives long to track her down and start asking questions.

The deceased was a rich guy named Alex Dunn: Sixty-three years old. Made a small fortune inventing software that streamlined electronic medical records in doctors' offices. Dunn was twice divorced. Father of three adult children. Grandfather to two teenagers. Once ran as a libertarian candidate for Texas governor in the 1990s, earning one percent of the vote. Lived in an exclusive neighborhood in western Travis County, outside the Austin city limits.

"And he was apparently a dedicated boob man," said Heidi, our largest client, on speaker via my iPhone. Heidi was a senior claims adjuster for a large insurance company, and she frequently hired us when she suspected fraud, or if an item of great value had been stolen and she thought we might be able to help get it back.

"Lot of that going around," said Mia, my partner, casting a glance my way in the rearview mirror.

"I don't get it," I said. "Here you have an older gentleman who pays money to have enormous breasts rubbed all over his face, or perhaps whacked upside his head, and you two ladies somehow make it sound sordid."

"Not necessarily sordid," Mia said. "Just...peculiar—if that's the only thing that, uh, gets you there."

Mia and I were parked in front of a Hooters on the north side of town, and our location, combined with our current conversation, said something—I'm not sure what—about our culture's fixation with breasts.

We were waiting patiently in the aging Dodge Caravan that sometimes acts as our rolling office. It's beige. So boring it's almost invisible. In other words, perfect. Mia was in the driver's seat and I was on the bench seat behind her, manning a video camera aimed through the tinted side window. Inside the Hooters was a 25-year-old motorcycle-riding pinhead who had filed a lawsuit in relation to an injury he had allegedly suffered. Our job was to prove he was a con artist.

"You might be surprised to learn that Serenity Sweet averages about a thousand bucks a night," Heidi said.

"Oh, you're kidding," Mia said.

"And she recently started a webcam subscription service. Big bucks there. People pay to watch her smash items with her boobs. Beer cans, a bag of potato chips, that sort of thing."

"Okay, you know I'm not judgey, but what is the thrill in that?" Mia said. "Men *pay* her for that?"

"The woman is a brilliant entrepreneur," I said. "And she should be congratulated on her innovative business model."

"Well, she was arrested instead," Heidi said. "Currently charged with prostitution, for starters, until they can confirm the cause of Dunn's death. But the cops suspect she might've smothered him."

"On purpose?" Mia said.

"I don't know the answer to that, but I do know the reason they're putting some heat on her—and the reason I'm calling you—is that the day after it happened, when his children were let into the house, they noticed that Alex Dunn's coin collection was missing. He owned an extensive collection of hobo nickels. At this point, you're wondering—"

"What the hell is a hobo nickel?" I said.

"Exactly. I'd never heard of them either. It's where you take a nickel—or some other coin, but usually a nickel—and you carve the face of it into something else, like a skull, or a man in a boxcar, or you put a top hat on the president."

Mia was already tapping away on her iPhone, and now she turned the screen to show me several examples of hobo nickels.

"We're looking at some now," I said. "That's actually pretty cool."

"It's a legitimate form of folk art," Heidi said, "going back about a hundred years."

I watched as three college-aged guys entered Hooters. Yesterday, we'd followed the motorcycle-riding pinhead around for the better part of the day, just waiting for him to make a mistake, with no luck. What we knew from his file was that he had supposedly torn the anterior cruciate ligament in his right leg after slipping on a wet floor inside a convenience store. Pinhead's limp was pretty good. Almost looked real.

He'd hired a lawyer, who'd sent him to a doctor, who'd said Pinhead needed surgery. And of course Pinhead wanted some money on top of that for pain and suffering, because the store shouldn't be allowed to get away with that kind of negligence, should they? It was a small case, but the insurance company for that particular chain of convenience stores had grown weary of getting shafted by cheaters. They'd begun fighting back.

"Was it actual hobos who carved these?" Mia asked.

"It was," Heidi said. "They typically used a buffalo nickel, for whatever reason. There are several famous carvers from back in the early days, although I don't remember any of their names."

"Nickelangelo, for one," I said.

Mia and Heidi groaned in unison, although I could see Mia's smile in the mirror.

"There are modern carvers, too," Heidi said, "but purists—like Alex Dunn—insist that anything after the Depression isn't a 'real' hobo nickel. He was a traditionalist."

"So they think Serenity Sweet stole the collection?" Mia asked.

"I don't know that for sure, either," Heidi said. "She says she didn't take anything, and when they asked how Dunn died, she said she had no idea. When they pressed too hard, asking if she was giving him a massage at the time—and the evidence says she was—she refused to answer any more questions. So they arrested her, and then she bonded out."

"How many coins are in Dunn's collection?" Mia asked.

"Last we knew, about three hundred—most of them tucked in little plastic sleeves inside a wooden curio box."

"How big was the box?" Mia asked.

"Oh, about the size of a 12-pack of Cokes."

The double-doors to Hooters swung open, and out walked a couple of tipsy businessmen. Bummer. Oh, wait. There was Pinhead, following right behind them. About time. He'd been in there for nearly three hours. Seriously, did the man have no sense of moderation?

"You said Serenity was on the security camera," Mia said. She'd seen Pinhead exit the restaurant, but she knew I had, too, so there was no need to point it out. "Was she carrying anything when she left?"

I had the camera rolling as Pinhead gingerly climbed onto his bike—a big cruiser—inserted the key, and hit the button for the electronic ignition. The big engine turned over, but it did not engage. Of course it didn't. That's because earlier, after he'd parked his bike, I'd noticed that his old Honda also had a kick starter. And a plan had taken shape in my nimble mind. Pinhead could gimp around on his bike and claim that it didn't put much stress on his knee—and he might even be right—but if he started kicking the crank with his right leg...

"According to Ruelas, it's hard to tell," Heidi said, "because you can only see her from the back."

Ruelas. Frigging great. Why was it always Ruelas?

Pinhead tried the electronic ignition again. No go. That was because, after he'd gone into Hooters, Mia had followed him inside and kept an eye on him while I disconnected his spark plugs. Mia hadn't been amused when the manager on shift had asked if she was there to apply for a job.

"So it's possible the collection disappeared earlier? Or later?" Mia asked.

"Unfortunately, yes," Heidi said.

Pinhead gave up on the electronic ignition and swung the kick starter into position. He glanced around the parking lot, but there was nobody to be seen. Nobody watching. Nobody about to ruin his little scam—as far as he knew.

"What's the collection worth?" Mia asked.

Pinhead kicked the crank hard with his right leg. Then again.

And again. Case closed. Mia was giving me a thumbs-up.

"About three hundred and seventy thousand dollars," Heidi said.

"Jesus H. Christ," Mia said. "For a bunch of carved nickels?"

"Yep. Are y'all free to take this one on?"

"You bet," I said.

# 2

The next morning, we took Mia's red 1968 Mustang fastback to the home of Callie Dunn, who lived in Tarrytown, not far from Mia's house. I had called Callie the previous afternoon, and, after explaining who I was and why I wanted to speak to her and her two brothers, she offered to arrange a meeting. She said it was very important to all of them to find out what had happened to their father.

Her home was much larger and newer than most of the homes in the historic Austin neighborhood. It was what many Austinites disparagingly called a "McMansion"—an oversized, often ostentatious, modern home on a small lot, where once existed a smaller, older, more tasteful residence.

Callie answered the door wearing black yoga pants and a hot-pink tank top. She was shoeless and her thick chestnut hair was pulled into a ponytail, à la Barbara Eden in *I Dream of Jeannie*. She was slender. Green eyes. In her late twenties. Obviously fit and healthy. As long as she didn't stand next to Mia, she might be the most attractive woman in any given room.

"Hi!" Callie said very perkily. "You must be…"

She'd already forgotten the name.

"Roy Ballard," I said, reaching to shake her hand. "And this is my partner Mia Madison."

"God, y'all look like those detectives from that TV show," Callie Dunn said. "What's the name of it?"

I shook my head.

Mia said, "Uh…"

Callie said, "Well, they're both gorgeous, so take it as a compliment. Anyway, come on in."

She swung the door open and stepped aside to grant us access to a small foyer that led into a large and well-decorated living room. Everything was very contemporary and sleek, including the matching red leather sofa and twin chairs. "Y'all want anything to drink? Max was supposed to be here, but he called ten minutes ago and said he can't make it. That's just like him, because he has two small kiddos and they totally rule his life. I can't even imagine. Doesn't really matter, because he probably wouldn't have been able to answer any of your questions. He's so disconnected from all of us lately."

"What about Cole?" I asked.

"As far as I know, he'll be here," Callie said.

I was glad to hear that. Some quick research last night had revealed that Cole was a problem child. He'd been busted four times in the past three years, including twice for possession of drug paraphernalia—in this case, used needles. The other arrests were for theft, which caught my eye. If Cole Dunn had a history of theft—

Then I realized Callie was looking at us inquisitively, apparently expecting one or both of us to say something. Oh, right, the drinks.

"Got any iced tea?" I asked.

"Sure! With sugar? Sweet'N Low?"

"Unsweetened is fine."

She looked at Mia.

"Nothing for me, thanks."

"Be right back," Callie said. "Have a seat."

She left in her yoga pants and I did my best not to watch.

"She's cute," Mia said. "Vivacious."

She looked at me. I nodded but said nothing. It took a lot of self-restraint.

We sat in the matching leather chairs and waited. I could see through a couple of windows into her backyard. She had a swimming pool. Small—more of a wading pool—because the size of her home used up the bulk of her lot. Just past the pool was a small pump house built from limestone to match the design of the home itself. Expensive, but it looked much nicer than your standard Home Depot metal shed.

"You usually put Sweet'N Low in your tea," Mia said.

"I do," I said. "Didn't want to bother with it."

We waited another minute.

"Beautiful place," Mia said softly. She was studying the artwork on the walls, and then her eyes lingered on a stunning metal-and-glass sculpture of a dragonfly in one corner of the room. "I think that's an Anne Woods."

"I was going to say the same thing," I said. "She expresses herself in ways I can't fully—"

Callie came back into the room carrying a tall, narrow glass filled with dark tea and two large, perfectly round ice cubes. I'd seen people use that type of cube in mixed drinks.

"Thank you," I said, rising to take it from her hands.

"You're very welcome," she said as she took a seat on the sofa and I sat back down on the chair.

"We're neighbors, sort of," Mia said. "I live two blocks over."

"How long have you been in the neighborhood?" Callie asked.

"A little over a year. The house has been in my family since the 1920s, and my uncle left it to me when he passed away. Do you remember a house fire earlier this summer?"

"That was you?"

"It was."

"I'm so sorry."

"Fortunately, the damage was minimal, thanks to a fast-acting neighbor. Now you can't even tell it ever happened."

"Well, that's good to hear," Callie said. "So, should we wait for Cole or get started? You said you wanted to ask questions. You're like investigators for the insurance company, right?"

"Sort of," I said. "Before we start, we just want to offer our condolences on the loss of your father."

"I appreciate that. It's been rough, but I'm trying to remember the good times and not dwell on the pain. It's what Daddy would want."

"He sounds like a good man," Mia said.

"He was. He really was. Not that he didn't have his weaknesses, like a lot of powerful men. He had a hard time resisting temptation. To be blunt, he liked women. All kinds of women. But he was a great father and I miss him a lot."

She looked at me.

I said, "To answer your question, technically, we aren't investigators," I said. "We're freelance videographers and we specialize in insurance fraud. In this particular case, we've been hired to see if we can find out what happened to your father's coin collection."

It might have been easier to simply say that we are investigators, but we aren't licensed. There were various legal hurdles we couldn't clear, the biggest one being my criminal history involving an assault on a boss at an old job. He called a female co-worker a disgusting name, so I broke his nose with a microphone stand. Ended up with probation. Shit happens, right? The man deserved it and I wouldn't change a thing. However, I would change the fact that I later had a separate charge for possessing some pills I used occasionally to stay awake on stakeouts. Dumb. More probation. Been on the straight and narrow ever since.

"Oh," Callie said in response to my last comment. She had a blank look on her face. Was she going to be reluctant to speak further? "I guess I misunderstood."

"Many times the work we do exposes all sorts of interesting facts," Mia said. "As we look into the disappearance of the coins, it wouldn't surprise me if we learn some things about your father's death."

Nicely done, Mia. Keep her interested.

"We're still waiting on the autopsy," Callie said. "It's just so weird. How do they not know how he died? That woman had something to do with it. It's so obvious. Why else would she run away? And it's not a stretch to think she stole the coin collection in the process."

"It must've been quite a collection," I said. "Frankly, I'd never even heard of hobo nickels."

"Yeah, ten years ago, I hadn't either. But a friend gave Daddy one on his birthday, and after that, he sort of became obsessed with them. It was like a hobby that went haywire, but he seemed to enjoy it so much. I'd go over to his house for dinner and he'd be checking his phone the whole time, keeping tabs on some auction on eBay. He was constantly buying and selling those silly coins. It's going to be a chore to go through his records and figure out what he currently owned. It wasn't until about a year ago that any of us knew how much the collection was worth."

"Who noticed that the collection was missing?" Mia asked.

"That was Max. Daddy has a big safe in his study, but he never puts the coins in there because, like I said, he's always getting new ones or selling old ones. He kept them in a big wooden box, and Max noticed that the box was gone. We looked in the safe and it wasn't there, either, so then we searched the entire house. No box, no coins."

"Can you think of anyone who might've taken the collection, other than Serenity Sweet?" I asked.

*Like your brother Cole*, I wanted to say.

She started to answer, but just then the doorbell rang.

"That must be Cole," Callie said. "Excuse me for a minute."

She rose from the couch, went into the foyer, and opened the front door. Standing on her front porch was a pair of uniformed Austin cops.

Their voices carried, so I could hear both of the cops introduce themselves, and then I heard one of them say, "Miss Dunn, may we step inside for a moment?"

"Is everything okay?"

"We have an important matter we need to discuss with you."

That wasn't good.

"What's happened? Did something happen?"

Both cops were casting glances over Callie's shoulder at Mia and me in the living room.

"It's a private matter, ma'am. Are your visitors family members or close friends?"

"They're friends. Please just tell me. Tell me right now."

After a pause, the cop said, "Yes, ma'am. I'm very sorry to inform you of this, but your brother Cole was found dead earlier this morning."

# 3

Mia's house was nearby, so we went there to regroup and figure out how we were going to proceed.

Callie Dunn had been in shambles after she'd heard the news, but there wasn't much we could do except offer additional condolences before we left. It was an awkward situation as we exited the residence, wanting to ask the uniformed cops how Cole Dunn had died, but knowing they wouldn't have given us even the tiniest bit of information. Callie herself asked them several times what had happened, but they wouldn't say anything while we were still there.

"Think it was an overdose?" Mia asked as I took a seat on her couch and she went into the kitchen to get some coffee started.

"The records I saw didn't say which controlled substance he preferred, but that's a good bet," I said. "Whatever happened, it raises a lot of questions."

"Such as?" she called out.

"If someone killed him, who and why? Was it related to his father's death or the disappearance of the hobo coins? If it was a suicide, why now? Did he steal the coins and then feel guilty about it? Or was he depressed about his father?"

"Or maybe it was completely unrelated."

"Maybe."

She came back into the living room, and the truth is, every entrance she makes is a grand entrance, simply because she is so damn beautiful. Tall—five-ten in flats—with long red hair, prominent cheekbones, and killer dimples. Even better, she is equally attractive in the ways you can't see right off the bat. Intelligent. Funny as hell. Compassionate. Always looking for the bright side of things.

Any wonder that I finally admitted to myself earlier this year that I am in love with her? I have been for quite some time.

Mia didn't know that yet, despite a recent vow I'd made to myself to tell her. My daughter Hannah had come to visit earlier this summer—the first time I'd seen her since she was a little girl—and I'd planned to tell Mia how I felt as soon as Hannah had gone back home. I didn't want to take that sort of serious emotional step until I had the time to handle Mia's response, whether it was good or bad. But by the time Hannah left, there was a reason I couldn't tell Mia the truth, and that reason was named Garlen Gieger. *Garlen*. Who the hell is named Garlen? I hadn't met him, but I already hated his guts. Not fair, I know, but still.

Mia sat at the other end of the couch and said, "What?"

"What what?"

"That look on your face."

I think she might've suspected on occasion that I'd fallen in love, or maybe she just thought I had a crush on her. Or maybe she thought I looked at her the same way I looked at Callie Dunn in her yoga pants. But it was totally different.

"Just thinking," I said. "Trying to decide what we should do next, and how much time we should commit. For all we know, the cops have already found the hobo coins in Cole Dunn's house. The dude—rest in peace—had a history of theft."

"If the cops find the coins in his place, I bet we'll hear from Heidi within a couple of hours."

"Yep. So I vote we slack off until lunch and see what happens."

Mia grabbed her laptop, which had been resting on the coffee table. "I want to check something real quick. Did the name Callie Dunn ring any bells for you before yesterday?"

"I don't think so."

Mia pecked away at her computer. I watched her, which was a good use of my time.

"Oh, this is interesting," she said. "I thought her name was familiar. Remember when a man here in Tarrytown complained that the person who bought his house had tricked him? The buyer said he was planning to restore the home, but he tore it down instead. Ring any bells?"

I shook my head. "I don't keep up with you ritzy Tarrytown types."

"Well, it turned out the buyer was actually a developer, and it looked like he'd planned all along to demolish the house and build a new one."

"Sneaky bastard," I said.

"A lot of people got pissed off about that, because the original house had earned an architectural award when it was built in the forties. It had historical significance, but the city granted a demolition permit anyway."

"Am I to assume the house in question is now Callie Dunn's abode?"

"The new house, yeah." She was reading and scrolling. "I didn't really keep up with this as well as I should have back then, but if I remember correctly..." She trailed off.

I sat quietly. The coffeemaker beeped, so I went into the kitchen to get us both a mug. Mia liked hers with one sugar and an ounce of hazelnut-flavored creamer.

When I came back into the living room, she said, "Check this out. The developer was a guy named Nathan Potter and guess who he used to be in business with."

"Carrot Top?"

"Alex Dunn. Wanna know how else they were connected?"

"A secret love affair?"

"Nathan Potter was Alex Dunn's brother-in-law at the time."

"So Potter was married to Dunn's sister?"

"No, Dunn was married to Potter's sister, Alicia. She was Dunn's second wife—his much younger wife, up until last fall. Apparently Dunn hired Nathan Potter to buy the old house, demolish it, and build the house Callie lives in now. So in the eyes of Tarrytown residents and the press, Dunn was as much the bad guy as Nathan Potter was."

Five minutes ago, I hadn't been much interested in this background information, but now I was starting to get drawn in.

"At one point," Mia said, "Dunn gave a really ugly interview in which he said, quote, 'Look, the bottom line is, I own that lot and I'm free to do whatever the hell I want with it. I plan to build a nice home for my daughter. Anybody that has a problem with that can go screw themselves.'"

"Nice. So the man might've made some enemies."

"I would think so."

"And you're thinking one of them might've somehow killed him?"

"Well, I'm raising the possibility."

"But why would somebody act on that now? Why wait so long?"

"Don't know."

We sat for a moment and drank coffee.

"Sure would make things easy if Heidi would call right now and say the coins were in Cole's place," I said.

"But then we wouldn't earn much money."

"True."

"Plus, you love a challenge more than anyone I know," Mia said.

She was right. My current challenge, other than this case, was named Garlen.

"Is that your way of saying I'm stubborn?" I said.

"Oh, I wouldn't sugarcoat it like that," she said. "You love a challenge, *and* you're stubborn."

"Thank you very much. Are you saying we should do something productive instead of waiting around?"

"I am."

# 4

Several years ago, after I broke my boss's nose, got fired, and became a freelance legal videographer, I worked for quite some time within the confines of that job description—meaning I shot video and that was about it. Most of the video I shot was of suspected insurance scammers. You know the type of covert video I'm talking about—grainy long-lens footage showing somebody who supposedly has a back injury doing the lambada, or some bro with whiplash playing rugby on the weekends.

It wasn't long before I realized I could do more than shoot video. No, I wasn't a licensed private investigator, but there really wasn't any law preventing me from talking to an alleged fraudster in the course of my work as a videographer, was there? If there was, I wasn't aware of it. Essentially, I had found a loophole—a way to investigate insurance fraud from many angles without being a PI. Then Mia became my partner and she did the same thing, as needed. Nobody had complained yet. It's like that old saying: It's easier to ask for forgiveness than for permission.

There were occasions, too, when we—mostly me—took steps that weren't strictly legal, like hiding a GPS tracking unit on a subject's vehicle, placing a covert camera on private property, or tampering with some poor guy's spark plug wires. It would be easy to rationalize this behavior by saying, "Well, everybody does it." But the truth is, I don't know how other investigators do it. I just know what works for me, and there hadn't been an incident yet where I regretted cutting legal corners. In fact, not long ago, those shortcuts helped me find and rescue a missing six-year-old girl. Hard to feel remorse for doing whatever it takes in a situation like that.

The question that often arises in the early stages of an investigation is: How should we approach it? When you're dealing with someone like the motorcycle-riding pinhead from yesterday afternoon, that's easy to answer. He claimed he was injured and we suspected he wasn't, so the most reliable method was to tail him discreetly until we could record evidence proving that his injury was either nonexistent or much less serious than alleged.

But this case wasn't nearly as cut and dried. There were a lot of players and several of them could have taken the coin collection. Plus, there wasn't much point in following any of them around. I doubted Serenity Sweet was going to walk out of her house toting a wooden curio box and head for the nearest pawnshop.

So why not see if she'd talk? Who knew what she might be able to tell us? Surely she and Alex Dunn had shared some personal moments from time to time, beyond the whole booby slapping thing. It was possible Alex Dunn had spoken to Serenity about his family, his coins, and other personal information. We should take a chance and contact her.

It was Mia's idea, so she's the one who called—and got voicemail.

"Miss Sweet, my name is Mia Madison. My partner and I have been hired by Alex Dunn's insurance company to find his missing coin collection. I'm sure the last thing you want to do at this point is answer questions from a bunch of nosy people, so let me assure you that we don't think you took it, and we don't think you killed Mr. Dunn. In fact, we can probably help you out. We're very good at what we do, which means we might clear your name by figuring out what really happened. If you'd give us a few minutes of your time, I promise we won't screw you around. You can ask us to leave at any time and we will respect your wishes. Thanks for your time. We hope to hear from you."

She left her number and ended the call.

"Sound okay?" she said.

"Perfect."

Mia placed her phone on the coffee table.

I checked my phone to see if Heidi had texted or called. Nothing.

"Know what I'm wondering?" Mia said. "What is the thief going to do with the coin collection? Every hobo nickel is completely original, meaning easily identifiable, so it's not like they can list them on eBay without expecting to get caught."

"This is where I point out that we encounter people exactly that stupid on a regular basis."

"Know what else I'm wondering?" she said.

"How I get my shirts so wrinkle-free?"

"What if Alex Dunn was dead when Serenity Sweet found him? It would be helpful to know that."

"It would," I said.

"And we know who'll be able to eventually answer that for us," Mia said.

Ruelas.

"He won't talk to us," I said.

"He might talk to me."

"Most men will. Hey, if you want to call him, go right ahead. He probably doesn't even have anything worth sharing yet."

She grabbed her phone off the coffee table, dialed his number, and got voicemail. She didn't leave a message.

"Any other ideas what we can do this afternoon?" Mia said. "Because I'm not sure what—"

Her phone rang. She checked it.

"Ruelas?" I said. I could picture him responding to Mia's call like an excited puppy.

"Nope. Serenity Sweet."

# 5

I didn't really have any preconceived notions about the type of home or neighborhood Serenity Sweet might live in, but I certainly didn't expect her to own a well-maintained American Craftsman-style bungalow in the Barton Hills area above Zilker Park in the heart of Austin. This was the type of neighborhood where she probably had a CPA on one side and a college professor on the other.

Her home had a lush front lawn and a wide, welcoming front porch with half a dozen ferns hanging in baskets around the perimeter. As we mounted the front steps, I felt the breeze of a ceiling fan spinning slowly overhead. This place sure as hell beat the apartment I was currently living in, and it even gave Mia's house a run for its money.

"Behave yourself," Mia muttered under her breath.

"But of course," I said.

I knocked, but before my knuckles even made contact a second time, the door swung open and there stood Serenity Sweet.

She was stunning.

Was I an ass for not expecting that? Well, sure. Who says a heavy woman can't be stunning? And this was a case where there was no need to add a qualifier, such as, "She's pretty, but she'd be even prettier if she'd lose weight." She was pretty exactly as she was, with gorgeous green eyes and thick shoulder-length hair that was a deep chestnut color.

In all honesty, I'll admit that I had been expecting to be overwhelmed by the attributes that earned her a living, but she was wearing a flowered knee-length muumuu that took the emphasis off her chest.

"My lawyer says I shouldn't be talking to y'all," she said as an introduction, and the skepticism was plain on her face. "She's probably right. I'll tell you this much. If it turns out that voicemail you left me was BS, I'll toss both of you out of my house. Fair enough?"

I liked her already.

"There must be some mistake," I said. "We're here to talk to you about annuities."


Her home had stained concrete floors throughout, and it appeared the paint was fresh on all the walls. From where I was sitting beside Mia on the couch, I could see into the kitchen, which was equipped with black appliances and granite countertops. Everything was comfortable and well decorated. Serenity offered coffee.

"No, thanks," Mia said.

I shook my head. "It'd keep me awake during this entire meeting."

Serenity smiled, then sat on a love seat at a right angle to the couch, so she could face both of us.

Mia said, "First thing I want to say, being completely up front with you, because you deserve it, is that we can't promise confidentiality. I wish we could, but the truth is, if you were to admit a crime to us—which you won't, because I believe that you're innocent—we'd be obligated to share that information with the police. And regardless of what we discuss, we could be forced by subpoena to reveal the details."

We hadn't discussed how we'd approach Serenity other than to agree that Mia would take the lead. I wasn't crazy about Mia being so blunt—and so honest—but Mia often seemed to have a sixth sense as to what would work with a particular person. She came across as trustworthy and empathetic, whereas my limited repertoire usually involved wisecracks, flirtation, or threats, depending on my audience.

"On the other hand," I added, "outside of those circumstances, I promise you can trust us to keep it between us."

"I have no problem with any of that," Serenity said, "but I might not even answer your questions. We'll just have to see. By the way, are you recording this?"

"No, we wouldn't do that without your permission," Mia said.

She looked at me.

I said, "I don't need to record anything. I have a pornographic memory."

"Roy," Mia said.

For half a second, I thought I'd blown it. Then Serenity gave me a small grin. "I bet that works a lot of the time, doesn't it?"

"What works?"

"That smart-ass routine. Always joking. You're cute enough to get away with it. Just barely."

"Imagine spending every day with him," Mia said. "Sometimes I'm tempted to buy a muzzle."

They'd found common ground—teasing me. I was fine with that.

"You could try a shock collar," Serenity suggested.

"That might work," Mia said. "He *is* a quick learner when corrected, I'll give him that."

I played indignant. "These dog metaphors are making me uncomfortable. Now if you'll excuse me, I saw a bush outside I need to pee on."

Serenity's smile widened, showing off a set of perfect teeth.

"The two of you put on quite a show," she said. "But we might as well get to your questions."

I looked at Mia, who said, "Okay, it would be helpful if we could determine whether Alex Dunn's death had anything to do with the missing coin collection. It's possible they're unrelated, and that would seem even more likely if he died in your presence. Is that what happened?"

Serenity took a deep breath, as if weighing whether she wanted to answer. Finally she said, "I'll tell you what I told the police, and if you're like them, you won't believe me. Whatever. I don't care. Alex was fine when I got there, and I did my thing, and right in the middle of it, his eyes rolled back into his head. At first I thought he fainted or passed out. That's happened before, especially with older men. Some of them are on all kinds of different medications and they just can't handle the excitement. Alex, if you don't know, had a problem with his heart and he took pills for it. That concerned me, and when I checked for a pulse, I didn't find one. So then I performed CPR for 20 minutes. I'm certified and I know exactly what I'm doing. But I got no response. He was gone."

Still, CPR or not, she should've called EMS.

I said, "Can you tell me what happens during a massage? I mean, I have a general idea, but, like, how much contact do you actually have with your clients?" I was getting a little tongue-tied, which was rare for me.

"Why do you need to know that?" Serenity asked. "You're looking for his coin collection, right?"

Mia said, "Sometimes we never know what will prove useful and what won't. So we ask any question that pops into our heads. If you'd rather not answer that one, we understand."

"No, that's fine," Serenity said. "Not like it's some big secret. Generally the client lies face up on the massage table," Serenity said. "I remain standing, and I work my way around the table, rubbing him all over with my breasts. Well, not all over. I avoid the crotch. I do the face, arms, chest, and legs. Some clients really like me to focus on their feet."

She gazed evenly at me. I smiled back.

"Do you know what kind of heart problem he had?" Mia asked.

"Sorry, no. One time he mentioned that he took some kind of pill, but that's it. That's all I knew."

"So what happened after you performed CPR?" I asked.

"I left," Serenity said. "There wasn't any sense in me hanging around. But I called 9-1-1 just a few minutes later."

"From where?"

"From my own cell phone. I blocked my ID."

"What did you tell them?" Mia asked.

"I gave them the address and said an older man inside the house had lost consciousness, didn't have a heartbeat, and didn't respond to CPR. Then I hung up. But I was caught on the damn security camera and the cops showed up here pretty quick."

"Who were you dealing with at the sheriff's department?" Mia said. "Guy named Ruelas?"

"Yeah. Very obnoxious man."

"That's him," I said.

"A real jerk."

"Your judgment is impeccable," I said.

"He has an ego," Mia said. "And he's stubborn as hell. Always thinks he's right. I know someone else like that, too." I opened my mouth, but she said, "He's also a really good investigator. The most important thing to him is finding the truth. I'm not saying you should talk to him, but if you do, he's not going to screw you around."

"Because I didn't do anything wrong," Serenity said.

"Exactly."

"Doesn't matter. I'm not talking to any more cops."

"I guess I don't blame you," Mia said.

"How long was Alex Dunn a client?" I asked.

"About a year."

"How often did you see him?"

"He had a regular appointment on the first Saturday of every month. And other times he would randomly call me and ask for a massage."

"How do new clients find out about your services?" Mia asked.

"Mostly though referrals," Serenity said. "Word of mouth."

"Did another client send Alex Dunn your way?" I asked.

Serenity nodded.

"Who was it?"

She shook her head. "That remains confidential."

"Sometimes details that seem insignificant turn out to be very important," I said.

"Sorry, no."

"Did you tell Ruelas?" I asked.

"He didn't ask."

I gave Mia a quick glance that said, *You sure he's a damn good investigator?*

"When you were at Dunn's house," Mia said, "did you ever see his coin collection?"

"He showed me a few of the coins, but I didn't pay much attention. I thought it was pretty boring."

"Did you know how valuable those coins are?" I said.

"I know he had one coin that was supposedly worth six or seven thousand dollars," Serenity said. "That blew my mind. Who would pay that?"

"So you didn't see any of the coins on the night he died?" Mia said.

"Nope, and I can't remember the last time he mentioned them. Generally, he was pretty eager for his massage. Not much small talk going on. And when I was done, like most clients, he wanted me to leave fairly quickly, so he could have some alone time."

She smiled at me again. Showing me how unabashed she was.

I, on the other hand, was a little bit abashed.

But I also believed every word she said.

We asked questions for another 15 minutes—most of them revolving around Dunn's health, his children, his business operations, and his coin collection—but Serenity had nothing of value to tell us about any of it.

# 6

"Think she's telling the truth?" Mia asked.

She hit Barton Springs Road and turned left, toward Zilker Park.

"I do, yeah. You?"

"I think so," Mia said.

I was disappointed that we hadn't learned anything that would drive our investigation forward. Heidi still hadn't called, so it was unlikely that Cole Dunn had taken the coin collection, or if he had, he'd already sold it or stashed it somewhere.

"I wonder how long she's lived in that house," I said.

"Meaning did she buy it with the earnings from her new career?"

"Can't help but wonder. Nice place."

It was a warm day, but not hot enough to keep visitors out of the park. To our left, a small group was playing a pick-up soccer game.

"It kind of makes me sad that she does what she does," Mia said.

I didn't respond.

"It's degrading. Don't you think?" Mia said.

"For her or for her clients?" I said.

"Come on. Don't joke."

"Yeah, okay, it probably is. But it's not up to me to make that decision for her. She seems to be doing fine."

"But that sort of thing just furthers the objectification of women," Mia said. "I'd rather see her succeed by working hard. By using her brain."

I was tempted for half a second to point out that Mia often acted as bait to make "injured" men exceed their alleged physical limitations. Put her in high heels and a tight skirt and men would volunteer to lift bags of concrete or change a flat tire. Did the ends justify the means? All I really cared about was that it worked. I didn't bring it up.

"Maybe we should talk to Max Dunn next," I said.

"Considering that his brother died just this morning, maybe we'd better wait a day or two," Mia said. She made the turnaround at Bee Caves Road and got onto Loop 1, the main north-south expressway in Austin.

"In that case, how about some lunch?"

She glanced at her wristwatch. "I'm supposed to meet Garlen in an hour. Remember? I told you yesterday I was taking the afternoon off. We're going to the San Antonio Zoo."

"Oh, that's right. Sorry."

Frigging Garlen. Everything she had told me about him was just so perfect it was sickening. I had gathered that he was handsome, funny, kind-hearted, charitable, and wise. It wouldn't surprise me if ol' Garlen volunteered at soup kitchens on the weekends, after picking up trash along the highways.

Mia exited on Enfield and stopped at the light.

"Hey, we'll probably grab some lunch before we leave for San Antonio. You want to join us?" she said.

"Thanks, but I'm going to do some research this afternoon," I said. "You crazy kids go have fun."

She looked over at me. There are times when I see something in her expression that almost certainly isn't there. It's all my imagination. Like this moment—the way she was holding my gaze. It almost seemed to say, *I'd rather be with you, Roy. Don't you know that?*

The driver behind us beeped. The light had changed.

* * *

"Research" consisted of a long nap, then lunch, and then, in the early afternoon, I sat down at my Mac—but I had researcher's block. What should I look for? I had no brilliant ideas.

So, instead, I clicked over to a website I'd visited last week. Real estate listings. This particular real estate agent was offering a home for sale on Raleigh Avenue. Which was in Tarrytown. Just a few blocks from Mia. Would it creep her out if I decided to move that close to her?

The home was still for sale—maybe because it was priced about ten percent higher than it should've been, in my estimation. And yet I was still considering making an offer, even though it was out of my comfort zone, budget-wise. Decent little house, though. Built in the '50s. Three bedrooms. Thirteen hundred square feet. No garage, just a carport. According to the tax assessor, the land the house was sitting on was worth three times the value of the house. That explained why so many homes in Tarrytown were getting bought and razed. It was the lot itself that was attractive to many buyers.

I closed that page. Back to work. I decided to take a closer look at the Dunn family and see if there was anything more to learn. I had discovered Cole Dunn's drug and theft arrests yesterday by visiting the county clerk's website, where you can search a database of misdemeanors for free, with records going back several decades. Callie also had an arrest—for driving while intoxicated eleven years ago. Not relevant. Alex Dunn's record was clean, as was Max Dunn's.

Now I clicked over to the Texas Department of Public Safety website, where you can conduct a statewide criminal background check, including felonies, for three dollars per search. What a bargain. I learned that Cole Dunn had two felony arrests—both for drug possession, and both within the past year.

My phone buzzed with an incoming text. I checked it and saw that Mia, now at the zoo, had sent me a photo of a chimpanzee, along with a message: **Ran into one of your relatives just now.**

I wrote her back: **Sure that isn't one of your old boyfriends?**

Next I visited the online archives for the *Austin American-Statesman*. Searched for anything of interest regarding Alex Dunn and his family members. I read for an hour but didn't discover anything surprising.

I did some reading about hobo nickels. The majority of the nickels, even vintage nickels, weren't worth much, but occasionally one might be worth several thousand dollars, depending on who carved it. There were a couple of carvers from the early days who were known as the best—namely Bertram "Bert" Wiegand and George "Bo" Washington Hughes.

I jumped over to eBay to see what some of the nickels were going for. A search for "hobo nickel" gave me 615 listings. I noticed that most of the nickels were modern-day carvings on old coins. Nothing from Bert or Bo here.

I changed the sort feature to show the highest-priced listings first. The one at the top had a "Buy it Now" price of $925. Not as high as I expected. I tweaked the search to show me completed listings, and I saw that a beautiful and highly detailed modern carving on an 1887 Morgan silver dollar had sold for $3,400. If a newer carving had fetched that much, I wondered how much a vintage engraving might cost. I opened a new tab, did a quick Google search, and discovered that one of Bo's coins had set a record by selling at auction for $24,200 in 2013. Damn.

I clicked back to the nickels currently for sale, but I added the word "vintage" to my search terms, which whittled it down to just 15 listings. The highest-priced listing had a buy-it-now price of $299 for a 1928 buffalo nickel. The description didn't say when the actual carving had taken place or which artist had done it. It didn't appear particularly masterful or detailed, but what intrigued me was that the seller was located here in Austin, and the listing had begun just yesterday. What were the odds? So I opened the folder of photos Heidi had provided of coins from Alex Dunn's collection.

And there it was.

# 7

It was the same coin. I was sure of it. A lot of hobo nickels appeared similar to me, but there was no way two of them could be exactly identical, since they were carved by hand. I looked very closely at both coins, side by side. No question. The same.

Okay. Now what?

This was a big find and I didn't want to blow it. Under "Seller Information" I saw that the person used the name "TexasLeo," and he—assuming it was a he—had completed 112 transactions on eBay, with a 98.2% rating. I went to his profile, where I could see details about his 112 transactions, and I learned that he had never sold a hobo nickel before, much less any other type of collectible. He had sold an assortment of unrelated, low-priced items, such as a set of Willie Nelson CDs, some silverware, a blood-pressure monitor, a life-sized metal armadillo garden ornament, a cast-iron skillet, a chess set, and a Barnett crossbow.

Weird. You know who would have possession of such a random collections of goods? A thief. He'd had one negative rating for the past six months, where the buyer said, "He took my money but never sent the item." TexasLeo had replied, "Post office fault. It will arrive."

Who was TexasLeo? How had he come into possession of one of Alex Dunn's hobo nickels? It was possible that Dunn had sold it at some point. He bought and sold frequently. And Heidi had mentioned that she couldn't be sure Dunn's catalog of photos was up to date.

I had to pursue this, though, and find out whether it was a dead end.

If I bought the coin, then I'd know who the seller was—right? Not necessarily. TexasLeo could mail the coin without a return address, or with a fake address.

But he was right here in Austin. Why not take advantage of that? I sent him a message:

**Hey, I love that nickel! Sharp! My dad's birthday is tomorrow and he's a big collector. Any chance I could pay for it and meet you somewhere, or pick it up at your house? I live in Austin, too. Sorry for the short notice. Let me know if we can work something out. I'd love to give it to him during his party tomorrow.**

I didn't want to pay for it before I heard from him, because if he had the money, and if he was a thief, he wouldn't want to meet in person. He'd insist on mailing it. So I'd just have to wait to see if he responded.

I heard another incoming text from Mia.

**What r u doing?**

She was probably feeling guilty taking time off while we were in the middle of a big case.

I said: **Solving the case while you goof around.**

As soon as I sent it, I felt bad.

She said: **Really? Making progress?**

If I told her what I'd discovered, she'd want to come back to Austin and work with me, thereby ruining her date with Garlen. I have to admit it was tempting as hell.

I said: **Nope. Have fun at the zoo.**

I went back to eBay and looked at all of the hobo coins for sale. There were no additional listings that raised my eyebrows, and none of the other sellers were from this area.

Fifteen minutes later, I received a reply from TexasLeo.


I arrived at the Walmart in Oak Hill 30 minutes early, because I wanted to watch TexasLeo arrive and possibly do a quick background check on him first. He'd told me he'd be driving a gold Mazda truck with a silver toolbox mounted in the bed. We'd agreed to meet underneath the big Walmart sign near the highway entrance. I knew there'd be parking spots that far from the store entrance, because your average American doesn't like walking any farther than the distance from the couch to the fridge.

I was driving my back-up vehicle—a little gray Toyota—because there were times when I didn't want to be seen in the van. Like now. If I needed to do surveillance on TexasLeo later, it would be better if he'd never seen the van before.

I parked about eighty yards from the sign and waited. I had $300 in cash in my pocket, and I was wearing a ball cap with a hidden camera built in.

This was probably a waste of time. Worst case, I'd end up with a hobo nickel that I'd have to resell on eBay, probably at a loss. No biggie.

Twenty minutes passed. No TexasLeo. What if he didn't show?

I wondered what Mia was doing right now. Still at the zoo? Maybe riding the little train that makes a circuit through Brackenridge Park? Garlen would have his arm around her, and Mia might have a hand on his knee. Was she serious about him? I hadn't asked and she hadn't given any indication.

Thirty minutes had passed.

Was Mia sleeping with him? That was the real question that had been preying on my mind. It was none of my business, was it? Nope. She could do whatever she pleased. In fact, so could I, and I frequently did, with a variety of interesting female companions.

Here came a gold Mazda truck that parked underneath the Walmart sign. Silver toolbox? Yep. I used my Canon super-zoom camera to take a closer look at the driver. White guy. Late twenties or early thirties. Ragged hair. Needed a shave. I snapped a few photos.

Earlier I had asked for his cell number, and he had surprised me by giving it, so now I sent a text:

**Hit some traffic. Be there soon.**

I watched as he checked his cell phone, then put it down and lit a cigarette.

I got the truck's license plate number. Used my laptop to access a website that identified the vehicle's owner as Leopold Julius Pitts. Leo.

In less than two minutes, I'd accessed his criminal history, and it was fairly impressive. Several drug charges, along with a long history of theft and burglary. Very typical pattern of behavior for a user desperately trying to raise cash for his next fix.

Sometimes, when I feel the need, I carry a handgun, but I wasn't today. I couldn't imagine I'd need one in the parking lot of a Walmart, with cars passing by just twenty feet away.

I waited one more minute, then drove over and parked on the driver's side of the Mazda truck. I came around the rear of my Toyota just as he was getting out of the truck.

"Leo?" I said.

"Yeah," he said. "You Bruce?"

I hadn't been entirely forthcoming with him.

"Yeah," I said. "Thanks for meeting me."

We shook hands. He was a slight man—slender and no more than five foot seven. He appeared nervous. He would meet my eyes, but only for a moment.

"You got the money?" he said.

"Yep," I said, pulling the cash from my pocket. "You got the coin?"

Why did this feel like a drug deal?

He pulled it from his pocket. The coin was inside a small plastic sleeve for protection.

"May I see it?" I said.

He handed the hobo nickel to me, but I didn't give him the cash just yet. The sleeve had a funky chemical smell to it—something familiar, but I couldn't place it.

"Your old man is a collector?" he said.

"Oh, you bet," I said. "He started about ten years ago. I'd never even heard of hobo nickels before that. Are you a collector?"

"Not really."

"So where did you get this one?"

"Bought it at a garage sale for fifty cents because it was kinda cool. Then I figured out it was worth some money."

"That's pretty lucky," I said. "How long ago was this?"

"Last year."

"Any idea who carved it?" I said.

"No way of knowing," he said. "I got in touch with some expert on the Internet, but he wasn't able to tell me for sure."

I turned it over and inspected the back. Nothing I hadn't already seen in the photos.

"Know when it was carved?"

"Nope. I'm no expert on these things. You're here to buy it, right? I didn't expect a bunch of questions."

"Sorry, yeah, I am," I said. "I just thought you might be able to tell me something about it, so I could pass that information along to my dad."

"That's cool, but I need to take off, so…"

He held his hand out for the cash.

I didn't move. I hadn't arrived here intending to provoke or confront him, but now I was thinking that might be wiser than letting him go. Did it really matter if I ruffled a few of his feathers?

"You know Cole Dunn?" I said.

I could see him deflate both physically and mentally. "Fuck, man. Are you a cop?"

That meant he *did* know Cole Dunn.

"Not a cop," I said. "Alex Dunn's insurance company hired me to find the coin collection."

"If you're a cop, you have to tell me," he said. "It's the law."

That wasn't true, but I didn't argue with him about it.

"Did you get the coin from Cole before he died?" I asked.

"None of your damn business," Leo said.

"Was he a friend of yours?"

"I got it at a garage sale," he said.

"Let me put your mind at ease," I said. "I'm going to give you the cash because I plan to keep the coin. And all I really care about is finding the rest of the collection. That's what I was hired to do."

I didn't mention that everything I had learned would be shared with the police.

"Okay, then give me the cash," Leo said.

"Just a few more questions," I said. "Did you get the coin from Cole?"

"I'm not answering your damn questions," Leo said. "I want the money."

"You realize this coin might be stolen, right? You could be in possession of stolen merchandise."

"Fuck if it is," he said. "Either give me the money or give me the coin back, asshole."

He was getting worked up.

"Did you steal the collection from Alex Dunn? Maybe you and Cole were working together?"

"You think I'm a thief?" Leo said.

I was just about to make a mistake.

"I *know* you're a thief, Leo," I said. "And a burglar. And a drug user. I already checked your record. The only thing that—"

Before I finished that last sentence, Leo hauled off and punched me hard right in the solar plexus. I hadn't seen it coming. The air shot out of my lungs and I doubled over. I couldn't speak. Hell, I could hardly breathe. Leo grabbed the cash from my hand, got into his truck, and drove away.

Slowly, my breath came back to me.

I decided I would not be leaving favorable feedback for TexasLeo on eBay.

# 8

By now, it was nearly five o'clock, and I was tempted to call it a day. Not that we keep regular hours, because we don't. But getting sucker punched sort of robs you of the motivation to work into the evening.

*Screw it*, I thought. Might as well plow forward. That way I could impress Mia with my industriousness when I saw her in the morning.

Only problem was, plowing forward meant I had to get in touch with Ruelas, because I needed to know if the medical examiner had determined how and when Alex Dunn died. So I got back into my Toyota, still there in the Walmart parking lot, and dialed the number. It went to voicemail, just as I expected. For reasons that I can't grasp, Ruelas seems to despise me as much as I despise him, which means he doesn't take my calls, or return them, unless he has to. In this case, he'd have to.

I left the same kind of warm, friendly message I always leave for him. "Hey, it's Roy Ballard. How are you? Fine, I hope. Ever get those hair plugs? A full head of hair might take the attention away from your beer belly. Anyway, that's not why I'm calling. I'm wondering how Alex Dunn died, and I bet you have the answer to that by now. I'm sure you'll want something in exchange, and I have something really good. Really good. So get back to me at your convenience."

I drove back to my apartment, had a snack, then sat down again at my computer and opened up Facebook. Good old reliable Facebook. Almost always helpful for a guy like me who needs personal information about people he doesn't know.

Using one of my fake accounts—a fictitious woman named Linda Peterson—I searched for Cole Dunn. Found him easy enough. The only posts visible to me on his timeline were cover photos, which meant he had tight privacy settings or he wasn't very active on Facebook. His current cover photo, dated two and a half years ago, showed him leaning against a sharp-looking Mercedes coupe. His only comment: "Check out my new ride." A friend had said, "Spoiled brat LOL." The cover photo prior to that one showed him on a cigarette boat with several scantily clad women.

I clicked on his friends list. You can hide your friends from strangers, but Cole hadn't done that. Was Leo Pitts on the list? Yep, but I'd already expected that. I went to Pitts's profile. Quite a few of his posts were visible to me, so I scrolled back at least six months. Didn't see anything interesting. I could confirm that he and Cole were close friends, but that was about it. I had to accept the possibility that Cole had given Leo the hobo nickel—maybe in exchange for drugs?—and that Leo knew nothing about the disappearance of the collection.

So now I clicked over to Callie Dunn's account, where I found limited commentary, but plenty of photos. Callie and her friends at happy hour. Callie and her friends at various concerts. Callie and her friends at charity-related events. She led an active social life, and she enjoyed documenting it. She passed along a lot of silly memes. If she had political views, she kept them to herself.

I scrolled further downward. More photos. More memes. A few photos with her brothers, and a couple with her dad.

I couldn't help stopping at a photo of Callie and her friends—

seven of them—in swimsuits around a beautifully designed and lushly landscaped swimming pool. This looked like a wealthy person's backyard, as opposed to a pool at a five-star hotel or resort. They were a lovely group of young women. Healthy. Happy. Not a care in the world. Callie had given it a caption: *Alicia's birthday party.*

Alicia? Wasn't that Alex Dunn's second wife? I checked the names tagged in the photo, and sure enough, it was Alicia Potter. I clicked on the name and was taken to her Facebook page. Again, not much of a privacy screen. Always good news for me, or for any sleazebag or stalker wanting to creep on a woman's page.

Potter had been on Facebook for about eight years, and it appeared all of her posts and photos were visible to the public. I spent an hour scrolling backwards on her timeline and learned that she and Callie Dunn were friends at least that far back, and they remained friends today. Maybe Alicia had met Alex Dunn through Callie. I saw quite a few photos of Alicia and Alex Dunn back when they were married, and I noticed that she smiled less and less in those photos as the marriage drew to its conclusion last fall. Even when she wasn't smiling, she was quite striking, with pale skin set off by bright red lipstick. In her most recent photos, her jet-black shoulder-length hair was asymmetrical—longer on the left side, where it curled in a gentle wave under her jaw to frame her face. I don't know why, but that hairstyle made her look European.

I wondered if Alicia Potter would be willing to speak to me. Maybe she could provide some objective insight into the dynamics of the Dunn family. Of course, I realized that even if she told me everything she knew, it probably wouldn't lead anywhere—but that's the way an investigation typically unfolds. It's like panning for gold; you have to sift through a bunch of useless background noise until you find that one nugget of critical information. Sometimes you have to pan in dozens of different streams, so to speak, before your efforts pay off. So maybe I should contact Alicia Potter.

Or maybe I should accept the very real possibility that Serenity Sweet stole the collection. Perhaps Occam's Razor—the idea that the simplest explanation is usually the right one—applied in this situation.

On the other hand, why not see if Alicia would talk? I switched from my Linda Peterson Facebook account to my real, and seldom used, Roy Ballard Facebook account, and sent her a private message. Cost me a dollar. That Mark Zuckerberg is one money-grubbing genius, isn't he?

After all that hard work, I deserved a cold beer, and just as I popped the top, Ruelas called me back.

I answered by saying, "Is this about that pizza I ordered?"

"You got something on the Alex Dunn case?" he said.

"You have no sense of humor."

"Only because you never say anything funny. You got something on Dunn or not?"

"Yeah, but I have no idea if it'll be useful."

"Surprise, surprise. What is it?"

"Well, let's talk about Dunn's cause of death first."

He let out a pronounced sigh. "One of these days—and this might be the day—I'm gonna file on you for withholding evidence."

"That would be rude."

"If you have something relevant to the case and you don't—"

"I know, I know," I said.

"You're not a cop, understand? You're not even a licensed PI. You're just some guy with a camera who snoops on people."

"I appreciate the kind words."

"And the only reason I haven't busted you yet is because I like your partner."

"She's probably flattered, while simultaneously considering a protective order."

He knew as well as I did that he'd never follow through with his threats. Mia and I gained a lot of valuable information during our investigations, which we often shared with Ruelas and other law enforcement officers. It was only fair that Ruelas should give us something in return. If he were to bust me, or to take the information I provided and not give something back, I'd never again share what I'd learned, and that would hurt him in the long run. I'm sure it pained him to admit this to himself.

"Most of the crap you give me is worthless," he said.

"Except for the ninety-nine percent that isn't," I said.

Another sigh. Then: "Okay, spit it out, hotshot."

This was the way it usually went. He'd make me share my information first—obviously a dominance thing—but I didn't care. Let him think he held the upper hand.

"Earlier today," I said, "I bought a hobo nickel from an eBay seller here in Austin. Turned out to be a friend of Cole Dunn's named Leo Pitts. I figure you recognize that name."

"Yep."

"It was one of the nickels photographed in Alex Dunn's most recent inventory of his collection."

"Doesn't mean it was stolen with the others," Ruelas said.

"Doesn't mean it wasn't," I said.

"You talk to the guy?" Ruelas said.

"Better. I met in person and bought the nickel."

"So you might be guilty of possessing stolen merchandise."

"Maybe, but I couldn't be certain it was the same nickel until I had it in my hands," I said. "Once I realized it was, I behaved like a law-abiding citizen and phoned the proper authorities, or in this case, you."

"I'm gonna need that nickel," he said. "ASAP."

"I'll drop it off tomorrow morning," I said.

"When you saw that listing on eBay, you should've called me. Now my chain of evidence is for shit. Did Pitts say how he got the coin?"

"Claimed he got it at a garage sale."

"Did he admit to knowing Cole?"

"He did not. How did Cole die, by the way?"

"That case is with APD, but they're telling me an overdose."

"Intentional?"

"Not as far as they can tell. He didn't leave a note."

"Which drug?"

"Heroin. You can get some of that shit for ten bucks a pop nowadays."

"Did he die at home?"

"You're gonna use up all your good will real soon."

"Oh, come on. This doesn't even count. Did he die at home?"

"He did."

"I assume the coin collection wasn't sitting there in plain sight."

"Nope. Still missing."

"So Serenity Sweet is still a suspect?"

"Absolutely."

"For the theft, or for Alex Dunn's death?"

"Right now, both."

"Any idea how Alex Dunn died? Was he smothered?"

Ruelas paused for a moment, so I knew he had something good to tell me. "Gotta be confidential," he said. "And I'm not bullshitting. Not a word to anyone."

"Absolutely. Just Mia and me."

I could hear him taking a sip of coffee and setting the paper cup down. Then he said, "Somebody fooled around with his heart meds. Emptied a couple of the capsules and filled 'em with cyanide."

## 9

I kept my word and left the nickel for Ruelas at his office the next morning, and then I showed up at Mia's house at nine o'clock. She peeked through the small inset glass window, grinned when she saw the bag of donuts in my hand, and opened the front door. She was wearing jeans and a red sleeveless top. Gorgeous without makeup. Stunning. Makeup only made her look different, not prettier. Her cheeks were just slightly pink from her outing yesterday.

"Glazed?" she asked.

"No, I'm perfectly alert," I said.

I handed her the bag. She had a weakness for glazed donuts.

"I shouldn't," she said.

"You should."

"I ate all kinds of junk yesterday."

"How was it?" I said. "Do zebras still have stripes?"

"It was fun," she said, turning to go into the kitchen. I closed the front door and took a seat on the couch. The scent of her perfume was strong. She must've just put some on. "There were a bunch of kids there," she said from the kitchen, "so it was kind of noisy. We left a little earlier than we'd planned and went down to the Riverwalk. I brought you something."

"Oh, cool. Did you get me a drunken sorority girl?"

"See that plastic bag on the coffee table? Open it."

I did, and inside was a T-shirt from my favorite San Antonio pub, Durty Nelly's. It was a lively place, with a piano player banging out classic songs while the patrons sang along. The floor was always littered with shells from the buckets of peanuts on every table.

"Hey, thanks," I said. "That was very nice."

"You're welcome," she said. "Coffee?"

"Sure."

She started the coffeemaker, then returned with four donuts on a plate and sat down beside me. She handed me a napkin, then took a bite of a donut. Her eyes rolled with pleasure. After we had each finished a donut, she said, "So...any progress?"

"Oh, just a little," I said.

I started by telling her about my eBay discovery and subsequent meeting with Leo Pitts. I even included the part where he punched me in the gut.

"And you didn't hit him back?" she said.

"One blow from me might've killed him."

She had other questions, which I answered, and then I grabbed my laptop and showed her that Pitts and Cole Dunn were friends, and that Callie and Alicia Potter were also friends.

She pointed at one photo and said, "That's Cole?"

"Yeah."

"Nice-looking guy. Not what I was expecting."

"The sense I get from some of these posts is that he was a player and a partier, and he managed to keep it under control until the last few years. That's probably when he started getting into heroin."

"Wait, how do you know he was using heroin?"

"Ruelas told me. And that's not even the biggest news. Somebody put cyanide in Alex Dunn's heart meds. That's what killed him."

"Holy moly," she said.

"Land o' Goshen," I said.

"I didn't see that coming. Isn't cyanide incredibly hard to get?"

"Here, yeah, it is. Not impossible, but close. At least we know Serenity didn't smother Alex Dunn, intentionally or unintentionally. I guess there's still the possibility that she might've poisoned him."

Mia said, "That seems so unlikely. If she wanted to steal his coin collection, she probably could've just walked out with it. Why kill him? Plus, the fact that this guy Leo Pitts had one of the hobo nickels seems like a big neon sign pointing toward Cole."

"And there's still the chance the murder and the theft are unrelated."

I grabbed a second donut and held the plate with the last remaining donut toward Mia. She grabbed it and took a bite. "This might be better than sex," she said.

I started to say that if that was the case, Garlen must not be doing it right, but I decided to keep that to myself.

Instead I said, "Another unknown is that the killer could've planted the poison capsule several days or even weeks ago. If they wanted to kill Alex Dunn and it didn't really matter how quickly it happened, that would've been a clever way to go about it. Obviously the killer had to have access to Alex's meds, and that can't be a very long list, can it?"

"You wouldn't think."

"And they had to have a motive—probably money," I said. "I wonder what his will says. I'm assuming the kids all get a fairly large amount."

"But there is that McMansion thing. Alex Dunn ticked a lot of people off. Maybe somebody did it out of pure hate. Then again, it doesn't seem likely that any enemies from that debacle have access to Dunn's heart meds."

"Unless they broke in," I said. "Or tampered with his meds when he was away from home. I wonder if he carried the prescription with him."

It occurred to me that we were making a mistake we often made—attempting to understand or untangle every aspect of a case, instead of simply figuring out the part we were paid to solve. It was only natural, I guess, but our task was to find the coin collection, or at least determine where it had gone, not to identify who had killed

Alex Dunn.

"I don't want to go off on any wild tangents or drag any unrelated facts into this investigation," I said, "but by my calculations, there are eight more donuts in the kitchen."

"No, Roy. No."

"Then think of it as sixteen much smaller half-donuts."

"No, thanks. I'm done. Really."

"Okay. I guess I am, too, then. Besides, I have to maintain my girlish figure."

We sat quietly for a moment drinking coffee. It was nice. The sitting, not the coffee.

Mia said, "What if Leo Pitts and Cole Dunn were in on it together?"

"The murder or the theft?"

"Either or both. Imagine this scenario. Pitts and Cole are drug buddies, and they constantly need cash because of it. Cole's daddy has plenty of cash, but he's cut Cole off, or at a minimum he isn't giving him enough to cover his habit. So then Cole and Pitts cook up a scheme to kill Daddy Dunn, which means Cole will score a nice inheritance, and they steal the coin collection to make it look like a burglary gone wrong. Cole knows enough about hobo nickels to know they can't sell them—not without getting caught—but after he ODs, Pitts is desperate for cash again, so he decides to sell one. That was him dipping his toe in the water to see if he could get away with it, except you came along and ruined his day."

She gave me a minute to ruminate on that scenario. So I ruminated.

"There are so many possibilities," I said. "Maybe Alex Dunn had a habit of giving his kids some of his less valuable coins. Or maybe Cole occasionally stole one to buy drugs and he had nothing to do with the theft of the entire collection. Maybe, at some point, Leo Pitts and Cole were in Alex Dunn's house, and Leo saw a loose nickel lying around, so he grabbed it, without Cole knowing."

"You think Ruelas will try to get a warrant for Leo's place?"

"He might. Don't know if the judge will grant one."

"What about Cole's place?" Mia said.

"Same. I'm sure the Austin cops had a good look around when

they removed his body, but they couldn't look into drawers and cabinets and so on."

"Not legally."

"Right. But we might be able to."

"Huh? How?"


Sometimes clichés exist for a reason. Like the one where an attractive woman uses her charms to talk some poor schlub into doing something he might not otherwise do. We've all seen that cliché in the movies. I've seen it in real life, many times, because when Mia does it, it works.

Cole Dunn had lived in a small, run-down apartment complex in the northeast part of town, in a neighborhood known for drug-related activity. There were two matching brick buildings in the complex, each with eight units, for sixteen units in total. One of the units served as the manager's residence.

We got lucky and found the manager at home—and he was a walking cliché himself. He was maybe thirty years old, average height, with pasty skin and a beer belly. He needed a shave, a shower, and a few more years in the public school system. In short, he was perfect.

He answered the door by saying, "Yeah?"

"Hi, there," Mia said. Big smile. "My name is Mia Madison."

She held out a hand. He shook it and took a quick peek at her chest. Couldn't help himself. "Doug," he said.

"And this is my partner, Roy Ballard," she said, gesturing my way.

Doug and I shook hands, but it was obvious he considered it no more than a task he had to complete so he could get back to talking with Mia.

"How can I help you?" Doug asked.

I'm sure it had been ages since those words had left his lips.

"Doug, we were hired to find a missing coin collection. It's sort of a long story, so I'll try to keep this brief. The coins were owned by the father of one of your tenants, Cole Dunn, who passed away recently."

"Yeah," Doug said. "The cops were here." The empathy was

palpable.

"In fact, Cole's father also passed away, just a few days before Cole did."

"Heard about that," Doug said. "Weird."

"Unfortunately, that means the father can't tell us where the coin collection might be. What we've been wondering—and this might be a long shot—but we've been wondering if maybe Cole was keeping the coins in his apartment for safekeeping."

"Safekeeping? In this neighborhood?" Doug asked.

Hey, who would've guessed? He had a sense of humor.

"The thing is, the coins are valuable, but they're all unique, so nobody would be able to sell them," Mia said. "Too easy to identify."

She was saying that as a precaution to prevent Doug from thinking he could score those coins himself.

"At least not without getting caught," I said, "and implicating themselves in what might turn out to be a murder case."

"Cole might've been murdered?" Doug asked.

"No, I mean his dad," I said. "And nobody knows for sure yet."

"Crazy," Doug said.

"So what we're wondering," Mia said, lapsing into a pseudo-flirtatious tone of voice, "is whether you could do us a big favor. Is there any chance you'd let us into Cole's apartment for a quick look around?"

"Is she pushy or what?" I said, laughing like the request was totally out of bounds. "I told her it wasn't cool to even ask."

"I promise it won't be more than a minute," Mia said. "And if we find the coin collection, we won't even touch it. We just need to know if it's in there."

"The man could lose his job, Mia," I said. A subtle little jab, implying that he didn't have the guts to do it.

"He's the manager, Roy. He can inspect an apartment anytime he wants." Then, to Doug: "Right? Isn't that the law?"

"Pretty much," Doug said. "If I have a good reason for being in there."

"And there's no reason we can't tag along, is there?"

"Jeez, Mia, give him a break. You're being a pain in the ass."

I was setting the stage for Doug to be her hero.

"I guess I could say there was a problem with the plumbing," he said.

**10**

It was a pigsty. Not a surprise. Drug addicts generally aren't meticulous housekeepers. The living room was littered with dirty dishes and fast-food garbage. The beige carpet had small stains all over it—some of which looked like blood. The sofa and mismatched love seat would've been turned away by any self-respecting charity.

The three of us were standing just inside the front door. Doug did not appear surprised by the condition of the apartment, which meant he might have been in there sometime after Cole Dunn's body had been removed. Or maybe he had worked in this industry—and in this part of town—long enough to expect this type of treatment from renters.

"Guess his estate isn't getting the security deposit back," I said.

Doug glared at me. He wasn't a fan.

"Why would he have an entertainment center," Mia said, "but no TV? No stereo or any other electronics."

"He was always selling his stuff to make rent," Doug said. "Or to get high."

"You talk to him about that?" I asked.

"No, but it was obvious he was a user."

I moved over to the entertainment center and checked the two drawers built into the base of the unit. They were empty.

Mia stepped toward the bedroom door, but Doug said, "Let's all stay in the same room, okay? No offense, but I don't know y'all."

"No problem," Mia said.

I looked around and shrugged, because there was no other place in the living room where the hobo coins might be stashed, even if they had been removed from the wooden curio box.

"May we?" Mia said to Doug, gesturing toward the sole bedroom.

He nodded and we went in, but there wasn't much to see. Just a queen-sized mattress resting on a box spring, with no frame or headboard. The sheets and bedspread were all tangled together, and there was a stale, sweaty funk hanging in the air. A sizeable mound of dirty clothes occupied one corner of the room, and more junk-food wrappers were strewn here and there. It was, all in all, a depressing scene. How does a person end up like this?

"He didn't even have a dresser," Mia said.

"Sold that, too," Doug said. "I saw a couple of guys hauling it out a few weeks ago. It was a nice piece of furniture. Teak or rosewood or something."

I walked over to the closet. The hollow-core door had a fist-sized hole in it. I swung the door open, hoping to see a wooden box on the upper shelf, but I was disappointed. The shelf was empty, and there weren't more than a dozen items of clothing hanging from the rod. Two large cardboard boxes rested on the floor, but they contained photo albums and various worthless odds and ends. No coin collection.

Mia pointed at something on the carpet near the pile of soiled clothes.

"Check it out," she said.

It was a tube of lipstick.

"Did Cole have a girlfriend?" I asked.

"Well, there was this one chick I'd see occasionally. She spent the night every now and then."

"How do you know she spent the night?" Mia asked.

"It's my job to make sure all residents are on the lease. I've gotta keep track of who comes and goes. Plus, my window looks right over at Cole's door."

"Tell me about this girl," I said.

"What do you want to know?"

"Anything. Height. Weight. Hair color. Shoe size."

"Well, she wasn't the kind of person you normally see around here, and not the kind I'd expect to hang out with a guy like Cole."

"How so?"

"Well, Cole was okay—you couldn't help but like him—but let's face it, he was a druggie. This girl wasn't from that crowd."

"How do you mean?" Mia said.

"She's more like a West Austin type. Drives a red BMW and wears expensive clothes. Or they looked expensive to me. I don't know."

"Do you know her name?"

"Nope. Sorry."

"What does she look like?"

"Pretty hot. Probably in her late twenties or early thirties. Skinny. Always carrying a purse. A lot of women around here don't carry a purse, but she does. She has very black hair that's, like, lopsided."

Oh, man. That sounded familiar.

"Longer on one side than the other?" I said.

"Yeah, exactly," Doug said.

"Hold on."

I took out my phone, opened Facebook, and went to Alicia Potter's page. I clicked her profile photo and showed it to Doug.

"Yeah, man, that's her," he said, looking at me like I was some sort of wizard.


"Alicia Potter and Cole?" I said. "I wonder how long that was going on."

We were walking back to the van in the parking lot. I saw a few pedestrians shuffling slowly along the sidewalk near the street, but other than that, there wasn't much activity. A neighborhood like this was busier, and more dangerous, after sundown.

"Callie would probably know," Mia said.

"I agree with Doug—why would Alicia hook up with Cole?"

"You never know what draws two people together," Mia said. "Cole was a good-looking guy, and judging by some of the comments on Facebook, he was a charmer. Maybe he was Alicia's type, regardless of his personal problems. And maybe they didn't have a serious relationship."

"You're saying she might've just been having fun with a party boy?"

"It's been known to happen."

"That offends my delicate sensibilities," I said, as we were getting into the van. "I forgot to mention—I sent Alicia Potter a Facebook message yesterday asking if she'd talk to me."

"What'd she say?"

"She hasn't responded. Hold on." I was checking my phone again. "It says she saw the message, but she didn't answer it. You'd think she'd at least reply. Now I have even more questions than I had before."

I backed out of our spot and pulled out of the lot.

"Like were Alicia and Cole seeing each other before Alicia divorced Alex?" Mia said.

"For starters. And did Alex ever know what was going on? If he did, was he mad about it? Did he and Cole have a falling out?"

"Think Alicia was a drug user?" Mia asked.

"I'd say there's a good possibility, even if just recreationally. Birds of a feather."

"On the other hand, we're making a lot of assumptions based on one tube of lipstick and the word of a semi-sleazy apartment manager," Mia said. "What if he has it all wrong?"

I was going south on Rundberg Lane.

"Only semi?" I said.

I'd given Doug $100 to keep it to himself that we'd entered the apartment. I doubted he would've mentioned it to anyone anyway, because what good could come of it? And it wasn't like we'd taken anything.

"If we noticed the lipstick," Mia said, "you can bet the cops did, too."

"Yeah," I said, "but it was a garden-variety overdose and I'm sure that's how they treated it. They wouldn't have been looking for clues in a homicide. Remember, Cole died in APD jurisdiction, but his father's death is with the sheriff."

"True. Ruelas, on the other hand, is going to want a search warrant for that apartment. And if he gets one, he'll see that lipstick and ask Doug the same questions we asked. And then he'll be as interested in Alicia as we are."

As I mentioned earlier, it wasn't our job to solve the Alex Dunn homicide, but figuring out where the coins had gone might lead us to the killer. That, in turn, would make Ruelas look bad—being upstaged again by "some guy with a camera"—and that was just a neat little perk of my job.

We went back to Mia's house and brainstormed on our next possible steps.

Idea number one: Interview Alicia Potter and see what sort of vibe we got. If she'd talk to us.

Idea number two: Talk to Callie again, and maybe Max Dunn, to see what they had to say about the relationship between Alicia and Cole.

Idea number three: Focus on Leo Pitts—but do what, exactly? Follow him? Harass him? Threaten him with assault charges unless he gave me some useful information?

We were debating the pros and cons of these possible approaches when, out of the blue, I found myself saying, "Hey, you know that little house for sale over on Raleigh?"

I knew she'd be familiar with it, because she routinely drove past it on her way out of the neighborhood.

"Sure. What about it?"

"I've been, uh, kind of wondering about it."

"Really? Like you want to buy it?"

She knew I'd been tired of my apartment for a very long time. I couldn't read her face. Was she freaking out?

"Maybe," I said. "I mean, it's just a crazy idea."

She surprised me. She broke into a big grin.

"That would be so cool. We'd be neighbors."

"I know," I said, "and, honestly, I was thinking that might bother you—me being so close. I'm sure you get enough of me during the day…"

"Well, it's not like you'd be right next door," she said, "which would be unbearable. Don't think I could stand watching the parade of women coming and going on a daily basis."

She was only joking, but it kind of stung.

"You know it's not like that," I said.

"Do you have a realtor?" she asked. "If not, my friend Abby is awesome."

"Well, I haven't even—"

"I should call her," Mia said, sitting up straight. "She could at least show you the house. Want me to do that?"

She was plainly excited by the idea, and that made me feel good.

"Like, right now?"

"I could call her, yeah. Then the two of you could figure out when to meet over there."

"She won't be mad if I don't buy it?"

"No, of course not. That's what they do for a living—show houses. Plus, she's cute. You've met her before, right?"

I don't know if I showed it on my face, but she had just punched me in the gut—metaphorically speaking—every bit as hard as Leo Pitts had. I didn't want to be set up with one of her friends. What did it say about Mia's mindset that she wanted to play matchmaker? What did it say about how she felt about me?

"What, you don't think she's cute?" Mia asked, because I hadn't responded.

"No, sure, she's adorable."

"Okay, now I know you're pulling my chain. 'Adorable'?"

"What are we even talking about?" I said. "I made a passing remark about a home for sale and suddenly I'm walking into the sunset with Abby?"

It sounded snarky. No two ways about it. It *felt* snarky.

Mia frowned and took a breath. "You okay? You seem out of sorts."

"Sorry," I said. "Didn't sleep well last night. Plus, generally speaking, I'm a jerk."

She didn't reply.

"You're supposed to argue with me about that," I said.

"Not in the mood," she said.

She leaned back. We remained quiet for a few moments. There would be no more discussion about the house for sale.

"So…what next?" Mia asked.

"Idea number four," I said.

"There is no idea number four," Mia said.

"I have one. Don't know if it's any good."

## 11

Not only did Max Dunn answer my phone call, he agreed to see us that afternoon, which was a surprise, considering his brother had died just the morning before. If Callie had described Max correctly—saying he was always too busy with his own family to interact much with his siblings—then he wouldn't be able to shed much light on the situation. Still, it couldn't hurt to chat with him for thirty minutes.

Max invited us to his home in a small, exclusive neighborhood off Bee Caves Road. We grabbed a light lunch, then got into the van and headed out to Weston Lane, which led into the neighborhood called Rob Roy on the Lake. It was a gated neighborhood, but the gate was open and we pulled through.

"Any idea who Rob Roy was?" I asked. "I know there's a drink called a Rob Roy. Think there's a connection?"

Mia was wearing sunglasses and showed no expression.

"And wasn't there a movie called *Rob Roy*?" I asked.

Mia grunted, meaning she didn't know or care. She appeared to be checking addresses on mailboxes as we slowly descended Weston

Lane toward Lake Austin. We passed three separate landscaper's trailers as crews mowed and trimmed. The neighborhood probably had a restriction limiting the use of power equipment to one particular day of the week. Rich folk couldn't be bothered to hear weed eaters all the time.

"How in the hell do people get so rich?" I said. "Some of these houses have to be worth three or four million."

Mia said nothing. It was clear that I had hurt her feelings earlier. She had been equally quiet during lunch.

"Think the Dunn kids got their money from daddy, or did they earn it themselves somehow?"

"No idea," Mia said.

"Max Dunn is a financial consultant," I said. "Is that vague or what? That could mean a thousand different things."

"Pretty vague," Mia said.

Okay. Enough.

"Sorry I snapped at you earlier," I said.

She didn't respond, so I looked over at her. Then she said, "What was that all about, anyway?"

"Just grouchy," I said.

"You'd rather I not set you up with my friends?" she said.

That was a difficult question to answer honestly. I was tired of ducking the issue—my feelings for her—but I damn sure wasn't going to get into it right now.

"That's complicated," I said. "But it was a nice gesture and I shouldn't have gotten uptight."

Mia is one of the most intelligent and intuitive people I know. Could she see through my dodge and understand exactly what was going on? Maybe. But in response, she simply nodded. Apology accepted.

We'd reached Max Dunn's driveway and Mia immediately said, "Check it out."

Right next to the stone mailbox was a for-sale sign.

I pulled in and stopped the van for a moment. Dunn's house, forty yards away, was beautiful, but also kind of disgusting. So perfect. Like something that might be featured in a magazine article about "gracious living." Two stories built from sandstone. A flat, sweeping expanse of flawless St. Augustine grass. There would be a pool in back, of course.

I whipped my phone out and took a photo of the for-sale sign. Then I continued up the driveway to a circular parking area in front of the house.

"I feel like Nick Carraway," I said.

Mia looked at me and raised an eyebrow. She was impressed with the reference.

"Hey, I can read," I said.

"Will wonders never cease?" she said. Then, looking at the house, she said, "Shall we?"

We got out, ascended the sandstone steps to the front door, and rang the bell. I could tell from the grain in the door that it was an exotic wood, probably harvested from some remote jungle. What's wrong with good old oak?

I heard footsteps, and the door swung open. Max Dunn looked just the way he did in Facebook photos: Trim, healthy, and handsome. But he also appeared fatigued and stressed. A harried executive with too many obligations, both business and social. Or weighed down by the recent deaths in the family.

"Roy?" he said.

"Yes, and this is Mia."

We shook hands all around and Max invited us in. The inside of the house was as fabulous as the outside. Max led us into a den with built-in bookcases occupying two walls and massive floor-to-ceiling windows filling the other two. We sat in leather chairs that were arranged around a circular coffee table built from the same wood as the front door.

"We're very sorry for your loss," Mia said.

"I appreciate that, but which one?" Max said with a rueful grin. "Been a rough week."

"I can't even imagine," Mia said. "It's just horrible. So we'll try to keep this short. I'm sure you have other things you need to tend to."

I glanced out the north-facing windows and saw that I was right—there was a pool in the backyard. In fact, I realized it was the pool in the photo from Callie Dunn's Facebook page—the one taken at Alicia Potter's birthday party. There was nobody to be seen back there now, and I hadn't heard anyone else in the house. If Max's wife and kids were home, they were keeping quiet.

"You said this is about dad's coin collection?" Max said.

"Right," Mia said. "We were hired by the insurance company to see if we could figure out where it went."

"Okay, but I have a question. What happens if you find it?"

"I don't understand the question."

"If you find the coins, won't our claim be rejected?"

He looked at me. That was an odd question.

"Well, yeah," I said. "But if we figure out where it went, then you'd likely get the collection back. Wouldn't you prefer that?"

He was shaking his head. "Honestly, I'm just so overwhelmed by everything right now, it's hard to care one way or the other. I think it would be easier to get paid for the loss than to hassle with selling the collection. Except, wait. I guess it would be great if you found the coins, because that would mean you'd found the killer, right?"

I said, "There's just no way of knowing if they're connected until we find the collection, so any help you can give us would be greatly appreciated."

That seemed to satisfy him.

"Sure thing. What're your questions?"

I said, "Do you know if your father kept his inventory of coins reasonably up to date?"

"Meaning the photos?"

"Right."

"I can't be sure about that. All I know is that he bought and sold them pretty regularly, but there was a core group of coins that were his keepers. In fact, that was the bulk of the collection. He loved those coins. At first I thought: What on earth is he wasting his money on? But then I looked into it and learned that the coins hold their value pretty well, and they can even increase in value. Plus, they're pretty cool. I wouldn't have said that when he first started, but I grew to appreciate the artistry. So I guess it wasn't such a bad investment, really."

Mia said, "That's your line of work, right? Investments?"

"Well, sort of. I'm a financial advisor."

"Where?"

"I'm self-employed."

"How is the real estate market in the Austin area nowadays?" I said. "I noticed your house is for sale."

"Oh, it's fine. We bought this place because of the lake, of course, but the kids don't have any interest in it. When I was their age, I'd be out on the boat all day long. But I can't remember the last time we went out, so I decided it was time to move on."

"How old are your kids?" Mia asked.

"Sixteen and thirteen. Two boys."

"Where are you moving to?" I asked.

I could tell he was getting a little impatient with the questions, because it was small talk and had nothing to do with the coins—as far as he knew—and he wasn't a small talk kind of guy.

"Lost Creek," he said. "Want to stay in the Eanes school district."

Lost Creek was a nice neighborhood, but not as exclusive or expensive as Rob Roy. For him, it would be a step down.

"I don't blame you," I said, and began to transition back to our reason for being here. "I need to ask a couple of things that, quite frankly, are going to come across as intrusive."

"Okay," Max said. Noncommittal.

"Who is the executor of your father's estate?" I asked.

"I am. Lucky me. Another chore to take care of."

"I assume the bulk of the assets and any life insurance goes to you three kids?"

"It does, yes."

"Equally split?"

"Yes."

"Has the will been probated?"

"Well, no, not yet. Of course not. We have to wait to see how the investigation goes."

The meaning was clear. He was acknowledging that he couldn't distribute the assets until his siblings—or, now, just his one remaining sibling—were cleared in his father's death.

"Were you and Cole close? I apologize for getting so personal."

Max didn't appear angry or offended, but he studied me for a moment, before he said, "Cole had his problems. I'm sure you know all about that, as do the police. The drugs wrecked his life—it's that simple. There were times when I could still see the old Cole in there, but for the most part, in the past year or so, he was like a stranger."

"Did he ever come to you for money?"

"Yeah, sure, he came to all of us, and we eventually had to agree to cut him off. That was rough. I know he kept badgering Dad and got really ugly with him at times." He must've caught the expression on my face, because he added, "I realize how that looks and what you must be thinking, but there is no way Cole had anything to do with Dad's death. Just no way. If you told me he stole the coins, I might say, yeah, he'd do that, which is sad, you know? But he wouldn't harm anybody, even for an inheritance."

I gave Mia a quick glance and let her explore the next area of interest.

"Did Cole have a girlfriend?" she asked.

"He had a lot of them over the years, but the most recent ones weren't exactly the kind you'd bring home to mom."

"Party girls?" Mia asked.

"That would be a generous description. They were drug addicts, and I suspect some of them were prostitutes when they needed money."

"So I guess you didn't know any of them?" Mia asked.

"Not really, no, but especially not any women he met in the past year or so."

We had debated whether we should bring up Alicia Potter, and had finally agreed that we'd wait and see how Max responded to our questions. If he seemed to be honest and forthcoming, there was no reason not to ask.

So Mia said, "Did the three of you kids get along with Alicia okay?"

"Yeah, sure," he said. "She was fine. I wasn't what you'd call close with her, but she and Callie have been friends for years—well before Alicia married Dad. That's how she met him—through Callie."

"How did your dad and Alicia get along after the divorce?"

"Well, he was upset, but it wasn't as contentious as some divorces. He got over it and moved on. She was too young for him, and they both should have known that from the start. Plus, my dad was not what you'd call an ideal husband."

"How so?"

"His eye wandered. I know he had at least a couple of affairs."

"So Alicia was the one who asked for the divorce?"

"Right."

"Did they have any sort of ongoing relationship afterward?" Mia asked.

"Not at first, no, because she was pretty angry about the cheating. But after he apologized and some time went by, I think they had dinner occasionally, but only as friends."

"How did Cole feel about Alicia?" I asked.

"I gotta admit, these are some weird questions," Max said. "Why this focus on Alicia?"

"Sometimes it helps if we can get a big picture of all the different relationships in the family," I said. "Most of it turns out to be irrelevant, to be honest."

"Well, Cole liked Alicia fine, I guess. There weren't any problems that I know about."

"Do you know if Cole and Alicia ever saw each other?"

For a second, he appeared genuinely puzzled. "How do you mean?"

"We're wondering whether they dated."

"Alicia and Cole? Why would you ask that? Where is this going?"

He looked at me, then back at Mia.

She told him about the manager at Cole's apartment complex identifying Alicia from a photo, making it clear that Alicia and Cole had had something going on.

Max reacted by sitting in confused silence. Then an expression I couldn't interpret slowly formed on his face. I had no idea what he might say, nor did I expect what he actually said.

"Alicia had an older sister who died several years ago."

He paused, apparently trying to recall the details clearly. Mia and I waited patiently.

Max said, "I can't believe I'm even pondering the possibilities here, but…Alicia's mother was terminally ill and didn't have much longer to live, which was sad enough, but then Alicia's sister died in an accident. Her mother passed away just a month later, leaving behind half a million dollars, which Alicia inherited all to herself. I never thought much about it, but now, considering how my dad died...I'm not saying Alicia had anything to do with it, but it just seems kind of coincidental, you know? Is that crazy, considering that my dad cheated on her? Maybe she hadn't forgiven him after all."

# 12

I prefer fraud cases that are more cut and dried. Give me, for instance, an alleged slip-and-fall accident in a Walmart, or a guy who files for disability while moonlighting as a stripper for bachelorette parties.

In my early days as a legal videographer, those types of cases made up the majority of my work. I would spend days, and many long nights, conducting surveillance, hoping to get video of a subject behaving in a manner that proved he or she wasn't actually injured. Basic stuff.

But then I began to work on more complex cases, because my clients needed it, and with those cases come more challenges. Like having too many suspects. That was the problem here. Too many people had a motive and the means to kill Alex Dunn, or to steal his coin collection, or both. Now we had to add Alicia Potter to the list. In fact, at this point, I had to wonder if she was the prime suspect.

According to Max Dunn, Alicia and her sister Glenda had taken a hike along the Barton Creek greenbelt, and Glenda had fallen to her death. Just a sad accident. Glenda got too close to the edge, slipped off a wet slab of rock, and fell 90 feet. If there had been water in the creek, she might've had a chance, but the drought had left the creek bed bone dry.

I'd gently prodded Max for his feelings about Alicia. Was she a killer? He said he had no idea, but sometimes people did crazy things for money. True enough. How was Alicia as a stepmother? He said it was weird, because she was a few years younger than he was, but they got along fine. She was sort of superficial and focused on material goods, but that described a lot of people nowadays. He certainly hadn't ever suspected that she was seeing Cole, and he still wasn't convinced. Perhaps the apartment manager was simply wrong.

An hour after leaving Max's house, we were back at Mia's place, and I was on my iPhone, verifying the facts of Glenda's death via the *Austin American-Statesman* archives.

"It was a Tuesday evening in December," I said, reading from the article that first reported the death.

"Not exactly prime hiking season," Mia said. She had her laptop open, doing some research of her own.

"They were on a lookout point above something called the Urban Assault Wall, a popular spot with climbers," I said. "It was ten minutes after seven when Alicia called 9-1-1, which is well after dark that time of year. Apparently she tried to find a way down to her sister, but there isn't one, so then she ran back to her car and called for help. She said she'd left her phone in her car."

Mia grunted as she continued her own search.

"Who leaves their phone in the car?" I said. "Especially when you're out hiking."

There wasn't much more to the article, and I saw no indication that Glenda's death had ever been considered suspicious, either then or later.

I closed my browser and opened the photo I'd taken of the for-sale sign at Max Dunn's house. The realtor was named Kiersten

Stanley and her cell number was included on the sign. I sent a short text:

> Saw your name on the sign at Max Dunn's. Need a realtor
> to show me a house in Tarrytown. Interested?

She didn't reply right away, so I slipped my phone into my pocket.

"Are we way off in the weeds on this?" I asked. "I mean, even if Alicia and Cole had something going on, that doesn't mean either of them stole the coin collection. I feel like we're on a wild goose chase."

Mia was too focused on her laptop to respond.

"Which raises a question: Are wild geese particularly elusive?"

Mia wasn't listening.

I lapsed into my best Marlin Perkins. "While I remain in the comfort of the vehicle, Jim wades through a marsh in search of the ever-crafty wild goose."

Finally, Mia raised her head. "What are you babbling about?"

"I think we need to step back for a second and take a fresh look at the case. I feel like we're spinning our wheels. I am overwhelmed, quite frankly, and I'd prefer to simply be whelmed."

She looked at me, then looked at her laptop again. "Then you might not want to know what I just found."

"Ah, man," I said. "What is it? No, wait. Don't tell me. You're probably right."

She shrugged. "Okay. It's probably not relevant anyway."

"You're lying."

"Of course I am."

She waited.

"Okay," I said. "Go ahead."

"Max Dunn filed for bankruptcy seven months ago."

"Well, crud," I said. "Of course he did. Why should he be the one person without a motive?"

"Chapter 11," Mia said, scrolling downward, "although to be honest, I don't really understand the difference between the chapters. Don't know if it really matters here."

"Chapter 11 is reorganization," I said. "And when an individual chooses that chapter, instead of chapter 13, it means he has a boatload of debt. Like more than half a million, I think."

"Okay. Bottom line is, he's broke, and I'd guess that's why he's really selling his house."

"Which means he's a liar," I said.

"That might be a bit harsh," Mia said. "In the scheme of things, it was a white lie to avoid embarrassment. He seemed like a decent guy to me."

"But I want to impugn his character, so I can leap to conclusions about his involvement with the coin collection."

She kept reading, but apparently found nothing more worth sharing.

I was restless. I always got this way when we were making no discernible progress on a case, or when there were so many forks in the road.

Too many suspects.

I stood up and walked to one of the windows facing east. I could see Mia's next-door neighbor Regina working in her garden between the two houses. What do you grow this time of year in central Texas? I had no idea. Mosquitoes?

Serenity Sweet.

Callie Dunn.

Cole Dunn.

Max Dunn.

Leo Pitts.

Alicia Potter.

Too many suspects.

Maybe Regina had a sixth sense, because she turned and saw me watching through the window. She gave me a small wave and a warm smile. I waved back. This was a woman who had saved Mia's home by extinguishing the flames when an arsonist had tried to burn the place down. A hero. I'd sent her flowers at the time, and it still didn't seem like enough. I moved away from the window and let Regina go about her business without me watching over her shoulder.

"Let's brainstorm," Mia said.

I sat back down.

"You storm first," I said.

"Max Dunn seemed to know a decent amount about hobo nickels, and I'm guessing the other kids did, too. Don't you think they'd understand that the coins would be hard to sell because they're so easy to identify?"

I was nodding. "I reached that conclusion myself, but look at Leo Pitts. He sold one."

"But we don't know if it was stolen," she reminded me.

Sometimes you're trying so hard to see the big picture, you forget the smaller details.

"Damn you and your facts," I said.

It was hot today, so Mia was once again wearing a sleeveless top, showing off her well-defined arms. The self-defense technique known as Krav Maga had become a regular part of her routine, and it was amazing what the exercise had done for her fitness—and her confidence. I wouldn't mess with her.

"My point," she said, "is that anybody who knew how hard they'd be to sell probably wouldn't have stolen them. Either that or, as we discussed, the theft was a cover for the murder, and they never had any intention of selling the coins."

"But that doesn't make much sense anymore, considering what I learned from Ruelas. The theft might've been a good cover if the killer wanted to make it look like an interrupted burglary. But it was a poisoning. A surprised burglar doesn't poison anybody."

Sometimes you're so focused on the details, you forget the bigger picture.

"Damn you and your facts," she said.

We sat quietly for several moments. The air conditioner had shut off for a few minutes, and I could hear the scrape of Regina's gardening tools in the soil outside.

"But I think you're right about the first part," I said. "The thief probably didn't know the coins would be hard to unload without getting busted. That, or they were so desperate, they were willing to take a gamble."

"You're referring to Cole?"

"Not necessarily, although he falls in that category. Maybe Max does too, depending on just how bad his finances are."

"But not Callie," Mia said. "As far as we know."

"Right. And Alicia is the wild card," I said. "I would think she'd know as much about hobo nickels as the kids do, so she wouldn't have stolen them. Assuming this theory we're working on is correct."

"I hate to say it, but that leaves Serenity Sweet," Mia said. "She probably didn't know much about the coins, except that they were valuable."

I try to avoid making decisions based on a gut feeling alone—because your gut will lead you astray—but my gut had told me from the beginning that Serenity had not stolen the coins. She just did not seem like a thief. Of course, that's the best disguise for a thief—not seeming like one.

"Don't forget Leo Pitts," I said.

He seemed like a much more viable candidate.

"Yeah."

"I'm guessing the Evil One has made his life miserable by now."

I was referring to Ruelas, and Mia knew that without asking.

"We could ask him," she said.

"Leo or Ruelas?" I said.

"Ruelas."

"*You* could ask him," I said.

Ruelas might've been forthcoming with me last night, but in general, Mia had much better luck getting information from him, especially when he didn't owe us anything. He had a soft spot for Mia, and had in fact asked her out once. She managed to turn him down without pissing him off.

"Want me to?" she said, holding her phone up.

"Sure."

She dialed and, yes, he answered. He rarely let it go to voicemail when he saw her name on the caller ID. She hadn't put the call on speakerphone—again, because he would be more cooperative if he didn't know I was around—so I could only hear her side of the conversation.

"Great, and you?" she said. Bubbly. Warm. Like two friends who had gone too long without talking.

Short pause.

"That's sweet," she said.

Pause.

"I do, yes, if you don't mind. I was just wondering if there was anything you could tell me about this guy Leo Pitts."

Longer pause. Mia nodded and murmured "Uh huh" every now and then.

Then she said, "Well, okay. Thank you."

She didn't seem particularly jazzed by what he had told her.

"I am, yes. His name is Garlen."

What a sleaze. Prying into her personal life.

"He does. Very much so. We went to the San Antonio Zoo yesterday."

He said something that made her laugh, and she looked at me.

"That's what I said! How funny. But we know that isn't true. Roy is all man."

Another pause.

"Okay, well, thanks again. I appreciate it." She disconnected the call and said, "Pitts admitted he didn't get the coin from a garage sale. He said Cole gave him the coin to pay back a loan. Ruelas suspected it was a drug thing, but Pitts wouldn't admit to that, and Ruelas didn't get anything else out of him. He said he can't get a warrant for Pitts's place based on what he has right now, and since nobody can prove the coin was stolen…"

"He can't charge Pitts with receiving stolen property," I said.

"Nope."

About what I expected. I'd rather solve the case without his help anyway.

"What was the bit that made you laugh?" I asked.

"Huh?"

"You laughed about something and told him you'd said the same thing."

"Oh. I mentioned the zoo and he asked if I'd seen your relatives, the chimps. Kind of funny that we made the same joke."

"Hilarious," I said.

"Hey, don't worry. You heard what I said—that you're all man." She was being playfully patronizing.

"It's true, you know," I said.

"I'm sure it is, Roy. I'm sure it is."

She was looking at me with that expression on her face again—

the one that said her silly comments were sincere, and that I was the world's biggest idiot for not acknowledging the connection between us. Was I misreading it? I had to be. She was just naturally a warm and affectionate person, and I shouldn't mistake friendship for something more. I could ruin everything that way. If I made a move and learned I was wrong, that could create an awkward tension that would ruin our partnership.

But she was still holding my gaze—holding it, holding it—until I lost my nerve and looked away, like an intimidated high school boy.

**13**

Shortly before six o'clock that evening, back at my apartment, I received a text reply from Kiersten Stanley, Max Dunn's realtor.

**I'd love to. When? Which house?**

I thought about it. Was I really prepared to move forward with this? Big step. But it wouldn't hurt to look, right? As Mia had said, that's what realtors are supposed to do—show houses.

**On Raleigh. My schedule is flexible.**

I took a gulp from the ice-cold Lone Star longneck resting on the coffee table.

**Short notice, but I'm free tonight. How about one hour from now?**

"The great thing about this house," she said as she swung the front door open, "is that it has the feel of classic Austin, but it has been maintained and upgraded all along. The plumbing and electrical were overhauled a few years ago, so there's no worries there. The foundation is solid, and of course you can't beat the neighborhood."

Kiersten Stanley was a petite blond woman in her mid-thirties, dressed in gray slacks and a red blouse. She was wearing flats and couldn't have stood more than five feet tall. Attractive, with sparkling blue eyes and great dimples. She had sort of a Kristin Chenoweth vibe going on, which was most definitely not a bad thing.

"Did they finally catch the serial killer in this area?" I asked as I followed her into the house.

That threw her for about half a second, and then she laughed. "I understand he was offed by one of the neighborhood gangs."

The house was empty. I hadn't realized the owners weren't living there anymore. The air was thick and musty, because the air conditioner had not been running. The interior was, simply put, gorgeous. Hardwood floors throughout. Great fixtures. Fresh paint on the walls in subtle but attractive colors. Crown molding.

"How old is the AC system?" I asked.

"Replaced last year."

She had obviously boned up on the highlights of the home in the hour before we met.

"What about the roof?"

"New shingles three years ago. The place really needs nothing. It's good to go, as is."

I stepped into the kitchen. Small, but functional. Stainless steel appliances.

"Nice," I said.

"And all brand new."

We followed a hallway past two small bedrooms, and then into the master bedroom. I looked around.

"Is there a dungeon?"

"Sorry, there isn't. You know how hard it is to dig in this area. It was cost-prohibitive."

"Max has a dungeon," I said. "Such a nice feature."

She kept rolling with it. "How long have you known Max?" she asked.

Old habit: I checked for a wedding ring and saw that she didn't have one.

"Actually, I just met him today. Some business stuff. Is he a friend of yours?"

"Yeah, but more like a big brother. I've been friends with his sister Callie since we were kids. Max even took me to my senior prom because I didn't have a date."

"*That*," I said, "tells me every other boy in your school was an idiot."

"Oh," she said. "That's very sweet."

She was blushing.

We moved down the hallway, back into the living room.

"It's a great house," I said.

"It is," she said. "This will sound like a sales pitch, but it'll go fast."

"I believe you."

"The schools would be Casis, O Henry, and Austin High," she said. "If you have kids."

"No kids," I said.

She nodded. "Me, neither."

I looked around one last time. "Hell of a lot nicer than my apartment."

"I bet. Any concerns? Questions?"

"Maudie's is right down the street. Want to grab something to eat?"

"That sounds nice."


"Were you close with Cole Dunn?" I asked.

"Not so much," she said. "He ran with a different crowd. I hadn't seen him in years. I wish I could say it was a shock the way he went, but I knew he'd been having problems for several years."

I could tell she wasn't enjoying this topic, so I let it drop.

"How long have you been looking for a place?" she asked.

"Not long. Just started."

Maudie's was crowded, as usual, and the food was tasty. Can't beat basic Tex-Mex.

"How many homes have you looked at?" she asked.

"Actually, just the one."

"Really? Well, you started with a good one."

"I think so, but that no-dungeon thing is really holding me back."

"Who can blame you? And what sort of activities do you participate in that require a dungeon?"

I like a woman who enjoys playing along.

"A little of this, a little of that," I said.

"Interesting."

"It can be."

"Let me ask you a question."

"Go right ahead."

"At this point, are we on a date, or is this a realtor buying a client dinner?"

"Do I get to make that decision?"

"You do."

"You don't have a boyfriend?" I said.

"Nope."

"Hard to believe."

"I had a somewhat unpleasant break-up not long ago, and now I'm just having fun."

"Then I'd say this is a date."

"I was hoping you'd go that way. In that case, I think I might have a second margarita."

I signaled for our waiter.

Afterwards, as we went to her condo on the 28th floor of a high-rise in downtown Austin, I got the sense that she was not in the habit of bringing men back to her place. She fidgeted nervously on the long elevator ride, and there was a self-consciousness about her as we kissed in the small entry foyer.

The kisses started slow and light and gradually got more intense.

If she wanted to slow the pace down, she'd pull back and offer me a drink or say she needed to use the bathroom. She did neither of those things.

I began to unbutton her blouse and she whispered into my ear, "I guess you know this means I can't be your realtor."

"At the moment, I'm fine with that."

I removed her blouse and placed it on a nearby credenza. Her bra, like her blouse, was red—made from satin fabric, with a small bit of decorative lace trim in the center.

She began to unbuckle my belt. The condo smelled faintly like vanilla, perhaps from a candle that had burned earlier in the day. Music played quietly from a stereo she had left on in her absence.

She reached for my zipper just as I unclasped her bra.

It was the most enjoyable evening I'd had in a long time.

**14**

Mia called at eight o'clock the next morning.

"I just got an email from Daniel Ivy asking if we have time for a case."

"What kind of case?"

"Construction worker with a neck injury. Another guy on the crew told the supervisor that the guy is faking it."

I was somewhat envious. This would be a straightforward case that would require only one person, and that person would be Mia, because she had been handling Daniel Ivy as a client for the past year or so.

"You should take it," I said.

"You sure?"

We'd bought Mia a used Chevy Tahoe for this type of situation, because she couldn't tail a subject discreetly in her classic Mustang fastback.

"Yeah. I'll keep working on this other thing."

Kiersten came back into the bedroom with a mug of coffee and set it on the nightstand. She was wearing a royal blue kimono-style robe that she casually slipped from her shoulders, letting it fall to the floor. Her naked body was stunning in the morning light—taut and toned in all the right places. Any self-consciousness from last night had disappeared. She got under the sheets and snuggled up beside me.

"If I have any luck, I'll get some video tonight," Mia said. "The coworker says they're supposed to play softball at seven. That's how he knows the guy is faking—he saw him playing two nights ago."

Kiersten began to rub the hair on my chest.

"Good luck," I said.

"Okay, then," Mia said. "I'll touch base later and see if you're making any headway."

Kiersten slowly ran a finger downward and began to circle my navel. Playful. She was intentionally trying to distract me.

"Roy?" Mia said.

"That sounds good," I said.

"What does?"

"The softball game."

"Are you surfing the Web right now?"

She got annoyed when I didn't give her my full attention. Bad habit of mine.

"Yeah, sorry," I said. "I'll let you go now."

"Hang on a second," she said. "What did you do last night? Anything interesting?" Her tone of voice was teasing, as if she knew exactly where I'd been and what I'd done. Had she seen me at dinner with Kiersten?

"Not a lot," I said. "Why?"

"Nothing in particular you want to tell me about?" she asked.

"Nope."

"Oh, come on, Roy. How was it?"

"Excuse me?"

Now Kiersten's hand went further downward and firmly gripped my erection. It was all I could do to stop from making a small moan of pleasure.

"I saw the van parked outside the house on Raleigh," Mia said.

Well, duh. Of course.

"Oh," I said, relieved. "Nothing gets past you, does it?"

"Remember, I am a trained surveillance professional," she said. "How was it? Did you like the place?"

Kiersten began to slide her hand up and down. My concentration was totally shot. "Hey, I got another call coming in," I said. "I'll tell you about it later, okay?"

"Sure, no problem."

I hung up.

"You little minx," I said to Kiersten.

"Can't help myself," she said.

"And I thought you were a respectable member of the real-estate community," I said.

"Speaking of which, I have a showing in one hour," she said. "So you'd better stop talking and start using this time wisely."


I showered at her place, and because I keep a spare set of fresh clothes in the van, I didn't need to go home before I started working for the day. So I went to a coffee shop on the ground floor of Kiersten's condo building and sat down to make a list of ways I might possibly move the Dunn case forward.

Ten minutes later I had nothing, which is a pretty short list.

I began to wonder if I should write an email to Heidi explaining that we'd put our best efforts into it and we didn't see much hope of finding the coin collection. Bail out. There wouldn't be any shame in it. Heidi would understand. Then I could take the day off, and maybe even meet Kiersten upstairs at noon so she could interrupt some more of my phone calls.

I liked her a lot. What wasn't to like?

I had learned that she was 28 years old, originally from Plano, but her family had moved here when she was four years old. She was a big college football fan. She read at least one novel per week— actual printed books, although she was tempted to buy a Kindle. She loved to travel and had most recently been to Mumbai for something called the Banganga music festival. She had a small scar on the back of her upper left thigh from when, at the age of eleven, she tried to vault over a chain-link fence and got snagged.

Admittedly, I hadn't been quite as forthcoming. Sure, I'd told her what I did for a living, but I hadn't fully explained my dealings with Max Dunn. I hadn't revealed that he was connected to one of my cases, because then she might have thought I'd only contacted her to fish for information about the Dunns. And that wasn't the reason. Nope. Not completely. When I texted her the first time, my primary purpose was to request a showing at the Raleigh house. Honest. But I figured if I happened to learn something about Max Dunn in the process, that would merely be a bonus.

I got up and got a second cup of coffee. This little shop wasn't as crowded as one would expect it to be, considering all the pedestrian traffic downtown.

I sat back down and continued working on my list.

Thirty minutes passed. Still nothing.

Time to change gears. Switch tactics. Come at it from a different angle.

Sometimes instead of trying to prove who did it, your best course was to prove who *didn't* do it. Rule the suspects out, one by one, until only one remained. Or maybe, in this case, nobody would remain, because all the suspects were innocent, and we'd never know who stole the coins. It could have been some random burglar, or maybe Alex Dunn had sold the entire collection without telling anyone.

So be it.

Who should I rule out first? And how would I do it?

I had Leo Pitts's address from the background check I'd done on him two days earlier, and it was only a fifteen-minute drive to his home in South Austin, so I swung by. His gold Mazda truck was parked in the driveway.

The house was nicer than I'd been expecting, considering who lived there. Nothing fancy—just a small frame home—but the paint was fresh and the lawn was mowed.

I parked along the curb and got out. Quiet street. The curtains on Leo's front windows were drawn tight. I walked up the driveway, and as I passed the passenger side of his truck, I dropped my keys.

As I scooped them off the ground with my right hand, I used my left hand to quickly tuck a small magnetic "slap and track" GPS device under the wheel well of his rear tire. It was a smooth and practiced motion, and the truck itself shielded the view anyone might have from inside Pitts's house, so I had no qualms about taking a risk like this in broad daylight.

Once I was on the porch, I pushed the doorbell button, but it made no sound, so I knocked. No response in thirty seconds, so I knocked harder. I heard movement inside, so I stepped back about three feet. Then Leo opened the door and recognized me instantly.

"What the fuck?" he said, and he began to close the door.

I held up my hands. "Relax, okay? I came to apologize."

He looked skeptical. "What're you talking about?"

"I was wrong the other day," I said. "I know enough about this case now to know you didn't steal the coins, so I wanted to say sorry for hassling you. I don't blame you for punching me. Nice shot, by the way. Totally had me sucking for air. You related to Jake LaMotta?"

"Who?"

"Never mind. Anyway, like I said, sorry for the static, and there's one other thing." I made a show of glancing over my shoulder, then spoke in a lower voice, saying, "You didn't hear this from me, but I happen to know the cops working the case are trying hard to get search warrants. You follow me?"

His eyes widened. "They're gonna search my place?"

"They've been hassling you, right?" I said.

"They asked me a bunch of questions."

"Dickhead named Ruelas?"

"Yeah. Exactly. Guy's an ass." Pitts said.

"You tell him you got that coin at a garage sale?"

"Nah, man, because what really happened was Cole gave it to me. He owed me some money. I didn't want to get into all that crap with you the other day, so I made up that stuff about a garage sale."

"Hey, I don't blame you, but I wouldn't be surprised if Ruelas didn't believe you about the money."

"But it's the truth."

I shrugged. "All I know is, he'll probably come after you pretty hard, so be prepared."

"So he *is* going to search my place?"

"Hey, man, I can't say for sure—you know what I mean?—because I could get in some serious trouble. But it never hurts to be cautious. That's all I'm saying. And the sooner, the better."

I winked at him.

He nodded like we had just shared a private message.

I turned and started down the porch steps.

Leo called out, "Hey, thanks, man."

I gave a wave over my shoulder without looking back. *No big deal. Just helping a bro out.*


An hour passed and Pitts didn't react.

I was parked two blocks away at a shopping center, monitoring the GPS unit on my laptop, and there was no movement. I was surprised, frankly. I figured, at a minimum, he had drugs or drug paraphernalia in the house, and he'd want to stash that stuff somewhere else for the time being. But nothing happened.

A tracking device could be tremendously helpful, albeit illegal. Cops could use them with a warrant, but a guy like me? No way. Didn't stop me, though, because I had never heard of a case where anyone had been prosecuted for using one.

Boredom began to set in, as it often does when you are on a stakeout.

I thought about Kiersten. Did I want to see her again? Sure. There was nothing wrong with a little no-obligation dating and associated fooling around, was there? I sent her a text:

**This is your neighbor in the building next door. You need better curtains. But that gentleman last night was a genuine hunk. Kudos to you, sister.**

If she hadn't put me into her contact list yet, she might get fooled for a second or two, and really, what more can a guy ask for?

She didn't answer right away. Probably at another showing. Or maybe still the first one. Or doing other realtor stuff.

I waited some more.

Kiersten returned my text: **lol. Right about the hunk part.**

I said: **Dinner tomorrow night?**
She said: **Aw, can't. The next night?**
I said: **Sounds good.**
Then, just before eleven o'clock, the GPS unit began to move.

**15**

Pitts went south on Lamar Boulevard.

I was tracking his progress via an app on my iPhone. The nice thing about the GPS unit is that I didn't have to keep him in sight. In fact, I didn't even have to follow him in real time. I could always check the app later and see where he went. But that wasn't ideal in this situation. What if he met with a particular person and I wasn't there to see it? The app couldn't tell me who that person was, of course. So I hung a few blocks back, knowing that when he eventually arrived at his destination, I would try to get a glimpse without Pitts seeing me first.

He came to Manchaca Road and took a left. He followed that down to Stassney, where he took another left. He drove for another minute or so, and then the GPS unit stopped moving. Several minutes passed, and he was still stopped, so I knew he wasn't waiting at a traffic light. I parked at a medical clinic and quickly hopped out of the van carrying a backpack. I was wearing sunglasses and a baseball cap—a master of disguise!

I followed the sidewalk east for forty feet, then stopped to check my phone. I looked just like any other douche bag who'd stop in the middle of a public sidewalk to check his phone. That was the idea.

According to the app, the GPS device was approximately 112 feet away, ahead and to my right. What was the next business I was coming to? I saw two matching stone buildings, but I didn't know what they were. Very few windows, so they weren't offices. I started walking again, and as I neared the end of the first stone building, I could see that there was a rolling gate between the two buildings, and now I could read the sign at the far end of the second building: Stassney Self Storage.

The app was showing that the GPS device was directly to my right, beyond the rolling gate. Pitts had entered this complex to access a rental storage unit. He had already been in there for several minutes, so now I had to act fast.

Still holding my phone, I checked Google Maps and saw that there were four more buildings behind the two stone buildings. A renter could drive through the gate and pull up right to his unit. Problem was, I wanted to learn which unit was Pitts's, but I couldn't see him or his vehicle. And I couldn't just walk onto the property, because it was gated.

I began to walk around the perimeter of the complex, hoping I might get a glimpse down the rows of rental units, but the entire lot was surrounded by a privacy fence. When I got to the rear of the property, along a quiet residential road running parallel to Stassney, I stopped and checked the app again. Now I was 97 feet from the GPS device. I walked eastward along the sidewalk and the distance dropped to 92...then 87...then back up to 94. I moved backward, to the spot where I was 87 feet from the device. This was as close as I could get on this side of the fence.

I slipped my phone into my pocket and placed both hands on the top of the privacy fence. I hoisted myself up just enough to see over the fence, and there, down a row of rental units, was the gold Mazda truck. I didn't see Pitts, but the door to a rental unit was open. There were no other vehicles or people on this row. I counted quickly. Pitts's unit was the fifth door down on the right.

I dropped back down to the ground and continued on my way

around the block. I returned to the van and waited. Five minutes passed. Then ten. Finally the GPS unit showed movement again. Pitts had exited the storage facility and was now driving west on Stassney. I stayed put, in the parking lot of the medical clinic, and a few seconds later I saw Pitts drive past.

Then I returned to the storage facility and rented a unit.


Sometimes I made Mia uncomfortable by crossing legal or ethical lines. Often, instead of not crossing those lines, I chose to leave Mia in the dark. She was aware that I did that sometimes, although she didn't know the specifics, which was the point. Sometimes she came down on me hard if she learned about my choices later, but she had never given me an ultimatum about not crossing those lines. Which was good, because that might've harmed our partnership. My view was that there were times when you had to push the boundaries, as long as you were prepared to live with your choices and could sleep well at night.

Like now. It was seven hours after I had tailed Pitts to the storage facility and I was about to break the law.

I pulled up to the gate in the van and entered the security code on the keypad. The gate rolled open and I entered, driving past the office, which was dark and unmanned at this hour. That's why I had waited. There were three hours in the morning and three in the evening when no employee was present but renters could still access the facility.

I drove between the two stone buildings and took a left, and then a quick right down the second of the four rows of storage units. My unit was one row over, but Leo Pitts's unit was up ahead on the left. Luckily, the row was empty of vehicles and people. I hadn't seen anyone else on the property yet.

I parked the van good and tight against the door to Pitts's unit. Before I did anything else, I checked the GPS tracking app on my phone. Pitts's Mazda truck was parked in front of his house, just as it had been an hour ago. If it moved, the app would alert me.

All systems go.

I got out of the van with a pair of bolt cutters in my hands. Acted like I belonged here. Went straight to the unit's roll-up door—which was like a garage door, but smaller—and popped the combination lock on the handle. Took the pieces of the lock and put them in the van, along with the bolt cutters.

I rolled the door upward and wasn't surprised to see a unit filled about halfway with dusty cardboard boxes and old furniture. Saw an exercise bicycle and a stack of obsolete stereo components. A rolled-up area rug and a washing machine. If Pitts had come here earlier today with the curio box containing Alex Dunn's coin collection, he had not left it in plain sight.

I took three steps forward. It was important that I leave things as I'd found them. I took two latex gloves out of my pocket and put them on, which was a bit of a chore, because my hands were somewhat sweaty.

I didn't care about anything except the coins. Where would he hide them? Would they still be in the curio box? Logic said no. Why keep that box? It would only serve as evidence to tie him to the crime. So...no box. Which meant the coins could be stashed in spaces that wouldn't necessarily have accommodated the box.

My phone was turned down, but it vibrated with an incoming text.

Mia said: **I am totally busting this guy.**

Cool. She was referring to the softball player. I gave her a thumbs-up and returned to my search.

First I tried a chest of drawers, which was shoved up against the left-hand wall of the unit. Your basic cheap dresser, about four feet high, with five drawers. The first drawer was empty. So was the second drawer. The third drawer contained what appeared to be a significant quantity of heroin. Holy crap. I glanced to my left—to the door of the unit—purely from nerves. Nobody out there. Just the van waiting there, filling up most of the space.

I did not touch the heroin. Actually, it could have been cocaine or even speed, because it was a white powder, but I was guessing it was heroin, based on Leo Pitts's ties to Cole Dunn, and because heroin was currently about as cheap and plentiful as it had ever been before. Maybe a narcotics investigator could identify the drug by sight alone, but I couldn't. Whichever drug it was, it was packaged inside small twist-tied pouches contained inside a zipped sandwich bag. Probably at least 20 or 25 grams, ready for individual sales. If I were caught here right now, in the presence of this stash, I'd be in serious trouble—like get-a-lawyer-quick kind of trouble.

I closed that drawer and checked the remaining two. Nothing.

Finding the heroin had deflated any optimism that I might discover the coins. The drugs were the reason Pitts had thanked me for alerting him about a possible police search, and why he had come to the storage unit.

I gave the rest of the place a quick search—working under the assumption that if the drugs were simply stuck in a drawer, the coins would be hidden in an equally uncreative manner—but I came up empty. The only other discovery of relevance was a stack of ten-year-old AARP magazines mailed to the attention of Phyllis Pitts. I was willing to wager that Phyllis was Leo's mom. Leo was stashing his drugs in his mother's rental unit, because if the unit was in his name, it could be searched right along with his residence. What a lowlife. Phyllis could get busted for the drugs. The charges might not stick, but they'd make her life hell for a good while. Not my problem.

I closed the unit. Then I got back into the van and searched through my collection of spare locks—which I keep for this purpose—and found one identical to the combination lock I'd cut off earlier. I snapped the new lock into place on the door, and then I got the hell out of there.

**16**

"He went three for five," Mia said. "That included a double where he slid into base headfirst. Then he made a diving catch out in left field. Good stuff. Got great video of it all."

We had just ordered breakfast at the Magnolia Café on Lake Austin Boulevard. It was jam-packed, as always. There aren't many genuine old Austin hippies running around these days, but our waitress was one of them. I knew this from discussions I'd had with her on previous visits to the diner. She was about 65 years old, slender from serving tables all day, and she moved about like a teenage girl. Her face was creased and weathered—a testament to the life she'd led so far.

"Have you sent the clips to Daniel Ivy?"

"Last night," Mia said. "Haven't heard back yet."

"I'm sure he'll be thrilled. Nice work."

"Thanks."

Mia's quick turnaround hadn't quite set a record for how quickly either of us had solved a fraud case, but wrapping it up within 24 hours was pretty damned impressive.

A couple of customers squeezed past on my right to get to a table in the back. They were youngsters. College age. Boy and girl. They held hands across the table as they scanned the menu.

"Roy?"

"Yeah?"

I realized she had said something before that, but I hadn't caught it.

"Boy, you are really distracted."

True enough. I was thinking about Leo Pitts's storage unit. Working theory: He was Cole Dunn's dealer, and Cole had paid him for dope with one of Alex Dunn's coins—the one I bought on eBay. But did he have more coins? Didn't look like it, because if he did have some coins, he would've hidden them in the storage unit, same as the dope. Right? Why would he hide them anywhere else?

"Sorry," I said. "The Dunn case has me brain dead."

"So what's up? Fill me in."

*Here we go.* Time to spill the beans. She needed to know this information, and there was no way to share it without revealing how I'd learned it. So I told her what I'd done.

"You really are nuts, you know that?" she said.

"Only in a clinical sense," I said.

Right then, the waitress showed up. "Here you go, hon," she said, setting a plate piled high with migas in front of me. "And French toast for you, sweetheart," she said to Mia. "Anything else?"

"I think we're all set," Mia said. "Thanks."

"Y'all enjoy."

When she was gone, Mia said, "What if you'd been caught?"

I sipped some coffee. "I have to say, that blouse really works for you. The color matches your eyes perfectly. You look lovely."

She gave me a look that said, *Don't try to derail the conversation with that bullshit.*

"I'm serious," I said. "Just because I'm ducking your question, that doesn't make it any less true."

"Roy," she said, sounding mildly exasperated.

"What?"

She shook her head. *Stop toying with me.*

So I stopped.

"What happens when Leo Pitts tries to open his locker?" she said.

"He thinks his lock is screwed up, or that he forgot the combination, so he cuts it off, finds everything as he left it, and is relieved nobody stole his dope."

"Does the place have security cameras?"

"Nope. Not a one. This place isn't that nice."

"The cameras could've been hidden."

"But that wouldn't make sense. They would mount the cameras in the most noticeable spot possible, along with signs drawing attention to them. That's what deters trespassers and thieves. There weren't any cameras. Hey, it's not like I don't think these things through beforehand."

"And yet you still do them anyway," she said.

I had to smile at that one.

"Seriously, Roy," she said, lowering her voice, "regardless of committing a jailable offense—forget about that part—now you've put us into a position where we know about the guy's drug stash, but we can't do anything about it."

"Like what? Report it?"

"Exactly. Somebody else could overdose."

"Well, if I hadn't done what I did, we wouldn't have known about the drugs, so we couldn't have reported them anyway."

She shook her head as a means of saying she wasn't going to argue about it. If she had continued, she would've said I was rationalizing. She said that a lot—because I did it a lot.

"In fact," I said, "now that he's a little nervous and thinks the cops are breathing down his neck, maybe he won't sell for a while. Maybe my little trespassing episode will prevent a tragedy."

"Don't forget criminal mischief. They'd slap you with that, too."

I let it go, chiefly because she had the moral high ground in this situation, as she usually did. I was the one willing to cut ethical corners if I felt it helped me accomplish a larger, more important goal, and if no innocent people were hurt in the process. I realize that philosophy is riddled with potential pitfalls. Luckily, I hadn't fallen into one yet. Matter of time, I guess.

We both ate in silence for a moment, until Mia changed the subject by saying, "Hey, you never told me about the house on Raleigh. Did you like it?"

I had a mouth full of eggs, but after I swallowed, I said, "Nice place. Wouldn't need any work at all. Beautiful inside."

"You'd love the neighborhood," Mia said.

She truly seemed excited by the prospect of living so close together.

The waitress came around again and refilled my iced tea.

Mia said, "Was it the listing agent who showed you the place, or do you have a realtor now? I didn't mean to force Abby on you the other day, but you should hire a realtor, if you're serious about the house."

I could feel my face flushing a bit as I thought about Kiersten.

"Actually," I said, "I called the agent who's selling Max Dunn's house."

Mia would immediately understand why I had done that. All else being equal, why not call Max Dunn's agent?

She said, "Oh, that was smart. Did you learn anything useful from him?"

"Her," I said. "No, not really. I poked around a little bit"—I almost laughed at my inadvertent choice of words—"but she didn't know anything about Dunn's financial situation, or if she did, she didn't share it. She's probably bound by a code of ethics not to discuss that sort of thing."

Mia was just about to reply when my phone began to play the opening notes of Loverboy's "Working for the Weekend," which meant it was a text from Heidi, our client.

It was early in the day for her to be contacting me, so I knew it was going to be good. Or bad. Or at least newsworthy in one sense or another. And it was.

**Call me**, Heidi said. **Serenity Sweet was arrested last night for theft.**


People play you for a sucker all the time. I know that from experience. They'll lie right to your face, or even steal something when you turn your head. Later, they'll swear up and down—convincingly—that they didn't lie, or they didn't steal, or they weren't faking an injury, or they had not slept with that particular man or woman. I'd hoped Serenity Sweet wasn't in this category, and maybe she wasn't, despite what we learned that morning. The facts were still somewhat sketchy.

Shortly after the text from Heidi, we went out to the van and called her. First thing she said over speakerphone was, "All I know at this point is that they found the curio box at Serenity's place."

"They got a search warrant?" I asked.

"Don't know. I assume so."

"Where did they find the box?" I asked.

"Don't know."

"Who searched the place—APD or Travis County?"

"Don't know."

"So that really was all you know," I said.

"Handsome," Heidi said, "but slow on the uptake sometimes."

"Handsome, eh?" I said.

"Don't let it go to your head."

"So they found the box, but not the coins?" Mia said.

"That's the situation as I understand it," Heidi said. "Ruelas left a voicemail earlier, but there wasn't much to it. I assume if they'd found the coins, he would've mentioned that part. I called him back and left a message."

"Interesting," Mia said.

"Obviously, this doesn't close the case," Heidi said, "but it gives us plenty of justification for denying the claim—until we know more."

"If she did steal the coins," Mia said, "won't you still have to pay out?"

"Sure," Heidi said, "but if she stole them, there's a good chance we can get them back. Maybe she still has them, or if she managed to sell them, we can get them back from the buyer."

"Or maybe she didn't steal anything," I said.

Mia and Heidi both remained quiet.

"It's still possible, you know," I said.

Heidi said, "Is it also possible, my dear, that you are overly enchanted by this woman and her attributes?"

Mia grinned.

"Well, sure it is," I said. "You're talking about her eyes, right?

Gorgeous. Only Liz Taylor had eyes that captivating."

"Let's just wait and see what Ruelas has to say," Heidi said.

"You mind if we call him?" Mia asked.

"Be my guest. Let me know if you learn anything."

We hung up and Mia immediately called Ruelas. No answer. She left a voicemail. Then we waited for ten minutes, hoping he would call back. He didn't.

So I said, "How about if we skip Ruelas and go straight to the source?"

"Meaning Serenity? You think we should call her?"

"Or just drive over there," I said. "It's not far. There's a good chance she's bonded out by now, or she will be in the next couple of hours."

"We might as well check," Mia said. "She'll probably actually be happy to see us."

# 17

Serenity's front door swung open and a very large man said, "Who the fuck are you? You're trespassing."

He stood about six-three and was broad enough that I couldn't see past him into the house. He had the enormous rounded muscles of a steroid junkie, and any exposed skin seemed to be glistening, perhaps with baby oil. He was in his late twenties, with a jaw like a tractor shovel. His hair was sheared to about a quarter-inch, and it was thinning on top, but he was trying to make up for it by growing a beard. Directly in the center of his forehead was a perfectly round scar—still somewhat red, so it couldn't have been very old. Bullet wound? If so, the man was lucky to be standing here.

"Uh, my name is Otto Preminger and I'm casting a new feature about the Visigoths. Ever done any work in front of a camera?"

He continued to glare at me for several long seconds. Then he looked at Mia for a moment. Then back at me. "I don't like it when people fuck with me. Are you fucking with me?"

"Never," I said. "Nope. No way."

Mia spoke up. "I'm Mia Madison and my wildly inappropriate

partner here is Roy Ballard. We work on fraud cases for insurance companies. We met with Serenity three days ago about the Alex Dunn situation. We understand she was arrested last night, and if she is innocent, we are still willing to help her."

"What the hell do you mean 'if she is innocent'?" the ogre said.

He took a half-step toward Mia as he spoke—body language that was plainly meant to intimidate. This was a guy who regularly used his size to cow people. I guess I couldn't blame him.

"Buddy," I said, "all we did was knock on the door. If Serenity isn't in there, just tell us and we'll leave. If she's in there and doesn't want to talk, that's fine, too. But if you—"

"Roy," Mia said.

I couldn't stop myself. "But if you make another move toward my partner, I promise you'll wish you hadn't."

By this time, my face and the back of my neck were burning hot. I could feel sweat beginning under my arms and in the small of my back. Adrenaline had kicked in hard and fast, and my own words had stoked my anger. I hadn't intended to get this worked up, but I also meant every word I said.

The big man was staring at me with a poker face. I couldn't tell if he was contemplating maiming me or wondering what he might have for lunch later. After two more seconds, he said, "Hang on."

He closed the door.

I let out a breath.

"One of these days, Roy," Mia said quietly. "But thank you."

"I might not be willing to die for you," I said, "but I guess I'd be willing to have my arms ripped from their sockets."

Now the door swung open again, and there stood Serenity. She laughed and shook her head when she saw us. "Did he scare you?" she said.

"Only in the sense that I thought I might die," I said.

"Sorry about that," Serenity said. "He thought you might be with one of the TV stations. Come on in."


Mia and I sat on the same couch we'd occupied three days earlier, while Serenity and the big guy, who was named Colin Kelly, sat together on the love seat. It was a tight fit. Serenity was wearing a muumuu again, and I began to suspect that this was her go-to outfit when relaxing at home.

"You still believe me?" Serenity said. "That I'm innocent?"

Mia looked at me, knowing I'd insist on answering that one, but no doubt apprehensive about what I might say.

I said, "Let me put it this way: I believe you, and I think Mia does, too, but we've both been fooled plenty of times. I hope you're telling the truth, because I know for sure that I liked you right off the bat, and nothing sucks worse than when somebody you like turns out to be jerking you around. Have you ever been in a situation like that?"

Serenity said, "Sure. I guess everybody has."

I looked at Colin. "How about you?"

He gave a slow nod, but he didn't appear particularly happy. Perhaps still stewing that I'd called him out. Or maybe that was just the way he was. I couldn't figure out the relationship between him and Serenity. Friend? Neighbor? Manager? Bodyguard?

"So all I can do is go with my gut, and yeah, I think you told us the complete truth when we were here last time. Of course, the bottom line is that we were hired to find the coin collection, and that's what we're trying to do, regardless of who took it."

"Meaning you'll bust me in a heartbeat if you find out I did it," Serenity said. She was grinning again. Colin was still doing an impression of Mount Rushmore.

"Absolutely," I said.

"Without question," Mia said.

"Well, the good news is, I *am* innocent. Maybe you can help me prove it."

"Baby," Colin said. "You sure about this?"

*Baby.* Not her manager, unless he was a manager with benefits.

Serenity took one of his large hands in hers. "Ronnie told me to stop talking to the cops, but he didn't say anything about insurance investigators." She looked at us again. "Ronnie is my attorney."

"So what happened yesterday?" Mia asked.

"I'd just finished lunch when the cops knocked on my door. It was that guy Ruelas, along with an officer from the Austin Police Department. He asked if he could search the shed in my backyard."

"Shoulda said no," Colin muttered.

"I know," Serenity said, squeezing his hand, "and I wish I had. They didn't have a warrant—it was completely voluntary—but I said yes, because I have nothing to hide. Stupid. They wanted me to stay in the house, so I watched through the back window. Ruelas opened the door and didn't even step inside. He pointed at something and the Austin cop looked in the shed, too. Then they took some pictures, and then they went inside and came out with Alex's wooden box—the one he kept his coins in."

"Somebody set her up," Colin said.

"It's just so stupid," Serenity said. "First, if I stole those coins, why would I hang onto that box? And second, if I did hang onto the box, why would I leave it in a shed in my backyard?"

"Because it was a set-up," Colin said.

"Which is what I told the cops," Serenity said, plainly frustrated, "but they didn't believe me. I still refused to answer any questions, so they left, and they came back a few hours later with an arrest warrant. I had to spend the damn night in jail."

Colin was seething. I could almost feel the heat coming off him.

"Any idea how they knew to look in your shed?" I asked.

"None at all. If they had asked to search my house, I would have said no, just on general principle. But the shed? That seemed so harmless. All I keep back there is junk."

"You should've said no, then searched the shed yourself," Colin said. "I wish you would've called me."

"Serenity," I said, "is there any chance they'll find your fingerprints on that box?"

I knew from photos that the box had a lacquered finish that would easily hold prints.

I could tell from the defeated expression on her face that the answer wasn't good. "It's possible. Alex would sometimes show me the coins he'd bought. I might've touched the lid of the box."

This was new information. Why had she not mentioned that during our first interview? She might not have considered it relevant, but it was.

"When was the last time you touched it?" Mia asked.

Serenity shrugged. "Could have been as recent as a couple weeks ago."

"None of this matters," Colin said, "because somebody planted that box in her shed. That should be obvious to any motherfucker with a brain."

Serenity gave him a sharp glance, presumably because of his language.

"I'm sorry," he said. "This is just such...bullcrap."

Obviously not his first choice of words.

"It's horse hockey, is what it is," I said. "Possibly even cow fritters."

He gave me the glare again, but only for a moment, and then he smiled—just a little, and it was a reluctant smile, but it was a smile nonetheless.

"He's right that it wouldn't have been hard for somebody to get back there," Serenity said.

She didn't have to convince me, considering I had broken into Leo Pitts's rental unit the night before.

"Was there a lock on the shed?" I asked.

Serenity shook her head.

"A lock on the gate into your backyard?"

"Yes, but the fence is only four feet tall. Easy enough for someone to jump over it."

"I've been saying you need to get a dog," Colin said.

"But the lock wasn't cut?" Mia asked.

"No," Serenity said.

"I never noticed—can you see the shed from the street?" I asked.

"You can, from one spot, looking through the trees."

"She needs some security lights," Colin said. "I've been meaning to install some, and maybe some security cameras. Considering her line of work, we don't need anyone thinking they can come around and pay a visit."

"Do you know if any of your neighbors have cameras?" Mia asked.

"I haven't ever noticed," Serenity said.

"I think the house on the corner has some," Colin said, pointing south. "The house on the right."

"Before or after the stop sign?" I asked.

"Before. The northwest corner."

"We'll check that out," I said.

Colin nodded.

"Did you see anyone hanging around lately that made you suspicious?" I asked.

She began shaking her head.

I was contemplating warning her that the cops would be back with a search warrant for her house—possibly any minute now, or this afternoon, or tomorrow at the latest. But her lawyer had surely told her that would happen.

I tried to think of questions we hadn't asked the first time we'd interviewed her.

"Have you ever met any of Alex Dunn's children?"

"No."

"How about Alex Dunn's second wife, Alicia Potter?" Mia asked.

"You kidding? My clients generally don't want me to meet their wives. Besides, isn't she his ex-wife now?"

"Yeah, she is. Did Alex talk about her much?"

"He mentioned her now and then, but nothing ugly. In fact, I think they had dinner occasionally."

"Did she come to his house?" I asked.

"That I don't know."

"Did he talk about his kids?" I asked.

"Some."

"Did he ever say anything that now, in hindsight, seems like it might've been related to his death, or to the disappearance of the coins?" I asked.

"Sorry, no. Nothing I can remember."

"Any chance you know a guy named Leo Pitts?" I asked.

"Don't think so. That name isn't familiar. Who is he?"

"One of Cole's friends," I said. "Nothing important. I'm just fishing. You haven't seen a gold Mazda truck in the area lately?"

"Not that I remember."

"How about a red BMW?"

"Same thing. Don't remember one."

"We'll definitely be keeping an eye out for scumbags now," Colin said. "I live way the hell out in Leander, but I'm gonna stay here for the time being. Let 'em try and come back. I'll be ready. I've got a shotgun in the bedroom."

It was hard to tell whether Serenity was happy with that arrangement. I didn't point out that it was unlikely that the person who had planted the curio box—if that was indeed what had happened—would ever return.

"Just, uh, don't, uh—" I said.

"You carry a gun?" Colin asked.

"I usually fight people off with my scathing wit."

"So you don't carry one?"

"Honestly, Colin, that's not something I discuss with anyone."

"Yeah, okay. That's cool. I gotcha."

He actually winked at me, like we were new pals sharing a secret. I looked at Mia to see if she had any other questions. She didn't.

"Thanks for talking to us," I said to Serenity.

"What exactly are you gonna do to help her?" Colin asked.

"Pardon?"

"That sounded shitty and I didn't mean it that way. What I'm saying is, whatever you're gonna do, if you need some backup, just let me know."

Mia cleared her throat. Her way of saying, *I'm his backup, you oversized cretin. And he is mine.*

"I will certainly keep that in mind," I said.

# 18

Colin was right. The house on the northwest corner of the nearby intersection did have at least one security camera. I could see it mounted in a corner of the ceiling above the covered porch. But when Mia and I ascended the steps, I was in for a letdown.

"Pretty sure that's a dummy," I said.

You could buy fake security cameras for about ten bucks online. Did they deter burglars? Possibly. But I was familiar enough with the most common models, both real and fake, that I could generally distinguish between the two.

"You sure?" Mia asked.

I got closer, craning my neck upward. "Yep."

"Well, that sucks," Mia said.

We turned around and left. We checked other homes in the vicinity, but we didn't see any other cameras. Disappointing.

"I think this might be the most frustrating case I've ever experienced," I said after we were back in the van.

Mia didn't say anything. I looked over and she was checking her phone, smiling.

"What?" I said. "Did Ruelas call back?"

"Oh, no, sorry. It's nothing."

'Nothing' probably meant a text from Garlen.

A moment later, she said, "Where are we going?"

"I don't know. Any suggestions?"

"Roy, what's the deal?"

"About what?"

"About *you*. For the past few weeks, you've seemed so touchy, like something's bothering you."

"Sorry. Must be the whole Mercury in retrograde thing."

She didn't say anything.

"Just moody, I guess," I said, dead serious now. "It'll pass. Now, any suggestions on what we should do next, because I'm at a loss."

We reached Barton Springs Road and I turned right, then left a minute later on Lamar.

"Based on what Max and Serenity have both told us, it sounds like Alicia and Alex had fairly regular contact after the divorce," Mia said. "Makes me wonder if she sometimes went to his house. Did she have a key?"

"You'd think she'd know those coins wouldn't be easy to sell," I said.

"We've had this conversation already about the kids," Mia said.

"Yep."

We crossed Town Lake—now known as Lady Bird Lake—and it was shimmering like a jewel with late-morning sunlight. Then I caught a green light at the intersection of Sixth Street and turned westward.

Then I totally changed my mind and hung a U-turn on Fifth Street, then went south on Lamar.

"Roy, where are you going?"

I turned west on Barton Springs.

"Roy? Are we going back to Serenity's house?"

"Let's take a break," I said. "Do something completely different. Maybe that will help."

Mia was always a sport in moments like these. She could roll with the flow with the best of them.

"And what might that be?" she asked.

We were now in Zilker Park, and I took a left, followed by another quick left.

"Are we going to the pecan grove?" Mia asked.

"Nope," I said.

Then she looked to her right, toward Barton Creek, and saw a banner that read: CANOE RENTAL IS OPEN. She began to grin.

Mia sat facing me, while I paddled slowly backwards.

"You can't see where you're going," Mia said.

"Warn me if I'm about to hit an iceberg."

"Don't you want to see the water ahead? It's beautiful."

"The view this way is pretty nice, too," I said, looking right at her.

"You're sweet," she said.

There were a few other canoes on the water, along with a handful of paddle-boarders, but the closest was thirty or forty yards away.

I stopped paddling for a moment and just drifted. We were on Barton Creek, east of the famous Barton Springs Pool. Roughly a third of a mile ahead of us, the creek fed into the lake. We'd go that far and turn around. There was no reason to rush.

"The sun feels great," Mia said. "Not too hot yet. And a nice breeze."

I could imagine being here under different circumstances. I could picture us tying up under a shade tree and eating lunch out of a cooler. Maybe pouring ice-cold champagne into plastic cups. Holding hands. Kissing. Slowly and gently at first. Then making out like a couple of teenagers until we couldn't stand it anymore and had to hurry back to the car.

Yeah, I could imagine that.

We hadn't spoken for several minutes when Mia said, "We're overlooking something, Roy. There's some connection we aren't making."

I didn't have to say anything. She knew I agreed.

"Have you checked eBay for any other hobo nickels?" she asked.

"Yeah. Several times a day. Nada."

I began to paddle again. It felt good to work my shoulder muscles.

"I wish Ruelas would call us back," she said. "Maybe the case against Serenity is stronger than we suspect."

"Guess we'll know more when they search her house."

"I'm a little worried about that, to be honest. If she's innocent and someone planted the curio box, what if they put something in her house, like a couple of the hobo nickels?"

"Don't know," I said. Frankly, the sun was making me drowsy and I wasn't inclined to think about the case just then.

"What are we missing, Roy?"

For some reason, I responded in a Humphrey Bogart voice. "Wish I knew, shweetheart. Wish I knew."

Four hours later, Mia received a text from Serenity that the police had arrived with a warrant and were currently searching her home. By then, Serenity had had plenty of time to search the house herself for any planted evidence, and to remove any documents that would implicate her massage clients, assuming she kept any records that could identify them.

The cops were gone in two hours. According to Serenity, also via text, the only thing they had taken—as far as she could tell—was her computer, but she was confident there was nothing of relevance on it and there never had been. The tone of her texts seemed upbeat, as if she'd been proven right.

So Mia and I explained to her that the cops wouldn't necessarily have to tell her if they'd found the hobo nickels or any other possible evidence that could have some bearing on the investigation of Alex Dunn's homicide. They could choose to keep the results of the search to themselves for the time being, if they thought sharing the information might impede the murder case. Serenity's response?

**Well, that sucks. When will this end?**

**19**

That evening, I set out to learn everything I could possibly learn about Alicia Potter.

Criminal history? She was once arrested for trespassing at the age of nineteen. The charge was ultimately dismissed. I Googled the address where the infraction was committed and found that a water tower stood at that location. So she—along with some friends, most likely—had climbed a water tower, or attempted to. Teenage shenanigans. Beyond that, she had nothing except a few traffic tickets.

Her credit was outstanding.

She was a registered voter.

The home she owned was hers outright, with no mortgage.

Alex Dunn had been her second husband. She had been married once before at the age of 23, for sixteen months.

At least 90 percent of the relevant links had to do with the death of Alicia's sister, but I didn't find anything new about that tragedy or the subsequent investigation. The widely held conclusion was that it was an accident.

I got lost in my work and the hours went by quickly. But I didn't make any real progress on the case.

Finally I went back to that message I'd sent to Alicia Potter on Facebook. Still no reply. So I sent another one, saying that I simply wanted to ask a few questions about Alex Dunn's coin collection, and promising that I would only take a couple minutes of her time. If she wanted to do it by phone or email, that was fine with me.

It was fifteen minutes after ten when I heard a knock on my door.

I wasn't expecting anyone, so I expected it to be someone at the wrong address. That happened occasionally in this apartment complex, especially later in the evening. Someone would think they were at Building B when they were at Building C, and they would be looking for the second door on the right down the breezeway on the second floor. Oh, wait. This isn't Sally's apartment. Sorry to bother you.

I opened the door and was met by a handsome face. The face was on a man in his mid-thirties, with a nice tan and white teeth. He was wearing khaki pants, loafers, and an expensive golf shirt. He stood about six feet tall, with a slender but athletic build.

I recognized him from photos Mia had shown me, but I pretended I didn't.

"Roy?" he said.

"Yeah?"

"Garlen Gieger," he said.

"Oh, hey," I said, shaking the hand he now extended. "How's it going?"

I'm sure I appeared slightly puzzled, which wasn't pretense, because I had no idea why he was here. For a moment I wondered how he had gotten my address, until I remembered that I'd invited him to a small barbecue I'd hosted a few months ago. Mia had come alone, which hadn't bothered me a bit.

"Hope I didn't wake you," Garlen said. "You got a minute?"

Right then I could smell the beer on his breath. I was guessing Garlen had been out to happy hour earlier, and that had turned into a longer evening, and now he was here, for some reason.

"Sure. Come on in."

I closed the door behind him, and he declined an offer to sit, saying this would only take a minute. I didn't bother offering him anything to drink.

"You doing all right?" he asked.

"Sure. You?"

"Not bad."

"Good."

"Look," he said. "I just wanted to come over and introduce myself, because Mia and I have been seeing a lot of each other lately. Obviously, I hope that continues, and if it does, I thought you and me should have a little chat. Kind of get to know each other. So we both know the lay of the landscape, as it were."

Perhaps Garlen was a little more inebriated than I'd first thought.

I said, "I, uh—"

"First things first," Garlen said. "I understand that the two of you are partners, and even more than that, you're friends. I totally respect that."

"You do?"

"Absolutely."

I could smell his cologne. It was honestly quite pleasant.

"That's comforting," I said.

Garlen swayed a little on his feet. Just a little.

"She thinks very highly of you, Roy," he said. "I think she even loves you in the same way a sister loves a brother, and I bet it goes both ways. Of course, I'm hoping that's—well, how can I say this? I'm here, right now, because—how was the canoe ride today?"

"The canoe ride?"

"She said you went on a canoe ride."

"Well, yes, we did, in the sense that there was a canoe, we were both in it, and it was on the water."

"That's cute."

"Thanks."

"But why?"

"It was cute because I have a clever way of looking at things."

"No, come on, Roy. You know what I mean. Why a canoe ride?"

"The kayaks were all taken."

He shook a finger at me, like I was quite the mischievous rascal. "She's told me you're funny—and she's right. But let's get serious for a moment, okay? Can we do that?"

"You go first."

"Okay, cool. Look, I guess I'm making this into a big deal, and that's not my intention at all. But going on a canoe ride—that doesn't seem like a partner thing, or even a brother-and-sister thing."

He stopped talking. I waited. He lowered his head and looked at me meaningfully.

"Roy?"

"Yeah?"

"What's the deal on the canoe ride?"

"Garlen?"

"Yes?"

"I'm not entirely sure what you're asking me. Are you under the impression that I took Mia out in the canoe today as some sort of romantic overture?"

"That's, yes, what I'm wondering. Am I off base?"

He was going to wake up tomorrow with a hangover and a lot of regret for having come over here.

"Yes, you are," I said.

He blew out a big breath of relief. "That's good to hear."

"Not that it's really any of your business," I said.

If this situation was going to get ugly, here is where it would start.

"I guess not," he said. "Fair enough."

"Besides, if I wanted to make a romantic overture, I don't think that's the way I'd go about it."

"Well," he said. "It seemed like—"

"What I'd do," I said, "is take her to her favorite restaurant, out of the blue, when she's having a crummy day and needs a little lift. I'm sure you know which restaurant that is."

He blinked a couple of times. His expression said, *But she likes a lot of restaurants. How would I know which one is her favorite?*

I said, "Or I might buy her a big box of a particular kind of candy, because it brings back good memories of hanging out at her grandparents' house."

I would bet money he didn't know I was referring to marzipan.

"Or I might ask her friends to record a short birthday message, and then put all those clips together into a video."

Even in his tipsy state, he had now figured out what I was doing.

"Or I guess you could take her to a zoo," I said.

"Hey, we had fun," he said. "She likes the zoo, in case you didn't know. I just want to make her happy."

I could tell that he meant it. Neither of us spoke for a moment. I'm sure Garlen was a decent guy. If he wasn't dating Mia and we met at a party, we'd probably get along just fine.

"She's just so great," he said. "I feel so happy when I'm around her."

"I can understand that," I said.

"I'm going to ask her to move in with me," he said. "Or, okay, I'm *thinking* about it. It's a big step. I don't want to freak her out."

I didn't want to know any of this, and it was difficult to refrain from telling him it was a bad idea, even though I didn't know if that was true. Maybe Garlen was Mia's perfect match—when he wasn't drinking and feeling insecure about their relationship.

"I think I'd better sit this discussion out," I said.

"Okay, yeah. I don't blame you. Would you do me a favor and not tell her I was here?"

"Only if you promise you won't come back," I said.

"Ha. You *are* funny."

"You probably shouldn't drive," I said.

"No, I'm okay," he said.

"Let me make some coffee," I said. "Just hang around for an hour. Then you can drive. Fair enough?"

He nodded.

"How do you like it?"

"Black is fine."

"Have a seat," I said, gesturing toward the couch.

I went into the kitchen and prepped the coffee pot. When I came back out, he was gone.

**20**

"The truth is, I'm ready to give up on this one," I said the next morning. "We can't solve them all."

"Wow. Good morning to you, too."

"Heidi knows we aren't perfect."

"Heidi would cast your likeness in bronze if the budget allowed for it," Mia said. "That's how highly she thinks of you."

"Yeah," I said. "That's probably true. Must be my modesty."

It was eight-thirty and Mia had called to see what our plan was for the day. I kept thinking about Garlen and his visit the night before. Weird. If it was driven by jealousy, I didn't think that boded well for their future. Then again, I'm no psychologist.

"Let's give it a little more time," Mia said. "Okay?"

"I have no problem with that," I said, "except for having literally no idea what else we can do to find those coins."

The line remained quiet for several moments. We did this sometimes—linger on the phone, hoping one of us would come up with something brilliant. I was sprawled on the couch in my living room. Mia, for all I knew, was still in bed, possibly with Garlen, if he had gone to her place after leaving my apartment.

"Give me a couple of hours to think about it," she said.

"'Kay."

"I still think we're missing something."

"Oh, absolutely. A clue."

"Hey, I was wondering about something yesterday and I forgot to ask. Did you ever remove the GPS unit from Leo Pitts's truck?"

"I'm glad you reminded me," I said.


We agreed that that would be my chore for the morning—retrieving the tracker—while Mia spent some time contemplating new approaches to the case. If she didn't have anything brilliant by lunchtime, I would call Heidi and proudly announce that we were miserable failures.

I logged onto the GPS tracking software and saw that Leo Pitts was currently on the move. Or his truck was. Could be someone else driving. Location: Way the hell out in Pflugerville, moseying along Grand Avenue Parkway. I sat and watched for a while. No sense in going after him right now. Let him get closer and stay put for a period of time. He stopped at a house on Liffey Cove and stayed there for less than five minutes.

Then he went farther north, up into Round Rock, and stopped at another house—again, for about five minutes. This is what the police would call "suspicious behavior," going from house to house and not staying long. The behavior of someone selling illegal products.

Finally, he began to move southward, coming down Loop 1, passing US 183, then 2222, and now I was hoping he was going home. Better yet, maybe he'd stop somewhere at a restaurant or grocery store, where I could remove the unit without stepping onto his property. Which meant it was time for me to get into the van and move in his general direction.

I was already dressed, so I grabbed my keys and my phone and went outside. As I walked to the van, I opened the GPS tracking app on my phone. Pitts was still moving, passing Windsor Road, and then he took the Enfield exit. So he wasn't going home. I started the van but sat for a moment, watching Pitts's movement on my phone screen. He went west on Enfield, took a few more turns, and stopped in front of a familiar address.

Callie Dunn's house.

"Let this be a lesson to us," Mia said when I called to tell her what I'd learned.

"Agreed," I said. "Always be willing to skirt the law to get results."

"No, you goofball," Mia said. "Never give up too soon."

I was back in my apartment. Obviously, we had no plans now to remove the tracker from Pitts's truck. Later, but not now. I just had to hope he didn't get a flat tire or need service on his truck in the meantime, because the unit would be easily visible to anyone working underneath the vehicle.

"Okay," I said, "we learned something new, but what does it mean? Leo Pitts was friends with Cole Dunn, and Callie was Cole's sister, so there could be a perfectly innocent explanation."

"Did Callie strike you as the type of person who would hang around a guy like Leo Pitts?" Mia said.

That statement echoed something else I had heard a few days earlier. "No, but does Alicia Potter strike you as the type of person who would hang around a guy like Cole Dunn?"

Mia made a noise indicating I had a point. "Is he still there?" she asked.

I checked the tracking app. "Yep."

"How long has he been there?"

"Thirty-seven minutes."

"He's just a few blocks away," Mia said. "I could go over there and knock on the door. Just to see what happens."

"Oh my god, that's tempting."

"That would shake things up, wouldn't it?"

"Possibly. Probably. But I think we'd better take advantage of the fact that she doesn't know that we know he's there. Hang loose. I'm heading your way."

* * *

We knocked on Callie Dunn's door three minutes after Leo Pitts had driven away. He had been at her place for just under an hour. It was apparent she didn't recognize us at first.

"Yes?" she said. "Oh, hi! It took me a minute."

"Sorry to show up unannounced," Mia said, "but we were driving by and we took a chance that you might be home."

"What brings you to this neighborhood?" she asked.

Apparently Callie Dunn did not have a great memory.

"I live two blocks over," Mia said.

"Oh, that's right. You had the house fire."

"That's me."

"I'm so scattered. Well, come on in," she said, opening the door wider.

She was dressed in a similar fashion as she had been four days earlier—black yoga pants and a colorful tank top, this one lime green. No shoes. Her toenails were painted the same color as her top, and I had to wonder if she applied new polish every day. Seemed like a big hassle to me.

She offered coffee and we both declined, and then we sat in the matching leather chairs, just as we had on our earlier visit, and Callie sat on the sofa.

"So," she said. "Here we are again. I just hope there isn't another knock on the door."

She was referring to the cops who had shown up last time to inform her about Cole's death.

"We're very sorry about your brother," Mia said.

"I can't say it was a complete surprise," Callie said, "but that doesn't make it any less difficult. I'm putting together a memorial service for later in the summer."

"I'm sure you have many wonderful memories of Cole," Mia said. She could generally find something suitable to say in situations like this one, which was a relief, because it meant I didn't have to risk saying something clumsy.

"We do, yeah," Callie said. "I'm trying to focus on the good times. He had a lot of friends." There was a short pause—a natural transition point in the conversation—and then Callie said, "I suppose you heard that woman was arrested. She had Daddy's curio box."

Callie had a habit of avoiding speaking Serenity's name. I had noticed that the first time we'd talked to her.

"We heard about that," I said. "And we—"

"Don't you agree now that she stole the collection?" Callie said.

"It doesn't look good, does it?" I said, which wasn't really an answer.

"Let me ask—do the police share information with you?" she asked.

"Sometimes," Mia said. "But not a lot. We are by no means insiders."

"So they haven't told you if they found the coins or anything else in her house?"

"I'm afraid not."

"Well, I'm assuming they didn't find the collection or we'd all know by now," Callie said.

Again, that wasn't necessarily true. The cops had no obligation to divulge the information right away.

"For now," I said, "we are operating under the assumption that the coins have not been found, and so the case is still open."

"She must've sold them," Callie said. "Or she panicked and got rid of them somewhere. But she still had the curio box. I guess I should just be grateful she was too stupid to get rid of it."

I didn't understand how she could be so convinced of Serenity's guilt, but Mia and I had nothing to gain by arguing with her about it, especially since Serenity could in fact be the thief. I didn't think she was, but she was still in the running, and if I had a hobo nickel for every time my intuition had been wrong, I'd be a wealthy man.

"You mind if we ask you a couple of questions?" I asked.

"Fire away."

"Some of these are going to seem kind of random."

"That's fine," she said. "Whatever."

"Did your father ever give any of his nickels to you kids? Like for birthday presents, Christmas, that sort of thing?"

"He did at first—I think we all got at least one—but I think he figured out pretty quickly that we weren't really into it. I mean, it was a nice gesture and everything, but it just wasn't our thing."

"You still have the coin he gave you?" I asked.

"I'm sure I do, but I couldn't even tell you where it is. Probably in one of my jewelry boxes somewhere."

"And Max and Cole each got at least one coin?"

"As far as I remember," Callie said.

"Would they have held onto the nickels?" Mia asked.

Callie frowned. "As opposed to what? Oh, I see what you mean. You're being diplomatic. You're wondering if Cole would have sold his. Right? Honestly, that wouldn't surprise me. I had to go over to his apartment yesterday and clean his stuff out, and I didn't find the nickel. There wasn't much in there at all. I took a few small things and paid the apartment manager to get the rest of it hauled away. Once Cole got really hooked, it was amazing how quickly all of his possessions disappeared. He sold it all."

I was wondering if she had noticed the tube of lipstick on the floor. Would the manager Doug have pointed it out and told her where it had come from? And what about Max? Would he have called Callie and relayed the conversation we'd had three days earlier? Possibly. But if he hadn't, I couldn't decide whether or not to ask Callie about Alicia. If we did ask, Callie would almost certainly tell Alicia about our questions.

"Do you know if Cole was seeing anybody?" I asked.

"Like, dating? He didn't do much of that in the past year."

"So you were in touch with him regularly?" Mia asked.

"More than Max or Daddy were. We agreed that we needed to stop rescuing Cole every time he needed money or a place to stay. Max's solution was to basically cut off contact, but I still talked to Cole fairly often."

"And he never mentioned any girlfriends?"

She held up her hands for a second. "Excuse me, but can you tell me why you're focusing on Cole?"

I gave her my best comforting smile. "Investigations generally take us down a bunch of dead ends, and I'm sure this is one of them. Here's what happened. A couple of days ago, we spotted a coin for sale on eBay that might have been one of your dad's. If it was, it's possible it was not one of the stolen coins. It could've been Cole's, so we're trying to figure out how it ended up on eBay. We thought maybe it ended up with a girlfriend."

"Oh," Callie said. "Okay. Well, if he was seeing anybody, he never mentioned her."

"Who were his closest friends?" Mia asked.

"Most of his friends bailed out on him a long time ago."

"What about a guy named Leo Pitts?" I asked, trying to sound natural.

Of course, Mia and I were both watching very closely. How would Callie react? Truth was, I was hoping she'd say she'd never heard of him. Lies often opened entirely new avenues of investigation. Lies can be a godsend.

Callie said, "Oh, sure, I know Leo. In fact, he was just here earlier."

"You and Leo are friends, too?" I asked.

"I guess you could say that, but he's also my pool guy. He cleans my pool."

# 21

We rode back to Mia's house in silence, thoroughly discouraged.

Leo Pitts had been cleaning Callie's pool for years—the one at her McMansion, and the one at her previous house before that. She said he did a good job, didn't charge much, and he was reliable. He and Cole had struck up a friendship several years earlier when Cole had been swimming and Leo had shown up to clean the pool.

Callie didn't seem to know that the friendship revolved around heroin. I would bet that Leo Pitts had been Cole's dealer almost as long as they'd known each other. Or maybe they'd really been just friends at first, until Leo Pitts offered Cole some smack. And because of that, Cole had eventually died. I decided I would take some steps to bring some karma down on Pitts. Get him arrested, if I could. I just had to figure out how to go about it. And I couldn't do it until I removed the GPS unit.

We sat for a few minutes in Mia's living room, brainstorming again, but coming up blank.

Mia glanced at her watch and said, "I have to meet Garlen in a little while."

"Lunch again?" I said.

"No, I have to pick him up from the body shop. He had a little fender bender last night."

You can bet my ears perked up.

"Is he okay?"

"Yeah, he's fine. He had to work late, and when he was going home, a deer ran out in front of him. He swerved and hit a small tree."

"He was coming home from work? What time?"

"He said it was about nine. Why?"

"Just curious. Did he report it to the police?"

"No, he said it wasn't worth filing an insurance claim. He's going to pay for the repair himself." She had already been looking at me, but now she turned and faced me full on. "What's that expression on your face? You look funny."

"I'm hilarious."

"You know what I mean."

She deserved to know the truth. Right? He hadn't wrecked on the way home from work. He'd wrecked after leaving my place, tipsy as hell. Last night and this morning, I'd been contemplating whether I should mention Garlen's visit, and I'd been on the fence, but this pushed me over.

"Okay," I said. "Here's the situation. Garlen came to see me last night."

Now she sat up straighter. "What?"

So I told her what had happened. All of it. I told her that Garlen had come by for a "little chat," and he said we needed to get to know each other. And then he began to make insinuations about the canoe ride, questioning my intentions. And, yes, I told her that Garlen had obviously been drinking.

"You sure about that?"

"Oh, yeah."

"He was buzzed?"

"I'd say a little beyond buzzed. Not sloshed, but I sure didn't want him to drive. I offered coffee, and he agreed to hang out, but when I came back, he was gone."

"What time was this?"

"A little after ten."

I could tell she was disappointed, and possibly on the verge of tears. But she didn't seem surprised. That wasn't a good sign.

"You okay?" I said.

She nodded.

"Should I have kept this to myself?" I said.

"Absolutely not." Then, after a pause, she said, "This isn't the first time he's done something like this."

"Oh, yeah?"

"I've caught him bending the truth before," she said. I waited for her to say more, but she didn't.

"Mia," I said gently. "It's also known as lying."

Now she wiped a tear that had begun to run down her cheek. I reached out and clasped her other hand. It was warm and soft and I could have held it forever.

"I'm sorry he said those stupid things," she said.

"It's okay," I said. "Not your fault."

"Make me a promise."

"What?"

"Don't stop taking me on canoe rides, okay?"


Mia went to meet Garlen, so I had some time on my own.

I checked Leo Pitts's location and saw that he was parked in front of a house in Westlake Hills. Google Maps in satellite mode revealed that the house had a pool, so I drove in that direction. Before I could get there, Pitts was on the move again, heading east on Bee Caves Road, then going south on Loop 1.

A few minutes later, I had his truck in sight, but I stayed at least fifty yards back. He eased into the left lane and took the exit to Loop 360 South, then exited onto Ben White, and turned south on Manchaca. Déjà vu. Shortly after that, he turned on Stassney.

Yep. Returning to his rental unit. Two days had passed and perhaps he'd decided the cops weren't going to search his house after all.

He pulled into the storage facility, so I drove past and found a convenient parking lot where I could wait.

I texted Kiersten. **We still on for tonight?**

She replied: **Absolutely. What r we doing?**

I replied: **Full contact badminton?**

She replied: **Full contact something ;)**

I liked the way she thought.

Seven minutes later, Pitts got back on the road and drove less than one mile to a pizza place on Slaughter Lane. Lunchtime for the busy pool cleaner and small-time drug dealer. After he entered the restaurant, I waited three full minutes before parking the van right beside his truck. I got out and removed the GPS unit. Then I went inside, sat down at Pitts's table, and said, "Hey, Leo."

"Jesus, fuck," he said with a mouth full of pepperoni pizza. The place had an all-you-can-eat buffet for $6.99, so you didn't have to wait. Pitts had five slices on a plate in front of him. He was seated in a corner, and there weren't many customers, so we had some privacy.

"You've always had a way with words," I said. "Mind if I join you?"

"Yes."

"You really should eat some salad, too," I said. "Your digestive tract will thank you."

"Look, man," he said. "I'm seriously starting to wonder what you're trying to accomplish. Why do you keep showing up?"

"The same reason your syphilis keeps showing up. You deserve it."

"That stuff about the cops was bullshit," he said.

"Well, yeah, maybe a little. Sorry about that. But we need to talk about something else."

"We don't need to talk about shit. Time for you to hit the road."

"Leo, don't be like that. I'm about to do you another favor. A *real* favor this time. Here's the situation. Just a few minutes ago, you went to your storage locker on Stassney, and it kind of freaked you out when the lock wouldn't open. Am I right?"

His eyes widened. Then he glared at me, knowing this conversation wasn't going to lead anywhere good.

"So you cut the lock off," I said, "and you were relieved to find that your stash was still inside, safe and sound. So then you decided the lock had simply malfunctioned. Still with me?"

"You aren't some damn insurance investigator," he whispered.

"Hey, believe whatever you want," I said. "Anyway, you took the stash from the unit—because you figured if the cops were going to search your house, they would've done it already—and now, the stash is outside in your truck. Just sitting there. Probably locked in your tool chest."

I gave that a moment to sink in. He looked ready to bolt.

"Now think about this hypothetical situation," I said. "Imagine that there are cops outside waiting for you. They might even have a drug dog ready to sniff your truck. If the dog alerts, well, you are seriously screwed, my friend."

"Are you a cop?" he asked.

Perfect.

"Nope. I am definitely not a cop," I said. "Representing yourself as a cop is a serious crime."

"I think you're a cop and you're trying to get something from me."

"I'm not a cop, but I do want something from you."

"What?"

"Information."

"About what?"

I could tell the pressure was getting to him. He was jumpy as hell. By now, he was under the impression I was a police investigator of some kind, and that I might bust him, or I might let him skate, if he'd cooperate.

So I said, "I'm not convinced you've told me everything about that coin I bought from you on eBay."

"Ah, man. Really? Are we on that again?"

"Well, see, it's kind of important, considering that the thief might've killed Alex Dunn."

"I got nothing to do with any of that. Cole gave me that nickel because he owed me some money. End of story. Then I sold it to you."

"Did Cole tell you where he got the coin?"

"No, but he said they were worth some money, and he was right. I didn't give a damn where he got them."

Wait a second.

"*Them*?" I said.

"Huh?"

"You got more than one hobo nickel from Cole?"

"Yeah. So what?"

Good god, it was irritating speaking to someone like Leo. How could he not have mentioned this until now?

"How many?"

"Probably six or seven."

A fly landed on Pitts's pizza. He didn't seem to notice.

"Where are the others?" I asked.

"I sold them, too."

"When?"

"Whenever I got 'em."

"Which was when? When did you get these other coins?"

"Different times, man. He gave them to me one at a time."

"Over the course of how long?" I asked. "When did you get the first one?"

"Jeez, I don't know. Maybe two years ago."

"Where did you sell them?" I asked.

"On eBay."

"But I checked your sales history. That was the only one you'd sold."

"Nah, man, I had a different account, but my feedback rating got too low, so I opened another one."

Damn. Why hadn't that occurred to me?

"And you never had any idea that Cole got the coins from his dad?"

"Nope."

Pitts picked up his half-eaten piece of pizza and prepared to take a bite, looking at me like, *Are we done?*

I was running out of questions. Then I thought of one.

"You know Alicia Potter?"

"Yeah, sure."

"What was the relationship between Cole and Alicia?"

"She used to be his stepmom, and after the divorce, they'd hook up now and then."

"Hook up, meaning they slept together?"

He grinned, like he thought I was naïve. "Yeah, man. That's what I mean."

"Did you hang out with her and Cole?"

"Nope."

"Is she a user?"

"Man, I got no idea. Why don't you ask her?"

Until now, I'd trusted every answer he'd given me. But he seemed evasive on that one, based on the way he looked down at his pizza when he replied. I decided not to pressure him. I already suspected that Alicia Potter used heroin. He might be able to confirm it for me, but I didn't see as how that would get me anywhere.

"I'm not a cop," I said. "I investigate insurance fraud. Just so we're clear."

He looked at me, still skeptical.

I got up and left.

As I drove, I realized I had no idea whether any of this new information was useful.

Perhaps Cole Dunn had routinely stolen coins from his father—a coin here, a coin there—before Alex Dunn limited contact. It was possible Alex Dunn knew what was happening and declined to press charges. That would be typical for a parent dealing with a child who was a drug addict. It isn't easy to practice tough love. Refusing to give a son money is one thing, but pressing felony charges is something else entirely.

I wondered if Cole had been recorded anytime recently by Alex Dunn's security cameras. Did he still have a key to his father's place? Could he come and go when the house was empty?

Square one. Again.

Time to get serious.

I went back to my apartment and took a nap.

When I woke up, I saw that Alicia Potter had answered my second Facebook message. Finally. Maybe this would lead to some real progress.

*I know nothing about the missing coin collection and I have no interest in answering any questions. I am in grief over Alex's death. Please do not contact me again. If you do, you will hear from my attorneys.*

Yikes. In that case, I figured it was probably better not to ask if she was grieving over Cole, too, considering that he had been her regular sleeping buddy.

A couple of hours later, I texted Mia: **Everything okay?**

She didn't reply.

I texted Kiersten: **Pick you up at 7?**

Ten minutes later, she said: **K. How about seafood? There's a good place two blocks away.**

I wasn't a big fan of seafood. **Sounds great.**

I took a shower, came out, and found a reply from Mia: **Yes thx. Lets talk tmw.**

I sent her a thumbs-up.

I shaved, spritzed a little cologne in strategic places, got dressed, went outside, and as I was walking toward the van, I saw Garlen Gieger striding across the parking lot toward me, looking like he'd caught me spreading rumors about his sister.

# 22

I'd already been punched once recently, by a weaselly little dope dealer, and I wasn't in the mood to get punched again, especially by some guy who'd been jerking Mia around.

I stood my ground and waited.

He marched right up to me, and I swiveled to face him with my left shoulder, ready to raise my arms in a boxer's stance, but he stopped short and said, "What the fuck did you do?"

"Care to narrow that down?"

He was plainly agitated. His face was a vibrant red. I couldn't tell if he had been drinking again. Possibly.

"You ruined everything," he said. "You understand that?"

"You did that on your own, Garlen," I said.

We were standing in an open area of the parking lot, not far from a row of parked cars. I didn't see any other residents in the area.

"What the hell does that mean?" Garlen said.

"You lied to her," I said. "Always a bad idea."

"That's none of your business."

"Sure it is. She's my friend and partner."

"And you want it to be more than that, don't you? That's the real issue here, huh?"

"You need to be on your way," I said. "I don't have time for this."

"I'm gonna kick your ass." His fists were balled up.

"Well, please hurry, because I have a date."

"Funny guy."

"I think perhaps humor is not your strong suit."

His body language—the way he was trying so hard to look like he was *not* about to throw a punch—told me he was contemplating throwing a punch. The truth was, guys like Garlen rarely had the nerve to take it past the mouthing-off stage. If they did get physical, they lacked the skills to do much damage, unless their opponent was equally unskilled. And, unlike the situation with Leo Pitts, I was fully prepared this time.

Garlen said, "You're thrilled about this, aren't you?"

I said, "Look—either be on your way or take a swing. Make a decision. Doesn't matter to me."

His face contorted in anger, and then he did take a swing. A big, looping, clumsy right cross that wouldn't have fooled my grandmother. I ducked under it and his momentum carried him around so hard, he almost lost his footing.

"You're telegraphing your punches," I said. "Do that against someone who knows how to fight and they'll tear you apart."

He had both fists up now, and he was breathing rapidly. As I'd suspected, he didn't know what he was doing. I'm no Sugar Ray Leonard, but I'd trained enough that Garlen would not be a great concern.

He shot out a jab—or his idea of a jab—but I leaned left and avoided it.

I knew what would come next. He'd lose his patience and rush me, wanting to wrap me up and take me to the ground, where he might have a small advantage. So I had to keep him off balance. I feinted left, then moved right, and he almost tripped over his own feet.

"Garlen, seriously, you need to take off," I said. "This is ridiculous.

We're grown men fighting in a parking lot. You think this is the way to win Mia back?"

But his anger was too much. He couldn't stop now.

He lurched forward, wanting to grab me, but I stepped to my right and backward.

He edged closer and faked a punch, then grinned when I flinched.

He said, "What's the matter, Roy? Worried I might—"

I slipped inside and popped him with a hard left jab to the nose. When his hands went up to protect his face, I drove a left hook into his exposed ribs. I held back—I didn't want to break anything—but it was more than enough. He backed away, covering his nose with one hand and clutching his side with the other.

"Jesus Christ," he muttered. Blood was dripping onto his expensive polo shirt.

I lowered my hands but kept my distance.

"Son of a bitch," he said. He removed his hand from his nose to gauge the blood flow. Nothing serious.

"If you get some ice on it, it won't swell too bad," I said. "Maybe take a couple of Advil."

He didn't say anything.

"Look, Garlen," I said, "it wasn't anything personal. I don't even know you. But if you knew someone was jerking Mia around, wouldn't you tell her?"

He pulled a handkerchief from his back pocket and pressed it to his nose.

I waited. I didn't want to leave him there until I was positive he would be okay.

After another half-minute, he glared at me, then turned around and walked away.


Despite the ugly incident with Garlen, Kiersten and I had nice evening. Turned out the seafood place also served an outstanding ribeye steak, a tasty cheesecake, and a fine glass of Irish whiskey, which helped settle my nerves, because even a small scuffle in a parking lot releases adrenaline.

After dinner, Kiersten and I went back to her condo and put all those calories to good use.

At midnight, as we were side by side in bed catching our breath, Kiersten said, "It's almost like you've done that before."

"Once or twice," I said. "But it was in prison and I don't like to talk about it."

"I guess your cellmate taught you a few tricks," she said.

"We still exchange Christmas cards."

We lay in silence for a moment. Her bed faced a wall of windows, and the blinds were open to reveal a blanket of lights south to the river. Stunning. It could've been a postcard.

"Thought any more about that house?" she asked.

"Yeah," I said. "Haven't decided. It's the only one I've looked at. Don't want to rush."

"I can tell you this much—that's a good price. Someone will grab it quick."

"Yeah, probably."

"I can hook you up with another realtor in my office, if you want," she said.

"Is it really against the code of ethics for you to represent me?"

"Well, technically, no, but I think it's probably for the best."

She had music playing softly—some satellite channel featuring soft-pop hits from the '70s and '80s. Carly Simon's "You're So Vain" at the moment.

"This song is about me, by the way," I said.

"I bet you think so," she said.

After another pause, I said, "That house is appealing because it's close to my partner's house, but that's also one reason I'm hesitating."

"I get that with younger clients and their parents. They want to be close to mom and dad, but not *too* close. What's your partner's name again? Mia?"

"Right."

"Afraid she'll get on your nerves?"

"Ha. No. The other way around."

"Oh, I doubt that," she said.

I had wondered whether I might hear from Mia over the course of the evening, but I hadn't. I assumed that meant Garlen hadn't told her about our bout in the parking lot. I couldn't blame him. I wasn't so sure I was going to tell Mia about it myself. If she'd broken up with Garlen and they remained broken up, there was no need for her to know. But if she showed signs of getting back together with him, I would tell her, because, quite frankly, his behavior concerned me. Did he drive drunk with her in the car? Did he get belligerent with her?

"The lease on my apartment is up in four months," I said. "I'm thinking about giving them notice that I'll be leaving, just because it will force me to do something. Plus, I hate the damn place."

"You should do that, Roy. You really should. Even if you don't buy that listing in Tarrytown. You could always go month to month if you haven't found a place by the time your lease ends."

More silence. It was so nice to just lie there. I knew I'd probably doze off soon.

"Maybe I should just buy Max Dunn's place," I said. "And take up yachting or something."

"Got a spare three million lying around?" Kiersten asked.

"Is that what he's asking?"

"Yep. Between you and me, it's overpriced. I've tried to get him down to two-five, but he won't budge, despite the fact that we haven't had a single offer."

I wondered if she knew about Max Dunn's financial difficulties. Did it matter? I also wondered if she was breaching the code of ethics by telling me this stuff. Did it matter?

"How long has it been on the market?" I asked.

"About four months," she said. "Ever since his wife asked for a separation."

"Excuse me?" I said.

**23**

The next morning, Mia and I convened in the spare bedroom in her house that sometimes acts as our conference room. "Sometimes" means exactly never, as far as I can remember. That's because we don't typically need a conference room in our line of work. We usually just gather in her living room and use our laptops as necessary.

But on this occasion, I wanted to take advantage of the large dry-erase board I had installed on one wall.

"What do we need a dry-erase board for?" she'd asked at the time.

"So I have a place to write my witty remarks," I'd said.

"Does that mean you have a dry wit?" she'd asked.

"Ooh," I'd said. "Well done."

We hadn't used the board since then. It still said, "Roy's witty remarks go here" in Mia's elegant handwriting at the top.

But now I felt the need to map out the Alex Dunn case in a visual manner and see if that could provide any clarity or untangle the cobwebs in my head.

"This has been a tough one," I said, "but we keep learning new information, and I think it's just a matter of time before we figure it out. Here's the question right now: Based on what we know, who would you say is most likely to have stolen the coin collection?"

Mia was seated nearby in one of two black faux-leather club chairs we'd bought at the same time as the dry-erase board. There were windows in the west and south walls, flooding the room with plenty of natural light.

I'd already told her about my conversation with Leo Pitts in the pizza joint, the message I'd received from Alicia Potter, and the juicy gossip I'd learned from Kiersten about Max Dunn's separation from his wife. The truth was, what had seemed like big news last night didn't seem all that relevant this morning. Really, there was no reason for Max to have told us about his marital problems—it was, after all, a personal matter, just like his bankruptcy.

On the other hand, he'd said some things that seemed intended to cover up the separation. Like the bit about moving to Lost Creek to keep the kids in the same school district. According to Kiersten, Max's wife and kids were already living in a rented house in Lost Creek, and the wife had no plans to let Max join them there. Was Max Dunn in denial about that, or had he intended to misdirect us? Could be either.

Mia said, "I'd say Cole Dunn or Max Dunn. Unless it was Serenity."

I wrote the three names as a list and said, "Okay, but that's three people."

"It's a toss-up," she said.

She hadn't said anything about Garlen this morning. I hadn't asked. However, it was obvious she wasn't her usually perky self. She hadn't even asked why I'd seen Kiersten again. I hadn't mentioned that Kiersten and I were dating.

"If you had to choose just one..." I said.

She was studying the names on the board. "Max Dunn, I guess. Between the bankruptcy and the split with his wife, he's under a lot of pressure. He needs money."

"Okay," I said. "Good. Makes sense." I wrote another name on the board, under the first three.

*Alicia Potter.*

"Thoughts on her?" I said.

"I think if she still had access to Alex Dunn's house, she would've been caught on the security camera. Ruelas would be all over her."

"But some of those systems only save a few days' worth of video," I said. "Or sometimes a week."

"They'd track the location of her cell phone and see if she went over there anytime recently," Mia said.

"If they could get a warrant," I said. "Which I doubt."

"There's zero evidence she stole the coins, Roy."

"But she might've killed her sister," I said.

"Zero evidence of that, too," Mia said. "I think you're grasping at straws. In fact, I don't think we have enough information to draw any conclusions about any of these people. We could sit here and build all kinds of wild scenarios that would make any of them guilty—or innocent."

"We're just brainstorming," I said.

"Yes, but I think we've done enough of that in the past few days."

"What do you suggest as an alternative?"

She looked out a window and contemplated that question. She was silent long enough that I thought she had gotten sidetracked by a daydream, or she was ruminating about her problems with Garlen.

"Mia?" I said.

"I don't know, Roy," she said. "Maybe you were right the other day."

"Of course I was. About what?"

"Maybe it's time to give up."

I sat down in the matching club chair. The faux leather made noises like real leather.

"You are seriously bringing me down," I said. "I was trying to be all optimistic and upbeat. Rah rah rah and all that."

She gave me a weak smile. "Sorry."

I set the dry-erase marker on the small table between the two chairs.

"I wasn't just blowing smoke, you know," I said. "I really do think we'll nail this one eventually."

"You were ready to give up yesterday morning," she reminded me.

This wasn't her typical mood. She was down, and I had no idea whether I should try to offer any consolation or not. But there was nothing wrong with a pep talk.

"Well, yeah, but that's me," I said. "A quitter. A loser. Always ready to throw in the towel at the slightest hint of difficulty. But you? Come on. We both know you're better than that. You're a force of nature. An ass-kicking machine. I rely on you to smack me around and tell me to stop being a wimp."

She gave me a look: *I appreciate your bullshit, but not right now, okay?*

I grabbed the marker and went back to the board.

"It's one of these four people," I said. "But I'm gonna concede what you said about Alicia a second ago and strike her from the list."

I drew a line through Alicia's name.

"Next," I said, "I'm gonna get all ballsy and say we can strike Serenity off the list, too. That's an executive decision on my part, you understand, based purely on instinct and perhaps a little telepathy. She appears innocent and I don't think she's lying. You okay with that?"

"Even though they found the curio box at her place?"

"That seems like a frame job. You don't agree?"

"I can only say probably. Or she did it herself, trying to make it look like someone was framing her. She's smart enough to do that."

"Yeah, she is," I said. "Do you think she did?"

"No, not really."

"Same here. So we can strike her?"

"Yeah, okay."

I drew a line through Serenity's name.

"Now we have two," I said.

"You always were a math whiz," Mia said.

Ah. A sign of life. Spunkiness.

"I'm going to make another bold move here, Mia. Ready for it? Because if you aren't, I don't want to blow your mind. So let me know."

She rolled her eyes, but nodded her head impatiently.

"Bam!" I said, drawing a line through another name. "Max Dunn is gone. Off the list. Want to know why?"

"The anticipation is killing me," Mia said.

"As we have postulated—excuse that high-dollar word—but as we have postulated several times, the three kids knew it would be very hard to sell the coins without getting caught. Max has big money troubles—and more coming, if he gets divorced—but he would've known the coins wouldn't have helped him. In fact, ipso facto, they would've gotten him arrested."

"Ipso facto?"

"Certainly, and habeas corpus maximus."

"But the same logic applies to Cole, who is the only remaining name on the list."

"Aha!" I barked, making her jump. "It doesn't apply to him. And here's the difference...Both men were desperate, but Cole was driven by addiction. And when you're an addict and you need your next fix, there comes a point where nothing else matters. You can't think rationally, and you take stupid chances. I think that's what Cole did. He'd been stealing his dad's coins, one by one, over the years—occasionally using them to buy dope from Leo Pitts—and he finally decided to go big and take the entire collection. The addiction was stronger than his fear of getting caught. Plus, he was willing to gamble that his dad would let it slide."

Mia thought about it. She said, "If he did it, he had to have access to his dad's house."

"Yes, and Callie said her dad hadn't been as stringent at cutting Cole off as Max had. Alex Dunn probably hadn't changed his locks or his security code."

"And you're assuming Cole stole the coins sometime shortly before his dad died."

"Right."

"Couldn't he have stolen the collection weeks or even months ago?"

I thought about that. "Yeah, I guess he could have, but at some point, Alex Dunn would have been committing fraud himself by continuing to insure an item he no longer possessed. He would've needed to either report the crime or remove the collection from his policy."

"Still, though, there's no reason Cole couldn't have stolen the coins, say, last month, or the month before that. We've been assuming the theft and the murder are possibly related, and so the coins must've been stolen recently—but that's not necessarily the case. Agreed?"

I was getting excited that we were discussing fresh possibilities that hadn't occurred to us before. Mia also seemed more invested in the conversation now.

"Agreed," I said.

"So let's say we're right. Cole stole the coins. Where would he have stashed them?" Before I replied, she said, "His apartment, right? Where else? He wouldn't have had the money to put them in a safe-deposit box or anything like that. He'd want them nearby and easily accessible for a quick sale, when he needed drugs. So what we need to do is create a separate list."

"People who could've taken the coins from Cole's apartment after he died," Mia said.

"Exactly."

"Whoever that might've been, they had to have planted the box at Serenity's house, yes?"

"Yes."

I wrote:

*Callie*

*Max*

*Leo Pitts*

*Alicia Potter*

Mia rose, took the marker from my hand, and wrote:

*Doug, the manager*

# 24

We found him squatting beside a condenser unit to the rear of the apartment complex. He had the housing removed and was working with a variety of tools and gauges that, quite frankly, surprised me. Here I thought Doug probably sat around all day eating potato chips and watching television. Maybe I was projecting what *I* would do if I were an apartment manager.

"Hey, there," Mia said as we walked up behind him.

He looked up at us, squinting into the sun. He still needed a shave. "Yeah? Oh. Hey."

"How's it going, Doug?" I said.

"Problem with the AC?" Mia asked.

"Yeah, and the residents ain't happy. At least the ones home right now. Gonna be mid-nineties today."

"You know how to fix stuff like that?" Mia said. "Impressive."

"I picked up a few things over the years," he said, standing up. "Better than waiting around for a service guy."

"Bet it's that round gizmo," I said, pointing. "Round gizmos are the worst."

"The run capacitor," he said. "You might be right. Air blowing, but it ain't cool. Good news, is, I keep an extra on hand."

"You mind a few more questions?" Mia asked.

"About capacitors?" It was his idea of a joke.

Mia laughed a fake laugh, then said, "We're still looking for that coin collection."

"Those hillbilly nickels?" he asked.

He was either confused or pretending to be.

"Hobo nickels," Mia said.

"You ain't the only one," he said. "Cops've been around a couple more times, and his sister came to get his stuff. She didn't find nothin' either."

"What we're wondering," I said, "is who had access to Cole's apartment on the day he died?"

"Same question the cops asked," Doug said. "And man, I wish I knew. Anybody could've been in there."

"Did you see anybody?"

"No."

"Did he routinely have a lot of visitors?"

"Not many."

"How did you learn he had died?"

"What happened was, I got back from Home Depot and this guy Leo knocks on my door saying he thinks Cole overdosed."

"Leo Pitts?" I asked.

"Yeah. He said he found Cole on the living room floor."

"Who called 9-1-1?" I asked.

"I did."

"And then what happened?" Mia said.

"The cops came, and an ambulance, and they checked him over, and then they put him on that rolling thing…"

"Gurney," Mia said.

"Right, and then they hauled ass."

"Where was Leo all this time?" Mia asked.

"Oh, he took off right after he told me what happened."

"He just took off?" I said.

"I told him he'd better hang around, but he said he didn't know any more about it than I did, and he said he had work to do. So he left. I told the cops, but I didn't know his last name at that point."

"How long were you gone to Home Depot?" I asked.

"About two hours. I had to go to the bank, too."

"Had you seen Leo before you left?"

"Nope."

"Did you see anybody else hanging around Cole's place?"

"Nope. His blinds were drawn. That always meant he was holed up in there."

"Getting high?" I asked.

He gave me a sharp look. "Man, I don't know anything about his drug use, okay? It was obvious he was a user, but it's not like I knew his personal habits, so I would appreciate it if you'd stop asking me questions like that."

"Fair enough," I said. "So his blinds were drawn and nobody was around when you left."

"Right. Then I got back from my errands, and five minutes after that, Leo knocks on my door. He was freaking out pretty bad."

"Had you ever met Leo before?"

"Well, I'd seen him around and said hi. I always try to do that with strangers, so they at least know I'm watching. He'd told me he was a friend of Cole's."

"So you have no idea how long Leo was in Cole's apartment before he came and knocked on your door?" Mia asked.

"Nope."

"You went into Cole's apartment to see if he was okay?" Mia asked.

"Yeah, of course. I found a heartbeat, but I couldn't get him to wake up. That's when I called for help. And there was drug stuff lying around."

"What kind of stuff?" I asked.

It was already getting damned hot out here on the southeast side of the complex.

"A syringe and some of that tubing. Plus a spoon. And some other stuff that I don't know what it was."

"Before that, when was the last time you were in that apartment?" I asked. I knew he wouldn't like that question.

His tone of voice changed. "At least a month. Why?"

I took out my phone and showed him a photo of the curio box.

"Did you ever see this wooden box in Cole's apartment?"

"Nope. I don't steal from the fuckin' tenants, if that's what you're asking," he said.

"I didn't mean that—"

"If I did that, I'd lose this job in a heartbeat, if I didn't get shot first. Somebody would pick up on what I was doing. It's not like I have the run of the place. There's always somebody hanging around, watching. They sit out in the courtyard for hours."

"Who does?" Mia asked.

"Just some of the residents. A lot of 'em sit out there during the day and bullshit or drink beer. I'm fine with that, as long as they keep it quiet and don't cause any problems. Point is, they know what I'm doing as much as I know what they're doing. They see me coming and going."

So the residents were, in effect, a security system. Not quite as good as a network of video cameras, but better than nothing.

"Were any of them sitting in the courtyard when Cole died?" I asked.

"Yeah, some."

"Do me a favor," I said. "Tell me who was out there."

We spent a solid hour knocking on doors—or door frames, because many doors were wide open, due to the AC problem—and interviewing residents in the complex. We talked to some of the people Doug had named, plus anybody else who was around.

We found that about half of the residents were home, which seemed high on a weekday morning. Didn't these people have jobs? Maybe they worked at night or on weekends. Yeah, right. Ever scroll through the mug shots on a police website? Those were the people living at this place.

It was a memorable morning, but ultimately we learned nothing more—until we spoke to the last person on the list Doug had given us. She was a tall, slender woman in her forties, originally from a small island in the Caribbean. Beautiful accent. Beautiful woman, for that matter. She looked out of place here.

We told her who we were and why we were there, and she was happy to talk to us. I got the feeling she was happy to talk to anybody about almost anything, because we knew, within five minutes, that she was an office manager at some sort of small manufacturing facility, and she was trying to get back on her feet after her husband had died suddenly of a heart attack. She was standing in her open doorway while we stayed outside. I'm sure she would've invited us in if the air conditioner had been working.

"You were in the courtyard when Cole died?" Mia asked when she finally had an opening in which to insert a question.

"I was. Horrible day, but it was no surprise. No surprise at all. Cole was a good man, but he had the demons after him." She leaned toward us and whispered. "Drugs. I don't know what kind. A lot of that in this neighborhood, you know."

"Did you see anyone coming or going from his apartment that day?"

"Just that man Leo. I saw him come out from Cole's place and walk straight to Doug's apartment, and then Doug hurried over to Cole's apartment, and then the EMTs and police officers arrived. It was easy to see that something unusual was happening."

"Did you see Leo arrive at Cole's earlier, or was that the first time you saw him, when he came out of Cole's apartment?" I asked.

Her answers came quickly, because she had already been asked the same questions by the police. "I didn't see him arrive. I don't know when he got there. He could have been there all morning, for all I know."

"Did you see anyone else coming or going from Cole's apartment other than Leo and Doug?" I asked.

She shook her head emphatically. "They were the only ones." Then her eyes widened and she half-turned toward the interior of her apartment, raising a hand into the air. She was smiling. "Feel that? Cold air. Praise the Lord."

Doug had come through.

* * *

"What now?" Mia asked.

Driving again—heading south on Loop 1. Amazing how much traffic there was at 11:37 in the morning.

I said, "I'm operating under the theory that our little exercise in deductive reasoning this morning was spot on, and that Cole did steal the coin collection. Now I'm further concluding that Leo Pitts was there when Cole shot up—because he'd sold him the dope—and he took off because he didn't want to get busted. And the kicker. He took the coin collection with him. Maybe the box was sitting right there on the coffee table, and Leo had gotten enough of the coins as payment from Cole to know he was looking at some serious money. So he grabbed it. Maybe he figured that even if Cole recovered, he wouldn't know who took the collection. Could've been one of the other residents, or the landlord, or even one of the EMTs. You on board with all that?"

"I am," Mia said. "It's a lot of guessing, but it all makes sense. Which would mean he's the one who planted the curio box at Serenity's place."

"Yep. He's seen her mentioned in the newspaper and it's obvious she's a suspect, so he tried to frame her."

One mile to the Enfield exit. Back to Mia's house. Home base.

Mia said, "When Leo stashed his drugs in the storage unit, why didn't he put the coins there, too?"

I moved into the right-hand lane and took the exit.

"Don't know," I said.

"You searched the unit well enough to know for sure the coins weren't there?"

"Yes." Then I added. "I think so. I mean, why would he stick the drugs in a drawer, but hide the coins better than that? Makes no sense."

"But you did look in other places, right?"

"Yes."

"So how sure are you that the coins weren't there?"

"About ninety-eight percent."

She didn't give me any static for not being 100% sure. Now I was wishing I had checked every square inch of that storage unit.

"So where are they now?" she asked. "Where did he hide them?"

We were just a few blocks from Mia's house now. As we passed the house on Raleigh, two cars were parked in the driveway. The for-sale sign was still in place.

Mia made a show of noticing the cars, then looked at me. "Got some competition, Roy," she said. "Better get on it."

## 25

We sat quietly in the conference room again. I had written a sentence on the dry-erase board:

*Why didn't Leo stash the coins in the storage unit?*

If we could answer that question, we'd be on the verge of a breakthrough.

Possibly.

Unless our theory was off base. And it very well might be.

Mia checked her phone for the second time in five minutes. Incoming texts, I assumed, but she had the volume turned off, so there was no audible alert. She tapped out a brief reply, then placed her phone flat on her thigh, screen downward. Her mood was souring again.

A question was on my lips, dying to be asked. I held back. Instead, I focused on the more important question.

*Why didn't Leo stash the coins in the storage unit?*

The AC shut off for the moment, and now it was dead quiet in the room.

There was an obvious answer to the question; we just hadn't

figured it out yet.

I glanced at Mia, and she just looked so sad, I couldn't help myself.

"How's Garlen?" I asked.

She shook her head. *Don't ask.*

I nodded back.

A minute passed.

"You deserve to be treated right, Mia," I said. "That's all I really want to say. Other than that, I'll keep my nose out of it."

"Thank you, Roy."

Another minute passed.

I said, "Were you thanking me for saying you deserved to be treated right, or for keeping my nose out of it?"

"Both," she said.

I grinned at her. "Okay." Then I looked at the board and recited the question: "Why didn't Leo stash the coins in the storage unit?"

Mia said, "Maybe he didn't stick the coins in the storage unit because he already had them tucked away someplace he considered safe."

"Interesting," I said. "Like where?"

"Don't know," Mia said. "Obviously not in his house or his truck."

"Why would he keep the drugs at home, but not the coins?" I asked.

"Don't know that, either," she said. "But we don't need to know. We can only hope we're right that Leo took the coins after Cole died, and if that's what happened, then it doesn't matter why he didn't keep them at his house. All that matters is where they are now."

She was right, of course.

But where? I had gone back and checked all of his movements from the moment I'd attached the GPS tracker to his vehicle, and there was nothing in his travel history beyond what we already knew.

I said, "Maybe he gave the coins to one of his friends to hold. Or even one of his customers."

Mia looked doubtful. "He'd have to have friends he could trust, and they'd have to trust him, too. Doesn't seem likely for a sleazebag dope dealer."

"True," I said.

"Let's be honest," Mia said. "We've made so many assumptions and guesses, the chances are slim that we're right."

I didn't want to give up, but only because I didn't want to leave Mia here to mope. Or to give Garlen a chance to come over and try to make up.

"Leo has those coins," I said. "I know it."

Mia didn't bother telling me I was full of crap. We both knew it. It was another frustrating moment in a case that was filled with them. It was a lesson I hadn't been taught in quite some time—that some cases can't be solved, and some criminals get away.

And then, in the blink of an eye—or, more accurately, in the half-second it took for Mia's expression to transform completely—everything changed.

"Roy," she said. "I think I've got it. I think I know where the coins are."

I was beginning to suspect that Callie Dunn had a limitless collection of black yoga pants, but who was I to question her wardrobe choices? Go with what works, right? The only difference this time, when she answered the door, was that the pants featured a floral-print waistband, and her tank top was a color of purple that the marketing people probably called Evening Eggplant or Rippling Ruby or Perfectly Plum.

We had called in advance, so she wasn't surprised to see us, but she was curious, because we hadn't said what we wanted. I'm sure Mia's tone of voice on the phone had sounded mysterious, despite her best efforts to conceal her excitement.

"Hi, again," Callie said. "Come on in."

We followed her inside, and before she offered drinks or a chance to sit down, Mia said, "Callie, from the very beginning of this investigation, you've been very helpful, and we're going to ask for your cooperation one more time."

"Okaaay." She drew the word out, apparently somewhat puzzled and wondering what might come next.

"This might sound like an odd request," Mia said, "but can we search your pump house?"

It was basically a small shed, measuring roughly six feet by six feet, but it was designed and built to complement the house. Same limestone exterior walls, same bronze-colored standing-seam metal roof. Not many homes were built to those specs.

The door—stained hardwood—had a keyed knob, but it wasn't locked. Mia swung it open and I stood next to her. The floor was plain concrete, and the left- and right-hand walls each had three built-in shelves that were crowded with various lidded plastic jugs, tubs, bottles, and buckets. Pool chemicals. The place smelled funny—like bleach combined with the mustiness of old books.

The rear wall had no shelves, but instead featured a medium-sized window that allowed plenty of light into the pump house. Just below the window was the pump itself, purring away. The unit comprised a round, gray cylinder about two feet tall, plus two smaller black cylinders attached at the bottom, and some PVC pipe exiting through the wall behind it. On the floor next to the pump was a coiled hose about two inches in diameter and maybe twenty feet long. For vacuuming the bottom of the pool, I guessed. Leaning in a corner was one of the nets guys like Leo use to scoop leaves out of the center of a pool.

Callie was ten feet behind me, standing not far from the pool itself, just watching.

Mia's theory—and it was a good one—was that Leo Pitts would've stashed the coins here because he knew that if they were discovered, the cops might think Callie had taken them. But if the coins were found in some other customer's pump house, that would implicate Leo and only Leo.

Mia entered the shed itself and I remained in the doorway. This was her moment. If the coins were in here, she deserved to find them. I can't tell you how much I was hoping she'd hit pay dirt.

Mia turned and spoke over me to Callie. "Does anybody else come in here?"

"No, just Leo. That's all pool maintenance stuff."

"What about these blow-up rafts?"

"I think I used those once when I first moved in, but not since then. I forgot they were in there."

Mia moved to the shelf on the left side and reached toward a square plastic bucket with a red lid. She jostled it. "Powdered chlorine, but it's empty." There were three identical buckets on the same shelf. Two were empty, one was half full. She lifted the lid and peeked inside. Nothing but powder.

On the shelf above that were five more plastic buckets, but these were round and had blue lids. From where I stood, I could read the label on the nearest bucket. It contained 35 pounds of three-inch chlorine tablets.

Mia checked the first bucket. Empty. Same with the second and third. Leo Pitts wasn't big on disposing of empties. The fourth bucket was full with tablets all the way to the top. Mia waved a hand in front of her face to disperse the odor. "Reminds me of your cologne," she said.

"I call it Eau de Michael Phelps," I said.

She checked the fifth bucket. It was filled halfway with chlorine tablets.

I was beginning to lose heart, because there weren't many other containers that could hold several hundred coins in plastic sleeves. Actually, there weren't any.

Mia spent a few minutes lifting various jugs and tubs, shaking them, and finding them full of liquid. No coins. She rattled the plastic two-inch hose. Empty. She got on her tiptoes and checked the highest shelf, just to make sure the sleeved coins weren't lying flat, individually, just out of sight. Nope.

"Anything behind the pump?" I said.

Mia leaned over, looked behind it, and shook her head.

She went back to the half-full bucket of chlorine tablets and removed the lid again. She tilted the bucket forward, causing some of the tablets to tumble toward the edge of the bucket, and giving her a glimpse to the bottom. Nothing.

She left the lid off that bucket and opened the completely full bucket of tablets. Nearby was a large scoop that was obviously used to remove tablets from the buckets. She began to scoop tablets from the full bucket into the half-full bucket.

After three scoops, she stopped. Looked inside. Shook the bucket. Then I saw her grin.

She dug in with the scoop again, but this time she dumped the contents on the concrete floor, and it was a mixture of chlorine tablets and hobo nickels in plastic sleeves.

# 26

We called it in, of course, to an APD detective I knew who handled theft cases. He passed it off to a detective named Rachel Cowan, who showed up fairly quickly with her partner and a couple of crime-scene technicians.

Neither of us had ever met either of these detectives, so we explained who we were and why we were interested in finding the coins. I knew they would end up questioning Callie Dunn pretty hard—after all, the coins had been found on her property—but we made it clear why we thought Leo Pitts had stolen the coins and hidden them in the pump house. There was an excellent chance they'd find Pitts's fingerprints on some of the plastic sleeves.

Finally, early in the afternoon, we were done—not just with the detectives' questions, but with the case itself.

While Mia drove, I called Heidi to give her the good news. She didn't pick up, so I left a detailed voicemail. Then I called Serenity. Same thing—voicemail.

When I hung up, I said, "Where are you headed?"

Mia's house was in the opposite direction.

"This calls for a margarita, doesn't it?"

"Oh, absolutely," I said.

She got on the Loop 1 feeder road and went south.

"Oh, jeez," I said. "I just figured something out."

"What?"

"The coin I bought from Leo Pitts in the Walmart parking lot had a familiar smell to it, but I couldn't place it."

"Chlorine?"

"Exactly. If I'd been a little quicker on the uptake, we might've wrapped this case up earlier. That's a pretty good clue."

She turned right on Lake Austin Boulevard.

She said, "Better late than never. At least that smell ties Leo to the coins. If he says he didn't know anything about the coins in the pump house, why did he have one in his possession that smelled like that? I bet the cops can even test the plastic sleeve for chlorine."

"I bet you're right."

She passed the Hula Hut, a popular restaurant and bar right on the banks of Lake Austin, and turned right to park in the overflow parking lot. The place was always crowded, even now, at two in the afternoon.

I wondered how quickly the APD detectives would be paying a visit to Pitts's house. They would probably request—and get—a search warrant for Pitts's house and vehicles. It would be great if they'd find some drugs. Pitts had probably provided the dope that killed Cole Dunn, and he deserved to do some serious prison time.

"I'm proud of you," I said as Mia pulled into a parking spot.

"Thanks."

"It was brilliant."

"It was obvious," she said.

"Hell if it was."

"Well, thanks. Let's go have a margarita."

"You'll have to lead me to the restaurant," I said. "I might not be able to find it on my own."

\* \* \*

We ordered margaritas, along with a variety of appetizers. Chicken quesadillas. Kawaikini stuffed avocado. Your basic Texas nachos. Plus another basket of chips with hot sauce. Despite the heat, we were out on the deck that extended over the lake, but the breeze and the shade from the palapa over our table kept us relatively comfortable. About half the tables out here were full, whereas the inside of the restaurant, in the air conditioning, was packed.

"Dare me to jump in the water?" I asked.

"I absolutely do not," Mia said.

"Because you know I'll do it."

"So would a ten-year-old."

My phone, resting on the table in front of me, lit up. Heidi had sent a text.

**You guys rock! In a long meeting. Will call later.**

I replied: **Better yet, join us at Hula Hut to celebrate**.

Our waitress came around again to see if we needed anything.

"What happens if I jump in the water?" I asked.

"I'm not sure," she said. "I don't think anyone's ever done that here."

"So I'd be a trailblazer. A trendsetter."

"A cautionary tale," Mia said.

"So…another margarita?" the waitress asked.

I looked at Mia, who said, "Sure."

After the waitress left, Mia said, "Garlen and I broke up. I broke up with him."

"Yeah, I figured as much. I'm sorry."

"Can't put up with a guy lying to me like that."

"And you shouldn't."

She was wearing sunglasses, so I couldn't tell if she was tearing up. I hoped not.

"He keeps calling and texting," she said.

I held my tongue for a moment.

"Last night, he came to my house and kept knocking on the door. I was this close to calling the cops."

I took a long, slow breath. I wasn't going to allow this to get under my skin. Mia could handle herself—including physically, if it came to that.

"You have that look on your face, Roy."

"Which one?"

"The one that says you might do something you shouldn't."

"I promise you," I said, "I won't do anything. Unless you need me to."

The waitress brought our fresh margaritas. "You're still dry," she said.

"No, no," Mia said. "Please. Don't encourage him."

We didn't discuss Garlen anymore after that, and we were able to enjoy the remainder of our visit. Mia asked again about the house for sale on Raleigh. I told her I still hadn't made up my mind. Mia said I should get on it before someone else did. How true, I thought. How very true.

Later, when I asked for the check, the waitress told me it had already been taken care of.

*Heidi.* What a gal.


Three days passed and I learned various tidbits from Heidi.

Leo Pitts had been arrested, but he was maintaining that he didn't know anything about the coins. Typical. They'd searched Pitts's house, but Heidi didn't know the results of the search, other than the fact that no more hobo nickels had been found. The quantity of coins hidden in the chlorine tablets was about a dozen shy of Alex Dunn's last inventory. Not all of them, but pretty damn close.

I left a message for Ruelas—just out of sheer curiosity—to see if he was making any headway on the Alex Dunn homicide, but he never called me back.

Where's a cop when you need one, right?

Meanwhile, no new cases came in, so I had a lot of time on my hands. I went out with Kiersten one night and stayed at her place again. I was getting spoiled.

I thought about Mia a lot and tried to check on her without being nosy. It was a delicate balance. She never said anything else about Garlen and I didn't press it.

I read. I napped. I went to a Texas Longhorns baseball game. I went for a weekday swim at Reimer's Ranch, where I had a long stretch of the Pedernales River all to myself.

Then I finally called Mia's friend Abby, the realtor.

"I'm surprised it's still on the market, to be honest, and I'm not just saying that," Abby said.

I was taking another look at the house on Raleigh. We were in the kitchen.

"If I was going to make an offer, what do you think that offer should be?" I asked.

She hemmed and hawed and quoted various comparables, but she finally spat a figure out.

It was doable, but I didn't want to go any higher. I told her so.

"They'll counter-offer, most likely," Abby said. "You should be ready for that."

"Could we start with a lower bid?"

"I wouldn't. They'll think you're not serious."

"Then what I'd want you to do," I said, "is present the offer as a take-it-or-leave-it type of deal. That's the way I prefer doing it anyway."

"I guess we could do that," she said. "Have you already pre-qualified for a mortgage?"

I could tell she was anxious to move this process along. She was a snappy dresser and an attractive woman, but she wasn't quite as smooth or professional as Kiersten had been when she'd shown me the place. I felt like she was representing herself, rather than representing me.

"I stopped at my bank yesterday," I said. "I'm all set."

"You qualify for the amount of the offer?"

"I was as surprised as you are. That's what happens when you drive a junker and live in a cheap apartment. You can save up."

She laughed, then said, "Well, what do you think? Got any additional questions or concerns?"

I pulled a quarter from my pocket.

"Heads we make the offer, tails we don't," I said.

She laughed again.

I looked at her.

"Seriously?" she said.

"Yep."

I flipped the coin into the air and let it drop to the floor, where it bounced and rolled and finally came to a stop next to the stove.

**27**

Two days later, we finally got another case, or I did. A fairly easy one, too, which is nice on occasion.

According to this client—who, like Heidi, supervised a claims department at a large insurance company—a shady chiropractor had devised a simple but effective scam.

The chiropractor's office manager would distribute coupons for a free 30-minute massage, and when a recipient redeemed a coupon, the chiropractor would gather the recipient's insurance information and later bill for a variety of services that weren't delivered—like traction, hot or cold packs, spinal manipulation, or myofascial stripping, whatever that is. Of course, the recipients were served by a variety of insurance companies, so the chiropractor probably thought the scam would be hard to catch. Only problem was, one of the "patients" worked in the medical-billing field and was savvy enough to understand the codes on the statement that followed her visit to the chiropractor's office. Now several insurance companies had banded together to sting this chiropractor and shut the scam down.

My client had gotten her hands on one of the coupons. My job was to go get a free massage and capture it all on video. When I called the number on the coupon to schedule the massage, what do you know—they had an opening that very afternoon. What were the odds of that?

Shortly after I hung up, Mia texted about another new case from Daniel Ivy. A woman had reported a valuable diamond bracelet as missing—either lost or stolen—but Daniel was skeptical, because this woman had a history of "losing" valuable jewelry. He wanted Mia to check into it—maybe shadow the woman for a few days—and see if she wore the bracelet in question, or any of the jewelry she had reported missing on earlier dates.

Perfect. Neither of these new cases required two people, so we both had one to keep us busy.

The chiropractor's office was on South Lamar, near Bluebonnet. Before my massage, I decided to made an impromptu stop at a certain bungalow in Barton Hills.

Colin Kelly answered the door again, but this time, after recognizing me, he was much friendlier. In fact, he stepped onto the porch and gave me a bear hug.

"Dude," he said. "You are awesome."

"Thanks."

I still wondered about that perfectly round scar in the center of his forehead—but I didn't wonder enough to ask about it.

"You nailed that little fucker," he said. "That Leo Pitts guy."

"Yep."

"But I heard he's denying everything."

"So far, yeah, but that won't work. His lawyer will advise him to accept a plea, and he will."

"Think he's out on bond?"

"Probably." I knew what Colin was thinking. "Best that you don't pay him a visit. You'll only get yourself in trouble."

"Yeah, okay. Wanna come inside? It's hot out here."

"Is Serenity home?"

"Not right now. She should be back in about an hour."

"Just tell her I stopped by to say hello, okay?" I said. "I'll catch her some other time."

Was that why I was here? To say hello? The case was closed. How come it didn't feel closed?

"You got it, bro. Thanks again."

I realize this probably makes me a pig, but I'd been hoping the chiropractor, named Stacy Belmont, would be a lithesome beauty with a soothing voice and tender hands. He was not. Stacy was about 50 years old, with thinning hair, a beer belly, and the stench of cigarette smoke in his clothes. He wore a white medical smock to give him credibility. Didn't work.

"Got any joint problems?" he asked. "Back problems? Pain or discomfort anywhere?"

I was already on the massage table, naked, on my stomach, with a towel draped over my backside. My face was in the circular ring thingy, which left me a beautiful view of the carpet below.

"None at all," I said. That's how the client had instructed me to answer.

"No aches or pain at all anywhere?" he asked.

"Nope."

"Never sprained a ligament or hurt any cartilage?"

"Nope."

"That's rare. Any surgery of any kind?"

"Had my spleen removed after I got shot in the chest," I said, because he was going to see the scar eventually anyway. "But it doesn't hurt."

Important to deny any pain, so he couldn't later claim that we'd agreed on any treatment beyond the massage.

"Jesus, really?" he said. "What happened?"

He placed his hands on my shoulders and began the massage.

"Long story," I said. "But it's all good now. Healed up perfectly."

"Wow. Okay. That's wild. I don't think I've ever met anyone who got shot."

My clothes were stacked in a chair in the corner, and on top was the baseball cap I'd worn. It had a built-in pinhole video camera that was recording all of this. Not the greatest quality, but it would do.

I was hoping to limit the conversation from here on out, but he kept at it, saying, "I feel a pretty big knot right there. Any discomfort?" He was working on a spot beneath my left shoulder blade.

"No, it feels fine," I said.

"You're carrying a lot of tension right there," he said. "Really bunched up."

"Funny, I don't feel it at all."

"Might be a pulled muscle," he said. "Been doing any lifting lately?"

"Nope."

"Sports? Tennis or golf?"

"My biggest exercise lately is reaching for the remote. I'm all good, though. No complaints. All I really need is the massage."

For ten more minutes, he probed—both physically and verbally—trying to build a good reason to bill my insurance company for treating an injury, whether I agreed to the treatment or not. I didn't give him one. Finally he shut up and just went about the massage.

I lay there in silence, and my mind wandered to the house on Raleigh Avenue in Tarrytown. The coin toss had come up tails, which meant I wasn't supposed to make an offer, but I'd made an offer anyway. The seller had turned it down in a matter of hours, without a counter-offer. Of course, I'd instructed Abby to tell them it was a take-it-or-leave it offer, and they must've taken me at my word. Abby had asked if I wanted to go full price, but I hadn't decided yet.

After the massage, I went back to my apartment and sent the video—which looked like footage from some undercover prostitution sting—to my client. Now it was simply a waiting game. Would Stacy, the cigarette-smoking chiropractor, file fraudulent claims after my visit? I figured he probably would, because anyone who thought he could get away with such an unsophisticated scam—especially in the digital age—wouldn't let a pain-free patient foul things up.

Just as I was finishing up, I heard a knock on my door. Strange, during working hours on a weekday. Turned out to be Rita, my neighbor directly across the breezeway. She was a cashier at Whole Foods and had an ever-changing work schedule.

She stood about five feet tall and had six piercings running up one ear, another piercing in her lip, and one in a nostril. I'd learned that she was 23, but she looked about 15. I knew from previous conversations that she was damn bright, but also kind of flighty.

"You doing all right, Roy?" she asked.

"Not bad. You?"

"Good, but somebody woke me up earlier banging on your door."

"Yeah? Any idea who it was?"

"Some guy."

"Seriously? Because I just saw some guy driving next to me on Barton Springs Road. Then I saw some guy riding a bike in Zilker Park."

She grinned.

"Yeah, okay. He was about your age, but not as cute. Wearing khakis and, you know, like those shirts golfers wear."

"So a golf shirt."

"If that's what they call them."

"Was he missing an eye?"

"What? No. I would've said that first. He asked if I'd seen you today, but I said no. Which was true."

I already knew who it was, but I asked anyway.

"Good cologne? Nice tan? Looks like he models for LL Bean?"

"Exactly. So you know him?"

"He's a hit man for the Texas Mafia. True story."

"You're so full of it."

"His name is Garlen," I said. "He's my partner's ex-boyfriend, as of just a few days ago. He's not taking the break-up well."

I figured he had continued to contact Mia, and she had probably put her foot down earlier today and told him to take a hike. That's why he was looking for me—to vent his anger.

"But why is he mad at you?" Rita asked.

"Well, I might've, uh, facilitated the split. Just a little bit."

"I've seen your partner," Rita said. "I don't think I'd let her go easy, either."

# 28

Of course, this news from Rita made me want to text Mia, and I had a good work-related excuse. So I said: **Done with massage. How's your case?**

Three minutes later, she called, sounding excited.

"Last night I checked this woman's Facebook page, but her privacy settings were too tight. So I randomly went to some of her friends' pages, and then to her sister's page, and I saw a photo from last week where I'm pretty sure she's wearing the missing bracelet."

"The woman or the sister?" I asked.

"The sister. The photo is kind of blurry, but I think this woman—the one who's claiming the bracelet went missing—gave it to her sister."

"What if they have identical bracelets?"

"That's a possibility, I guess, but the sister is insured through the same company, and she doesn't have a bracelet like that on her policy. Makes me wonder if that's what happened to the other items that went missing—she gave them to her sister, who may or may not know what's going on."

"How blurry is the photo?" I asked.

"Enough that I can't be sure. So right now I'm sitting outside the Four Seasons, waiting for her—the sister—to finish with brunch or whatever she's doing. When she went in, it looked like she was wearing the bracelet. I've got the super-zoom ready."

We both had kick-ass Canon cameras with a 50-power zoom lens. If Mia could get a good photo of the bracelet, and if it appeared identical to the one that was missing, she and her client would then have two options: offer the sisters the chance to stay out of trouble if the bracelet was suddenly "found," or turn the photo over to the police and let them turn up the heat.

"Don't let me screw up your shot," I said.

"I'm on speaker," Mia said. "Believe me, the camera is ready to go. What's going on with you?"

I told her a little more about the persistent chiropractor, then changed the subject by saying, "I hate to pry, but I'm going to ask anyway. What's the status on Garlen?"

"Any particular reason you're asking?"

"Actually, yeah. My neighbor said a guy matching his description was knocking on my door earlier this morning."

Mia let out a sigh. "I'm sorry."

"Hey, it's not your fault—but can you tell me what's up?"

"I saw him drive past my house a couple of times this morning, so I went outside and waited at the curb. When he came by again, I stopped him. I said what he was doing could now be considered stalking, and that I had reached the point of zero tolerance."

I groaned.

She said, "I reminded him that I'm great at gathering evidence, and that I'm also damn good at defending myself. He tried to talk and I said nope, we're done, and that if I saw him again, it would be the worst day he'd had in a long time. Then I went back inside. He drove away and that was it, I thought. I'm sorry he showed up at your place."

She wasn't emotional. Just hard-nosed and matter of fact. I was glad about that. She was done with him, and there would be no going back. I knew her well enough to be confident about that.

"I can handle it," I said. "In fact, I had to handle it once already."

"What're you talking about?"

I hadn't told her about the incident with Garlen in the parking lot outside my apartment the previous week, but now I shared every detail.

Mia immediately said, "Why didn't you tell me before now?"

"I was hoping you were done with him, in which case there was no reason to upset you with it."

"Damn it, Roy. That's not fair. You need to tell me these things."

"You're right. I'm sorry."

"So that's why his nose was red and swollen. You know what he told me when it happened?"

"What?"

"That he'd been stung by a bee."

"Well, in a manner of speaking, I'm kind of—"

"Not in the mood for it," Mia said.

"Okay," I said.

I waited for her to say something. She finally said, "I should probably remind you that he has a concealed carry permit."

"I remember. You think I should be concerned?"

"Hang on." There was a short silence. Then she said, "Sorry, wasn't her. Honestly, no, I don't think there's anything to worry about—but then again I didn't think he'd take the break-up as badly as he has. I didn't think he'd be such a jerk. Just be careful, that's all. Especially since you already kicked his ass once."

"I will," I said.

Another pause.

Then Mia said, "I just don't understand how there can be two sides to a person like that. He was so sweet and thoughtful."

*And also a liar and a stalker,* I wanted to say, but I kept quiet. She already knew what he was. No need to make her feel worse about it.

Instead, I decided to invite her to dinner tonight. Get her out of the house. Take her mind off Garlen.

"Mia, why don't we—"

"Oh, there she is. I'll call you later."

She hung up, and I waited.

Less than five minutes later, she texted me: **Boom! Done!**

I replied: **Got your shot?**

**Yep. Compare. Here's a pic from the client.**

She sent a photo of a bracelet with a lot of diamonds. It was impressive, but, honestly, I had a hard time believing how much it was worth. I can never see much difference between a piece of jewelry that's worth a few thousand bucks and a similar one that's worth a hundred thousand bucks. And what about fakes? Who could tell whether the diamonds were real without using a loupe or a microscope?

Now Mia sent the photo she had just taken.

**Twins,** I said back. I might not be able to judge the value of jewelry, but it was easy enough to see when two pieces appeared identical.

**I'd say I'm done then,** she said.

**I agree.**

**What were you about to say earlier?** she said.

**Want to grab some dinner tonight?**

A full minute passed. What was she doing? Sending the photo to Daniel Ivy? Or deciding whether she wanted to say yes?

Then she finally said. **Sounds good.**

**Got something I want to discuss,** I said.

And it was true. Not Garlen, either. Not anything personal.

**The Raleigh Street house?** she asked. Then she added: **I talked to Abby,** followed by a smiley face.

**No, something else,** I said.

**What?**

**The Alex Dunn murder.**

**What about it?** she asked.

**I think we should try to solve it.**

I picked her up at seven and took her to Salty Sow on Manor Road, because we'd driven past it a few weeks earlier and she'd said she wanted to try it sometime. They billed themselves as an "American gastropub" that served "contemporary farmhouse fare" which was "mindfully sourced," and they also pointed out that the place was "unpretentious." Something smelled good, I'll give it that much.

"So…" Mia said, scanning the menu. The place was packed.

Mia had already ordered a "Rosemary's Piglet," which was a drink of some sort. I'd requested a Miller beer, and our waiter informed me that they primarily focused on craft products from regional breweries. So I'd asked him to bring me whatever he liked best. He told me what it was, but I'd already forgotten the name of it, although I think it was a lager. We'd also ordered some truffled deviled eggs for starters, although Mia had expressed interest in the bacon and gruyère roasted bone marrow. I'm pretty sure she was pulling my leg. Hope so.

"So…" I said in reply.

"The Alex Dunn thing, huh?" She was looking at me over the top of her menu.

"I don't know," I said. "Maybe. Why not?"

"Because we aren't being paid to solve it?" Mia said.

She was absolutely gorgeous tonight, meaning she looked like she always did. She was wearing a red-and-white striped button-down shirt, a denim skirt, and sandals.

I said, "How dare you be so profit-driven and financially responsible."

"Gotta pay for all these meals we've been eating," she said. "First the Hula Hut, and now this. You're spoiling me."

"You deserve to be spoiled," I said.

"Thank you." She looked at her menu again, but she was smiling with satisfaction.

I said, "I'm not talking about spending a massive number of man-hours on it. But we have some free time yet again, because we're both so damn good at our jobs."

"But, seriously," Mia said. "Why do you want to solve it?"

"Curiosity, I guess. And just to prove we can."

"Trying to keep me busy so I won't think about Garlen?" she said.

Our waiter arrived just then with our drinks and the deviled eggs, which were topped with bacon and chives. "Have you decided on your entrées?" he asked.

"Just need a few more minutes," I said.

"How's the candied pork belly?" Mia asked.

"Divine," said the waiter.

When he left, I pretended I hadn't heard Mia's question. Instead, I said, "The fried chicken looks good, but when they say 'neck bone gravy,' do they really mean it? Wait. Never mind. Don't tell me."

We put our menus down. Mia sipped her drink, nodded approvingly, and sipped again. I took a drink of my beer. Not bad, whatever it was.

"But we drop it if new work comes in, right?" Mia said. The room was loud enough that we were leaning over the table.

"Sure. Or if it appears we're spinning our wheels."

I gestured toward the plate of deviled eggs. Mia picked one up and took a dainty bite. I took one and popped the entire thing into my mouth.

Mia said, "You understand that Ruelas and his team have access to phone records, emails, texts, social media posts that we can't see..."

"Yeah."

"They've gotten several search warrants, and they're the only ones who know exactly what they found..."

"Right."

"They've got the footage from Alex Dunn's security camera..."

"I know."

"And they still haven't figured out who killed him."

"That obviously means they need our help," I said.

Mia laughed. "Got any bright ideas how we should go about it?"

"Have you ever known me to have a bright idea?" I said. "I prefer the fumble-around-and-get-lucky method, like my junior prom. Look at it this way: there's absolutely no pressure. If we strike out, we strike out. Damn, these eggs are good."

"They are."

I put another one in my mouth, and as I was chewing, I looked across the room and saw a familiar face looking right at me, before she quickly looked away.

When I was younger, and when Austin was smaller, I would always see at least one person I knew—sometimes several—almost anywhere I went. For instance, a trip to the grocery store could turn into a miniature high-school reunion. If I went to a nightclub with friends, I'd see many of the same people I'd seen the previous weekend, or the weekend before that. But that had changed as the population had grown, and now it was the norm to feel anonymous in my own hometown.

Except this time.

Kiersten was seated at a small table against the far wall.

"What?" Mia said. She looked in the direction I was looking.

Kiersten's dinner companion was, by any standard, a handsome gentleman. Mid-forties, dressed in an expensive, well-tailored suit. He looked familiar.

"You recognize that guy?" I said.

"With the red tie?"

"Yeah."

Mia watched him discreetly for a moment, and when he turned to look for the waiter, she said, "I think he used to be a state senator. I can't remember his name right now. You know him?"

"No, but he's rubbing knees with the woman I've been dating lately."

"Oh," Mia said, in the way one says it when you hear some juicy gossip that is titillating and unexpected. *Ooohhh.*

"Not a big deal," I said. "We've only gone out a few times."

Kiersten was doing her absolute best not to look this way again.

"What's her name?" Mia asked.

"Kiersten Stanley."

"Max Dunn's realtor?"

"Yep."

"So you asked her out after she showed you the Raleigh house?"

"During, actually," I said. "And I only did it because she couldn't keep her eyes off me. It was inevitable that she was going to throw herself at me, and I wanted to help preserve her dignity."

Mia wasn't listening very closely. She was too busy watching Kiersten and the former senator out of the corner of her eye.

"Based on body language—and this is just a guess—I'd say he's been seeing her a little longer than you have."

I took another drink of my beer.

"She's wearing a bandage dress," Mia said, "and she's getting away with it, too. She's pretty hot, from what I can see."

Mia turned her gaze back to me.

"Is that an amused grin on your face?" I said.

"No, not really," she said.

"Looks like one."

"Okay, maybe a little. But it's not a big deal, right?"

I shrugged.

Over the years, Mia had teased me a little about my dating habits, and I had never figured out quite why, because she wasn't the judgmental type, and she certainly didn't disapprove of two consenting adults engaging in whatever behavior might please them. Was it jealousy? I'd wondered about that on occasion, but if so, why would she attempt to set me up with Abby? That didn't make any sense.

"I'm curious," Mia said. "Will you see her again after this?"

I was surprised to realize the answer was probably no.

"Don't know," I said.

"Had the two of you talked about dating exclusively?"

"Nope. In fact, she doesn't know who you are, so she might think you're my date tonight."

Mia said, "Wait a sec. Are you saying I'm not your date?"

Being playful.

"Well," I said.

"I'm a really fun date," Mia said.

"You don't have to convince me."

"And I don't go floozing around with politicians," she said.

"To be fair," I said, "I wouldn't say she's floozing around."

Mia didn't look convinced. "I guess that depends on how your dates with her went."

"Not as well as this one," I said.

"So it *is* a date?" she asked.

"You tell me," I said.

Our eyes met again, and we both held it for a long moment.

"Oh, Roy," Mia said.

"What?"

"Nothing. Hey, I have an idea! Let's set her and Garlen up on a blind date. They'd be perfect together."

**29**

The next morning, at nine o'clock, we stood on a slab of limestone rock and looked down to Barton Creek, 90 feet below. I was five feet from the edge, and that was as close as I was going to get. I wasn't scared of heights, per se, but the idea of falling gave me enough anxiety to make my palms damp. There was water in the creek below, so if a person slipped—or jumped—they might survive. Or they might not. Of course, when Alicia Potter's sister had fallen, there hadn't been any water in the creek because of a drought. She'd had no chance at all.

"Beautiful view," Mia said.

Both of us were dressed in T-shirts, shorts, and running shoes. The trail to the ledge was smooth from all the foot traffic over the years, but we were the only people out here this morning. From what I'd read, climbers didn't tackle this wall much during the summer because it was too hot and exposed. There were more enjoyable climbs nearby.

"I wonder if Alicia and her sister had ever been out here before,"

I said.

It had been my idea last night at dinner to start here, because we had to start somewhere. Better than sitting around with coffee and notepads. Sometimes, as with taking an impromptu canoe ride, you had to look at things from a different perspective, both literally and figuratively.

"If they had," Mia said, "surely she would've remembered that the rock tilts slightly forward. It wouldn't take much to lose your footing, especially if the surface was damp."

"Lose your footing or get shoved over," I said.

We were no more than a hundred yards from houses along Bluffview Drive to our east, and we could see traffic crawling along Loop 360 and Loop 1 in the distance, but the slab felt strangely isolated.

"I gotta say it would be ridiculously easy to commit a murder here," Mia said. "Especially if your victim trusted you."

I sat down on the flat rock and Mia did the same. The sun was low in the sky behind us, casting our squat shadows to the edge and over the ledge. The warmth on my back felt great and was making me drowsy.

"It would still be good to know what kind of relationship Alicia Potter and Alex Dunn had after their divorce," Mia said. "Max Dunn said they had dinner now and then, but what does that mean? Once a month? Once a year? Did she have access to his house? Did she have a key? When was the last time she was over there? We've never gotten good answers."

I said, "More important, did she think she was still in the will? According to Max, she wasn't, and if she knew that, then what motive did she have to kill Alex? What did she stand to gain?"

"Surely she was in the will when they were married, right?"

"I would assume so."

"So Alex must've changed it at some point after the divorce. But when did he change it? Is it possible she came up with this scheme to kill him while she was still in the will—maybe even several months after the divorce—but he revised it before he took the poison pill?"

A pair of ravens soared low over the creek, calling back and forth.

"I can't remember how long ago they got divorced," I said. "Do you remember?"

"I gathered it was near the end of last year."

"Well, let's find out," I said, pulling my phone from my pocket.

I surfed to a Texas public records website that included a divorce database. Fast and easy. Had the answer in about 20 seconds. "Eight months ago," I said.

"Meaning it's a stretch to think Alex Dunn hadn't revised his will yet."

"Not necessarily. Sometimes it's easy to overlook stuff like that, especially if the divorce wasn't particularly ugly."

Gnats were now buzzing around my head. My shirt was starting to stick to my back. I should've brought a couple of bottles of water.

"Max Dunn seems like a much more likely suspect," Mia said.

"Or the McMansion angle," I said. "We never really looked into that. He pissed a lot of people off."

"Again, though, it would have to be someone who had access to his home."

"Maybe, but what if he regularly carried his heart meds with him in his car?"

"We need to do what we did that morning in the conference room last week—rule some people out, instead of trying to figure out who did it. You agree?"

"Sure. Why not? But how do we do that? We need more facts. More raw information. We have a lot of questions, but what we need is more answers, and I'm not sure where we can get them."

Now it was Mia's turn to reach into her pocket for her phone.

Would you believe Callie Dunn was not wearing yoga pants this time? She opened the door of her father's house dressed in green Capri pants and a sleeveless white-and-green-striped blouse. The kind of outfit that would make her friends say, "Oh, don't you look cute! I couldn't get away with that."

"Come on in," Callie said, and we stepped into the spacious foyer, which had a marble floor and ten-foot ceilings. Stunning place. No surprise.

It was now three in the afternoon. Earlier, on the ledge above the creek, we'd had no idea how Callie would respond to Mia's request—which was to allow us to search Alex Dunn's home—but she had agreed. She'd only placed one condition on it: We'd get one search, just the one time, because she and Max had hired a firm to conduct an estate sale for most of the possessions in the house. Other items would be donated to charity and some stuff would simply be trashed. The firm would be starting the process in two days.

Callie closed the door behind us. "Honestly, I can't imagine you'll find anything useful after the police have been through everything, but you're more than welcome to look. I owe you one for finding the coin collection."

"Thanks, but you really don't owe us anything," Mia said. "That's our job."

"Well, I'm very grateful. Those coins meant a lot to my dad, so it's good that we got them back. Now..." She spread her arms in a gesture that meant, *Look wherever you want.*

"You mind a couple of questions first?" I asked.

"Sure. What's up?"

"Did the police get a warrant for this place, or did you and your brothers grant them permission to search?"

"We gave them permission. Max and I did."

"Did they have you sign a document?"

"They did, yes."

"Any chance I could see a copy of that?"

It would be important to know whether Ruelas and his team had searched Alex Dunn's computer.

"Sure. It's at home. I can send you a copy later."

"Perfect. Do you know if they got warrants for your dad's phone records?"

"They did, but I have no idea what they found. They haven't told us much about their investigation so far, to be honest."

"Detective Ruelas can be sort of a tyrant," I said.

"Really?" Callie said. "I find him kind of charming. Like you."

Mia let out a laugh and faux-whispered to Callie, "They don't get along. Imagine two brothers squabbling."

"The difference," I said, ignoring Mia, "is that his charm is part of an evil plan."

Callie said, "And what is the objective of his plan?"

"I haven't figured that out yet. Probably world domination."

"Sounds dastardly," Callie said. "Do y'all want anything to drink before you start?"

"No, thanks," I said.

"We're good," Mia said.

"Need anything at all?"

"I assume your dad had a home office or den…" Mia said.

"Down that hall, last room on the right," Callie said, pointing.

"Perfect."

"I know you already know this," Callie said, "but I don't want you to take anything without telling me."

"We absolutely will not," I said.

"And if you find anything that is unrelated to my dad's murder— I would want you to keep that confidential."

Mia said, "We realize it takes a great deal of trust to let two people you hardly know rummage around in your father's possessions. I promise you we won't violate that trust."

Callie nodded and smiled. "I appreciate that."

I said, "I assume your dad had a computer here at home."

"He did. It's still in there."

"Would it be okay if I were to copy the hard drive?"

Now she frowned. "Quite honestly, I'm not comfortable with that."

"No problem," I said. "I won't do that."

"Surely you can understand."

"I can."

"Anything else?" she asked.

"I think we're all set."

"Okay, well, I'll just hang out in the living room, so holler if you need anything. I need to leave in about an hour."

We both thanked her again, and then we went down the hall to the office, which was more of a library, and an impressive one at that. Two walls were filled floor to ceiling with books in built-in shelves.

Another wall, to the left, had three large windows looking to the rear of the property, which consisted of a heavily wooded and overgrown hillside sloping down to a creek. No manicured lawn and swimming pool for Alex Dunn.

I turned toward the large mahogany desk and was thrilled to see a Macintosh. I'm no computer guru, but I'm much better with a Mac than I am with a PC. While Mia went to a file cabinet and began to explore, I took a seat at the desk in front of the Macintosh. The screen saver appeared to be a random slideshow of Alex Dunn's vacation photos. I held my breath and hit the spacebar to bring the Mac out of sleep mode. Another bit of luck—no password required.

Alex Dunn maintained a clean desktop. Instead of keeping dozens of files and folders all over the screen, he had one folder called, "Alex's Files." I double-clicked it and found two more folders—"Personal" and "Work"—and each of those folders contained hundreds of additional folders. I expected as much, but now I really wished Callie was willing to let me copy the hard drive.

I spent about 15 minutes clicking through the Personal folder. Nothing jumped out at me, but then again, I was only perusing. It would take several hours to check each file within each folder.

I spent another 15 minutes poking around in the Work folder, which had three or four times more content than the Personal folder. There were folders about various business deals, proposals, feasibility studies, market analyses, and so on. Again, nothing of interest popped up, but, admittedly, I could have been looking directly at a vital piece of evidence without knowing it, and it would have taken hours, or even days, to review it all thoroughly.

Mia and I had been mostly quiet, focused on our searches, when she said, "Your luck as bad as mine?"

"Yep. Too much stuff."

I opened the web browser, Safari. Like most people, Alex Dunn had hundreds of bookmarks contained in a dizzying assortment of folders and subfolders. I started with the Favorites list, which was mostly business-related sites, plus various financial institutions, including Merrill Lynch, Capital One, and Scottrade.

Then I saw what I was looking for—a bookmark called "Security Camera." The camera at his front door streamed to the web, which allowed him to access it and review footage by logging in from anywhere. I clicked the link and was greeted with a sign-in page asking for a password. Crud. I tried a few random guesses but got nowhere. I was disappointed, but also kind of relieved, because how exactly would I go about reviewing what could be a month's worth of vidco?

I went back to Dunn's bookmarks. Most were fairly self-explanatory, except for one simply called "Riley2." I double-clicked it and was confused when I was taken to a log-in page for a Hushmail account. Again, there was a sign-in page that asked for an email address and a passphrase. Of course, I didn't know either.

I clicked over to Apple Mail and went to Dunn's preferences to see if there was a Hushmail account listed. There wasn't. That meant Dunn did not automatically receive emails from that account. He had to log in via the website.

It appeared Alex Dunn had a secret email address.

**30**

Mia must've seen the expression on my face, because she said, "Got something?"

"Possibly," I said. "But I'm not sure." I explained about the bookmark and where it took me.

"Riley two?" Mia said. She was still rooting through the file cabinet.

"Have you come across the name Riley in any of his documents?" I said.

"Not that I recall," Mia said, "but I wasn't specifically looking for it."

"Probably nothing," I said. Many people keep an extra email account to use as a throwaway of sorts when giving the address to some business or website that might send spam later.

The log-in page had very little text on it. I clicked on a link that said, "Can't remember your passphrase?"

The resulting page informed me that the security features of Hushmail were designed in a way that even Hushmail staff members couldn't recover a lost passphrase. Basically, if you forgot it, you were screwed. But there was a chance I might at least be able to figure out the email address itself. I typed the letter "a" into the box for the email address—and nothing happened. It did not auto-populate, meaning the email address did not start with an "a." That, or the page had been designed to prevent auto-population—just one more layer of security.

I deleted the "a" and entered a "b." Still nothing.

So I entered the remaining letters of the alphabet, one at a time, deleting the previous one before entering a new one, all to no avail. Then I did the same with the numerals from 0 to 9. Zilch. Time to give up and move on, because our hour would be up soon.

I scanned through the remainder of Dunn's bookmarks and found none that seemed odd or out of place.

Fifty minutes had passed.

Then I had one of those ingenious ideas that only comes to those with creative and razor-sharp intellects, or, occasionally, to me.

I went to the Hushmail page where Alex Dunn, or anyone else, would sign up for an account. This was not the log-in page, it was simply the account registration page, and I wondered if the security features would be less stringent.

In the blank where you were asked to "Choose your new email address," I did the same thing I'd done earlier—I entered the letters of the alphabet, one at a time, deleting the previous one before I entered a new one.

One by one, my hopes were dashed.

Then I typed in "m" and the blank auto-populated with Alex Dunn's Hushmail address—MaxCallieCole@hushmail.com.

"Damn, I'm good," I said.

"What?"

"I figured out the email address."

"Cool. Anything interesting?"

"Well, I still don't know the passphrase."

"Oh."

Now, of course, I tried entering letters individually into the "Create your passphrase" blank, but when you typed into that space, you didn't see a letter, you saw a dot, because it was encrypted. I was fairly certain that meant it would not auto-populate—and I was right. My luck had run out.

"How's it going in here?" Callie Dunn said, appearing in the doorway to the library. She was her typical friendly self, but her tone had just a hint of *Are you done yet?*

"Does the name 'Riley' mean anything to you?" I asked.

Callie thought for a moment, then said, "I don't think so. Should it?"

"Just a name I stumbled across," I said. "Actually your dad bookmarked an email account with that name, which doesn't seem to have anything to do with the site he marked."

Callie was shaking her head. She had no idea.

"He didn't have any friends or business associates named Riley?" I asked.

"None that I know of," Callie said. "Sorry."

"I'm curious," I said. "Did the police ask you that same question?"

"About someone named Riley?" she said.

"Right."

"Nope. They asked me a lot of questions, but not that one. Do you think you found something important?"

I didn't want to get her hopes up, only to dash them later, and I had no idea whether I had actually found a clue, so I said, "Probably not. But if you think of any connection between your dad and that name, please let us know."

"Will do."

She stood in the doorway, and it was obvious we had reached our time limit.

"Okay, then," I said, standing up from the desk. "We really appreciate your cooperation."


"Feeling pretty good about yourself, huh?" Mia said as we got into her Mustang.

"Because of my brilliant find?"

"Yeah."

"It didn't lead anywhere, though," I said.

"You know what I'm talking about," she said.

"Oh, you mean the fact that I found something that Ruelas and his team of rank amateurs overlooked? Yes, that is somewhat rewarding, but not surprising, given my history of surpassing him in every measurable way."

"Including ego," Mia said. She was backing onto the street now.

"Sure, I'm self-confident," I said. "It's simply the result of my many achievements over the years."

"Okay, Mr. Achiever. Where are we going now?"

She put the car into gear and began to ease forward.

"Did you see anything in his files about the McMansion brouhaha?" I asked.

"When he built Callie's house?"

"Yeah."

"Some letters from attorneys, but nothing I wouldn't expect. Some neighborhood groups threatened to sue, but nobody ever did. I'm sure Alex Dunn could afford more legal firepower than any of the neighbors would've been willing to match, and it appears Dunn did everything aboveboard anyway. He ultimately had a right to build that house, whether anyone liked it or not."

"I need to go over this in my head, to make sure I remember all the details," I said. "Alex Dunn bought an existing house in Tarrytown, and as far as the owners knew, he was planning to renovate the house. But instead, he demolished it and built Callie's McMansion. That sums it up, right?"

"Right. The owners thought he deceived them. Otherwise, they wouldn't have sold. Where are we going? My house?"

"How about we just drive for a while?"

"Sounds good." She headed east, back toward town.

My phone vibrated with a text. Kiersten said: **How's it going, stud?**

I wasn't sure how to react. Was she going to pretend she hadn't seen me at Salty Sow last night? I wasn't going to play that game. I said: **Will call you later.**

She replied with a thumbs-up emoji.

I put my phone back into my pocket.

"What is the process for demolishing a house like that?" I asked Mia. "What are the specific steps? Because you can't just do it, obviously. It has to be approved."

"If the home is more than 50 years old—and this one was—the demolition permit has to be sent to the Historic Preservation Office for review. They decide whether or not the home is historically significant. If they think it is, they can put a hold on demolition."

"What does 'historically significant' mean, exactly? That's pretty vague."

"It usually means there is something unique about it, like it was designed by some well-known architect, or something important happened there, or somebody famous lived in the house."

"So what happens if the preservation office decides the house is significant?"

"They pass the demolition permit—along with a recommendation, I think—to a city commission that deals with historic landmarks."

"And the commission decides whether the home gets demolished?" I asked.

"They vote on whether to give the house landmark status, which would halt demolition, and then pass their recommendation along to the city council."

She went north on Loop 1.

I said, "So the commission can decide that a house does or does not deserve landmark status, but ultimately the city council has to bless their decision?"

"Yes, because it's a zoning change. That's what the council has to approve—the zoning change—and I gather that some people think the council is less worried about the historical aspect and more worried about giving away too many tax breaks. See, historical homes get a tax break. Some critics say it's just another way for wealthy people to dodge taxes."

The issue of a tax break didn't apply to Callie Dunn's situation, because tearing down the old house meant she lost the break—and I doubted she was too concerned about the difference in taxes anyway.

Mia continued: "Another thing that happens is, when these old homes are bulldozed and a new home is built, not only are they taxed at full value, they're usually worth a lot more than the previous home. So property taxes can skyrocket—not just for the owner of the new home, but for everyone in the neighborhood."

That hadn't occurred to me. "Which is another reason for neighbors to be angry at the Dunns and anyone else who builds a McMansion," I said. "So that means the pool of possible suspects includes just about everyone in Tarrytown. Wonderful."

"It does create a lot of resentment," Mia said.

She took the 35th Street exit and went west.

I said, "I don't want to sound like a cynic, but wouldn't the people in charge of approving or denying landmark status or granting a zoning change be ripe targets for a certain type of financial inducement?"

"My heavens, Roy Ballard, are you suggesting bribery?"

"Just thinking out loud, for now."

The road forked at the water treatment plant and Mia stayed to the left, went several hundred yards, and turned right.

"Mount Bonnell?" I said.

"Why not?" said Mia. "I'd like to enjoy a view without fear of falling off a cliff."

# 31

The Historic Landmark Commission had twelve appointed members and the Historic Preservation Office had three staff members.

"I guess I don't totally understand the difference between the commission and the office," I said, looking at my phone. "But I'm also not certain it matters. This page says the office 'protects and enhances neighborhoods, buildings, and sites that reflect elements of Austin's cultural, social, economic, political, and architectural history.' Doesn't the commission do that, too? Because this other page—hold on—this page says the commission 'promotes historic preservation activities in Austin.' Sounds redundant to me."

We were seated around a concrete picnic table, enjoying one of the finest panoramas in Travis County. It made the ledge above Barton Creek look like amateur hour, quite frankly. Mount Bonnell is a prominent point high above Lake Austin, providing sweeping views up- and downstream. I hadn't been up here in several years, and the increased development to the west was noticeable. We were the only visitors here at the moment. I could see a dozen boats zooming along the narrow lake below, with at least half of them pulling skiers.

"I'm no expert," Mia said, "but I think the office has much broader duties than the commission. I think the staff reviews all the applications that come in and handles all the administrative stuff. And only some of the cases have to go to the commission."

"Bottom line," I said, "it sounds like anyone wanting a house designated as historical—or wanting to demolish a house that might be historical—has to jump through quite a few hoops, starting with the historic preservation officer. Right?"

"Right."

"So who is that? The preservation officer."

She grabbed her phone and we were both silent for a moment as she surfed. She was cupping the screen so she could see it better.

"A man named Albert Strauss. It appears he's been in that position for about ten years."

She kept reading and I sat waiting.

"Here's an article about a house that was up for a vote on historical zoning, and it sure sounds like the commission decides what is designated as a historical landmark. The preservation officer presents them with an application, and then they decide, and the city council votes whether to approve the zoning change."

"Is it the same way with demolitions?" I asked.

She kept reading. I was glad our table was in the shade. It was getting muggy up here. "I think so," she said. "There are dozens of articles about all this stuff—McMansions, the landmark commission, Albert Strauss, taxes, and so on. Lots of controversy, or at least some debate about, well, just about everything. Then you have residents who feel the same way Alex Dunn did—meaning they don't want the city telling them what they can or can't do with their own property." She began shaking her head. "Too much to read right now."

She put her phone down on the table. A cloud was blocking the sun at the moment, and I noticed, before the screen went dark, that she still had a photo of Garlen as her wallpaper. He was smiling at the camera, looking like a typical jerk. I was hoping she'd simply been too busy lately to change the photo, or perhaps it had been on there long enough that she didn't even notice it anymore. It also made me think of Kiersten, who had texted me earlier in the afternoon. I hadn't replied yet, because I wasn't sure what I wanted to say.

I pushed all that from my mind and said, "I think we need to talk to that Strauss guy and maybe some of the commissioners."

"Maybe, but if we're exploring the possibility of bribery, how would that have resulted in Dunn's murder?" Mia said. "I mean, if Dunn bribed someone, or several people, what happened after that? He got his demolition permit, so if there were bribes involved, it would appear they worked. None of the people bribed would have a motive to kill him. Right?"

I didn't answer, because I didn't know.

"Now, if Dunn offered a bribe and then didn't pay up, that might be different," Mia said.

"I think," I said slowly, "when a couple of people begin to conspire, there are a lot of things that can go wrong."

"Such as?"

"One of them gets paranoid and thinks they're about to be busted. Decides to kill the one person who can implicate them."

"Not bad. What else?" Mia said.

I could hear voices carrying in the breeze—several people coming up the long concrete staircase to the top of the lookout point.

"Did I say 'a lot'?" I said. "I meant at least one."

"What about Nathan Potter?" Mia asked.

"What about him?"

"Dunn hired him to buy the old house, demolish it, and build the new one, so wouldn't he have to be right in the thick of any type of bribery situation?"

A group of seven people—all in their fifties and sixties—reached the top of the staircase, and now I could tell they weren't speaking English. German, possibly, or Dutch. A couple of them glanced in our direction, and one man smiled and gave a small wave. Mia waved back. I noticed that none of them were out of breath, or overweight, for that matter. Damn foreigners. The group gravitated toward the little viewing pavilion twenty yards uphill from where we were sitting, and then they emitted the requisite oohs and aahs as the lake below came into view.

"That's a good point," I said. "I had kind of forgotten about Nathan."

"We had no reason to think about him when we were looking for the coins. But now…"

"No, you're right," I said, "and that introduces a third party into the mix. It's like that old saying: Three people can keep a secret, if two of them are dead."

"Who said that?"

"I did. Just now. Weren't you listening?"

"I mean originally, doofus."

"I think it was Ben Franklin. Point is, I know bribery is a big leap, but if that's what happened, then we have to wonder if Nathan Potter was in on it. The more people involved, the harder it is to keep it from unraveling."

The foreigners were snapping all kinds of photos now, and taking turns posing in various pairs and groups. It was quite a production. I was noticing that, just as they hadn't been bothered by the hike up here, they didn't seem bothered by the heat. It was nearly five o'clock now, but the temperature was still at least 95.

"It all sounds reasonable to me," Mia said, "and we should at least see if we can rule it out. But how would we go about proving any of it, or even determining if it's plausible?"

"Like I said earlier—talk to Strauss and some of the commissioners."

"Just go right at 'em, huh?" Mia asked.

"Why not? We've got nothing to lose."

"If they'll even talk to us," she said.

"They will if you call. Work your magic."

Mia always had better results with cold calls than I did.

"I'll start tomorrow morning and see if I get anywhere," she said.

Obviously, we wouldn't come right out and ask these people whether there was potential for corruption in their business dealings, but we could ask some general questions about the process of gaining a demolition permit for an older home. Who knew what we might learn in the process? Maybe one of the commissioners had a reputation for cozying up to developers more than he should, or for suddenly changing his mind on a particular application.

We got up to leave, and as we walked toward the viewing pavilion, one of the foreigners, a lean man of about 65, saw us coming and asked if we would mind snapping a photo of his entire group. Mia stepped right up and took his camera from him.

After she had taken at least a dozen photos from different angles and distances, the man walked over to get his camera and thanked us.

Mia said, "Where are you from?"

"A small city in northern Germany called Wilhelmshaven. It is on the North Sea, a short drive from Hamburg."

He spoke better English than many people I encountered on a daily basis.

"Well, we hope you are enjoying your visit," Mia said.

"We certainly are. Texas is quite beautiful, and may I say, so are you."

"That's very sweet of you," Mia said. I could see that she was blushing.

One of the women in the group called out to him in German. I couldn't understand what she said, but it was obviously some good-natured cajoling, because several others in the group laughed. I gathered that this man was known either for being overly friendly or for flirting outrageously.

The man ignored them and said to me, "You are a fortunate man."

I could feel Mia looking at me, and I knew she was smiling, enjoying the way the man had put me on the spot.

"I sure am," I said.

It was true, and I needed to remember that more often, and enjoy the good moments, because my day was about to take a most unfortunate turn.

# 32

We went back to Mia's house, where my Toyota was waiting, and after agreeing to touch base in the morning, I headed toward my apartment, driving directly into the teeth of rush-hour traffic. Loop 1 was almost at a standstill, and as I crept along, I couldn't help ruminating about the case.

Was the bribery idea valid? I figured it was probably as feasible as one of the Dunn kids offing their dad for the inheritance. Then there was Alicia Potter, but what was her motive? She was out of the will and had to have known that. Was she angrier about Alex Dunn's cheating than she had ever let on? Did she kill him for revenge?

A massive SUV was directly in front of me, obscuring my view, so I had no idea why we were all going five miles per hour. Behind me, an Audi was right on my ass, impatient as hell, as if I could go any faster or even move aside to let him pass.

I wondered if anyone on the landmark commission would be willing to speak to us. I'm sure Ruelas and his team had already spoken to all of them. Ruelas was no super-sleuth, but surely he had explored the McMansion angle in regard to Alex Dunn's murder. Maybe Ruelas had even speculated that bribery was involved—in which case the commissioners might be gun shy at this point.

Now the SUV in front of me came to a complete stop. The Toyota's air conditioner was laboring to keep the interior cool. I had a suspicion that the little car wasn't going to last more than another year or two. Then I'd have to buy another equally nondescript back-up vehicle that nobody ever noticed. One without any discernible—

My thoughts were interrupted by a small jolt from the rear. I looked in the mirror. Had the Audi just bumped me? Honestly, I wasn't sure. It felt as if he had hit me. There was too much glare on the Audi's windshield for me to see the driver's reaction. Screw it. What did I care? If he'd bumped me, it wasn't going to hurt the old Toyota any.

We finally began inching forward again, and I suddenly got a wild hair and merged into the exit lane for Bee Caves Road. Some barbecue from The County Line would be nice tonight. I could get a couple of pounds of brisket and ribs to go. A pint of potato salad and a pint of beans.

Traffic through Westlake was heavy, but not as bad as Loop 1, and soon I was moving along at a blistering 30 miles per hour. I realized the Audi was still behind me, and still tailgating. What a first-class jerk.

By the time I reached Walsh Tarlton, the Audi had had several chances to pass me, but he hadn't taken them.

Weird.

Now I was wondering: What did Garlen drive? Had Mia ever mentioned what kind of vehicle he owned?

Just for grins, I turned right a minute later on Westlake Drive.

The damned Audi stayed with me. This was not a coincidence.

I could get a glimpse of the driver, but the most I could tell was that it was a male.

I was tempted to call Mia and ask what kind of car Garlen drove, but what if it wasn't him? I'd look like an idiot, and it would also get her worked up for the evening. She didn't need that.

When I reached Buckeye Trail, I turned left. The Audi followed. I drove slowly—lots of deer on this thickly wooded hillside—and the

Audi stayed right on my tail. There was no question now that this person was following me. Not just following, but harassing. The only question was, was it Garlen or someone else? Who else would it be?

I took it easy on this narrow, winding residential street, and after a few minutes, I reached Bee Caves Road again. At this intersection, when you look left, oncoming cars appear suddenly from around a tight curve. No traffic was coming right now from the left, but I waited anyway, intending to take a right. The Audi was behind me. Still I waited. The Audi honked at me. Finally, a truck came from the left. I hit the gas, taking a sharp right onto Bee Caves, with the truck zooming up behind me.

I gunned it, gaining speed as quickly as the little Toyota would let me. It wasn't long before I was up to 60 in a 45-mph zone. Westlake Hills cops were always patrolling this stretch of road, or sitting with radar running, but that was a chance I was willing to take.

There were plenty of vehicles ahead of me, so I had to change lanes frequently, darting back and forth, like an obnoxious teenage driver. When I reached the intersection with Loop 360, the light was red and I had to stop behind a cluster of waiting vehicles.

And here came the Audi. I could see him back there, four cars behind me, in the other lane. There was no way I could outrun or outmaneuver him in the Toyota.

I opened the glove box—just to reassure myself, I guess—and my handgun was in there. It hadn't magically disappeared. Nobody had stolen it. It was a nine-millimeter Glock. Full magazine, empty barrel. I wasn't crazy about driving around with it, because I didn't have a concealed handgun license, but the laws about carrying a handgun while "traveling" were ambiguous enough that I kept one in my vehicle when I felt the need. And I'd felt the need lately, considering Garlen's strange and aggressive behavior.

The light changed and the traffic began to move forward slowly. The Audi switched lanes and was now three cars behind me.

I got into the left-turn lane, and when there was a break in the traffic, I turned onto Castle Ridge Road, then swung an immediate right into the convenience store on the corner. I drove to the far side of the parking lot, away from the store and the gas pumps and waited.

A moment later, the Audi was able to make the left off Bee Caves and, as expected, he turned into the convenience store. I didn't budge. He pulled up behind me and the driver's door opened.

Out stepped Garlen.

Of course it was Garlen. Who else was it going to be?

He walked toward the Toyota, his hands empty—no weapons that I could see—but I sure as hell wasn't going to get into another brawl with him here. I dropped the Toyota into gear and goosed the gas, heading for a different exit that would put me back onto Bee Caves Road. I could see in the mirror that Garlen was waving his arms and yelling at me. Then he got back into the Audi and came after me.

Son of a bitch.

Maybe it was time to call the cops. I had dash cams mounted front and rear—same as on the van, as well as on both of Mia's vehicles—so I'd be able to show footage of Garlen following me, and probably bumping me on Loop 1.

The road was divided here, so I had to go east, back toward town, but I took the first available U-turn and went west again.

Passed the County Line. No barbecue for me.

Passed Barton Creek Country Club Road.

Passed Riverhills Road.

Garlen was back there, keeping pace with me.

Passed Cuernavaca Road.

Three minutes later, I reached Highway 71 and turned right, heading northwest. After I passed Hamilton Pool Road, traffic began to lighten up, despite all the recent development out here in recent years.

I was just going to drive. Hell, I didn't have any plans. I'd go all the way to Llano if I had to. There was plenty of good barbecue out there. A nice drive through the Hill Country right before sundown.

I passed Bee Creek Road and the highway began a long descent. This had always been a dangerous stretch, just curvy enough in some places to limit the vision of drivers pulling out from smaller roads. I was keeping it at 60 miles per hour, and now Garlen was right behind me, tailgating again.

We crossed Bee Creek and the highway began a long ascent. We passed Bob Wire Road, RO Drive, and Crawford Road, and now the Audi was less than ten feet off my bumper. I was tempted to jam the brakes and make Garlen hit me. I figured there was a pretty good chance he'd been drinking, and having a wreck while intoxicated would result in some serious charges. But our speed was too great. One or both of us might get injured. Plus, the dash cams actually worked against that idea. I couldn't just slam on the brakes without a good reason. It would be obvious I had caused the crash.

We crossed the bridge over the Pedernales River and I sped up to 70. Traffic was sparse here. Surely we would pass a sheriff's deputy or a state trooper sometime soon. The cop would see Garlen tailgating and pull him over, especially if I flashed my headlights to attract attention.

I was starting to get seriously angry. What was Garlen thinking? What was he going to do? Try to fight me again? Was he armed? Did he consider the possibility that *I* might be, and that I would have solid legal grounds to defend myself?

Without thinking it through, I hit the brakes suddenly and whipped a hard left onto Fall Creek Road. Garlen followed. I had driven this county road plenty of times. It was narrow, with lots of curves and dips, and no shoulders. Right now I was moving at 45 and that was pushing it.

I realized it had been a stupid move to leave the highway. I couldn't maintain a decent speed without endangering any possible oncoming traffic. I dropped down to 35.

Garlen hit my bumper.

I held the steering wheel tight. I wasn't going to let another impact swerve me off the pavement.

He bumped me again, harder this time.

I was officially done. This was insane. Time to call for help. I grabbed my phone to dial 911, but my heart dropped when I saw that I had no signal. That left one alternative. I had to stop the car, grab the Glock, and prepare for whatever might happen next.

I needed to find a decent place to stop—a long stretch where traffic from either direction would be able to see us. Unfortunately, the road was too curvy.

He hit me a third time, the hardest yet, and I almost lost control. It was clear that Garlen was in a rage—the type of fury that would make him come at me even as I aimed a handgun at him. I didn't want it to end that way, but I wasn't going to put myself in harm's way by hesitating to stop the threat he presented.

I could see him dropping back, but only so he could build some space between us and gain speed to ram me again. He was ten yards behind me. Now twenty. And then he came rushing toward me, rapidly growing larger and larger in my rearview mirror.

I couldn't outrun him, and I couldn't outmaneuver him, but I had an advantage. I knew this road. I knew there was a hairpin turn just ahead, almost invisible, due to the high grass on the shoulder of the road.

Just before the nose of the Audi slammed into my bumper, there was a break in the grass and I cranked the wheel to the left, left, and left some more, practically flinging the Toyota onto Old Spicewood Road. My tires squealed for mercy, and for a brief moment, I thought the small car wasn't going to hold the turn. I just knew I was going to flip or spin out. But the moment passed. I made it, and I hit the gas.

I assumed Garlen—who had been accelerating to ram me—would have no choice but to miss the turn and make a U farther down the road. But the idiot was too stubborn. He tried to make the turn, and even in a car that was much more nimble and performance-oriented than mine, he was simply asking too much of it. His speed and momentum were too great.

I was watching in the mirror—and it happened quickly.

In the time span of half a second, the Audi came screaming around the corner, the tires began to slide on the pavement, and then they hit the grass on the side of the road. The change in surfaces—and the difference in friction—was a killer.

The Audi began to roll.

The driver's-side tires rose into the air, the passenger door hit the ground, and then the car disappeared from the reflection in my mirror.

I braked hard, came to a stop, then slammed the Toyota into reverse and screamed backward.

I reached the spot where the Audi had left the road, and I could see it seventy feet away, on the other side of a flattened barbed-wire fence, resting upright, but with the roof crumpled.

*Stay cool. First things first.*

I checked my cell phone. Still no service.

I killed the engine, left the Toyota parked in the road with flashers on, and began to run.

Slowed for a moment to pick my way over the fence, then sprinted again through the grass and weeds.

As I neared the Audi, I could see that all the windows were broken. I ran to the driver's side and Garlen was still buckled in, slumped in the seat, unmoving.

"Garlen!"

Nothing. Not even a soft grunt.

I saw no blood. No bones protruding from flesh. No obvious injuries. Didn't necessarily mean he was going to be okay.

I put two fingers to the side of his neck and managed to find a strong pulse.

Best thing I could do was get him some help. The nearest house was at least a hundred yards away. Then I saw his cell phone, somehow still clasped in a little mounting bracket on the dash. I leaned in and grabbed it.

No passcode required. That was lucky.

And the luck held when I saw that he had a different carrier— and a strong signal.

I made the call.

# 33

"I'm sorry, Roy," Mia said.

"Not your fault."

"I should've known he was capable of something like that."

"How? How would you have known that?"

"I just should've known."

"People can fool you," I said.

She didn't answer. She hadn't been talking much.

We were sitting in my apartment, five hours after Garlen Gieger had flipped his car. We were on opposite ends of the couch, facing each other, both of us with a longneck bottle in hand. Our second. Last we heard, Garlen was in serious but stable condition at Brackenridge Hospital. His troubles were only beginning. He'd be arrested as soon as he was fit to leave the hospital.

Mia had had to drive out and get me, because the Blanco County deputies had impounded the Toyota, which was standard procedure. I'd get it back in a few days. I'd forgotten that the first mile or so of Fall Creek Road was in Travis County, but then it entered Blanco

County. Fine by me, because I figured the case would get more attention from a smaller sheriff's department, as well as stricter punishment from a Blanco County judge and jury, and I wanted Garlen to be prosecuted to the fullest extent of the law. What's more, Mia and I were both going to apply for protective orders that would prevent him from having any further contact or communication with either of us.

I said, "I dated a girl once who hit me with a croquet mallet when I broke up with her. Before that, she was a total sweetheart. I never told you that story?"

Mia shook her head.

I said, "We were at a party at her friend's house, and while we were playing croquet, she brought up the idea of moving in together. This was like the fourth time she'd suggested it, and I wasn't going to lie or lead her on. Not only did I not want to live together, I thought it was time to split up. She totally lost it and whacked me over the head. We're talking blood, stitches, the whole thing." At this point, I couldn't resist feeling for the small, lumpy scar buried in my hair on the left side of my scalp. "Sucked, because I was just about to win the tournament. I think the grand prize was a gift certificate to Bath & Body Works, and at that point in time, my supply of mango-scented body lotion was running low."

Mia grinned. A full minute passed as we sat in silence. I could hear a car starting in the lot to the rear of my apartment.

"When was this?" she asked.

"A long time ago," I said. "I think I was 19."

"Why did you break up with her?" Mia asked.

"Because she had the type of friends who actually played croquet," I said.

Mia laughed, but said, "No, really. How was she under the impression that living together might be a possibility, and at the same time, you were ready to cut her loose?"

I didn't really want to talk about it, but if it kept her from thinking about Garlen...

"Well, for one thing, we had only been dating for about three months."

"And for another..." Mia said.

"On paper, we should've been a great match," I said. "But I just didn't feel it."

Her expression revealed that she knew exactly what I was talking about. Maybe she felt that way about Garlen, or about any of the dozens of men who had pursued her.

I gulped down the last of my beer. "Want another?" I said.

"No, thanks. I should go. It's nearly midnight."

"Let's, uh, blow off the Alex Dunn thing for a few days," I said. "I'm sure you don't want to—"

"Forget it, Roy. There's no reason to wait. I'll call Albert Strauss first thing in the morning and let you know how it goes."

She rose off the couch, so I stood, too.

We stared at each other, and now I couldn't read her expression. Exhaustion? Stress? She suddenly came toward me and wrapped me in a hug. I hugged her back, and we both just held it for several long seconds. On one hand, it felt wonderful to have her body pressed against mine, but on the other, I wasn't sure how long I could stand it. There was a melancholy pain to wanting more than friendship and a hug.

"I'm so glad you're okay," she murmured into my ear. "Talk to you tomorrow."

Then, before I could respond, she let me go, turned, and was out the door.

**📷**
# 34

At nine o'clock the next morning, I called the Blanco County chief deputy—a woman named Lauren Gilchrist I'd met at the scene of the crash—but I got voicemail. I left a message saying I wanted to make sure they'd been able to download and view the footage from my dash cams. That video would be the nail in Garlen's coffin. It would provide incontrovertible evidence that I had not baited him in any way. I hadn't even retaliated once he'd begun to hit my car.

I realized I hadn't called Kiersten yesterday as promised, so I texted her. **Hey there.**

A couple of minutes later, she replied: **Showing a house.**

I'd decided to come right out and tell her I'd seen her on a date, but I wasn't going to do it by text. I wanted to talk, even if only by phone. I didn't know where the conversation would go from there, but I suspected that we were done, and if I were honest with myself, I'd admit that Mia's breakup with Garlen likely had an impact on my attitude.

I replied: **Good luck. Talk to you later.**

I ate two hardboiled eggs, took a shower, and when I got out, Mia had sent a text: **Albert Strauss, 11:00, his office on Barton Springs. Pick me up in the van**?

"Not everyone cares about our past," Strauss said. "Most people drive past older homes in Tarrytown or Hancock or Old Enfield and they have no idea they are driving past *history*. These are the *roots* of our city. These old homes and buildings can *speak* to us if we listen. They can tell us stories about our cultural heritage."

I got the sense that Strauss had used some of those phrases, or maybe those complete sentences, in previous conversations or speeches, every bit as passionately as he had just now. He was a short, slender man with rimless glasses, medium-length gray hair, and a well-groomed goatee. He wore khakis and a black silk shirt. I judged him to be in his early fifties, and his accent told me he had been born and raised in central Texas.

Earlier, on the phone, Mia had told Strauss that we were working for a large insurance firm and we were looking into the death of Alex Dunn. That was all true, of course, but Strauss might've gotten the impression we were licensed investigators trying to legitimize a life insurance claim, rather than videographers who had no real authority to nose around in a homicide. Oops. Naughty Mia.

"I'm a Tarrytown resident myself," Mia said. "I live in a house that's been in my family since the 1920s." She told him the address.

"Oh, I know that home! It's darling. Didn't you have a fire not long ago?"

"I did, yes, but it wasn't major, thank God."

"It was arson, if I recall correctly," Strauss said.

"It was, yes, and we caught the woman who did it. She was a suspect in one of our investigations."

"Well, that's positively frightening. My job is stressful, but not like that. I'm glad everything worked out okay."

We'd agreed on the way over here that Mia would do most of the talking, because she'd done more research on this landmark home stuff than I had, and because men often responded to her more positively than they would to me. Go figure.

Mia said. "Thanks. Do you live nearby?"

"In Bryker Woods," Strauss said. "We bought a small cottage there in the early nineties. Love it. There's no way we could afford to buy the same house now."

The small talk was making me antsy, but I cleverly covered my impatience by gazing out the window. Strauss's office was relatively small, but he was on the fifth floor of the One Texas Center building and had a nice view of the lake.

"What can you tell us about Callie Dunn's house?" Mia said. "From what I read, it sounded like a great candidate for landmark status."

"The Walton home," Strauss said. "The original resident was named Walton. And, yes, it *would* have been," Strauss said, "because it had been left largely untouched over the years. Some older homes go through various stages of remodeling, and before you know it, it's not even the same house it was originally. You walk into a home like that and it feels...modern. That's not the type of property landmark status is intended to protect. But the Walton home was largely unmodified—almost identical to the day it was built. It had been maintained, but not greatly altered."

"So you recommended landmark status?" Mia asked.

"I did. See, there are generally two ways that can happen. The owner can submit an application himself or herself, or I can open a case myself, usually over the owner's objections."

"And that's what happened here?"

"Exactly. Alex Dunn had applied for a demolition permit, and I was trying to stave that off by filing for landmark status, which is very often a losing battle. As you know, in this state, private property rights are treated as sacrosanct, in most cases. And, to some degree, I can understand that. This office has to strike a delicate balance. We have to know when to push and when to recognize that the owner is just that—the owner." He paused for a moment, frowned, then added, "I have to say, I'm having a tough time understanding how this could be related to Mr. Dunn's death. Of course, I'm sure you can't share much information with me about that."

"That's true," Mia said, "but trust me when I say this information is helpful, and we appreciate it. So you initiated the application for landmark status, and then what?"

"It goes to the commission, where they generally have three options: they can approve the application, deny it, or pass it to the council with no recommendation. That's what happened with this one."

"They simply passed it along?" Mia asked.

"Yes, exactly, and then it goes to the council, and don't get me started on that. Some of those people—this is just between us, please—some of those people have no understanding at all of what we do and why we do it. They make their decisions based on politics, not on the merits of the application. Anyway, even with some friendly faces on the council, an application that is opposed by the owner has to be approved by a supermajority, and that doesn't happen very often—especially when the commission hasn't favored landmark status."

I said, "A supermajority is..."

"Nine out of ten council members."

"Yikes."

"When can you get nine out of ten people to agree on anything?" Strauss said. "My wife and I can't even agree on where to go to dinner."

"So the council rejected the zoning change?" Mia said.

"They certainly did. The vote was seven to three."

"Seven voted in favor?" Mia asked.

"Ha. One would hope. I would consider that great progress. But, no, seven voted against, and that cleared the way for Dunn to demolish the home."

"I assume the vote is a matter of public record," I said. "So we can go online and see which members voted against it."

"Yes, definitely, but you don't need to bother with that," Strauss said. "Here, I'll make you a list."


We went back to Mia's place and studied the seven names on the list.

Kathy Burton

Eric Keselowski

Ignacia Gonzalez

Kerri Holt

Scott Easley

Marcus Hardy

Alejandra Solis

I started with Kathy Burton and Mia took Eric Keselowski. We were on the couch, using our laptops, surfing in relative silence.

After five minutes, Mia said, "This is interesting. Keselowski's little bio says he used to be the marketing director for McMahon Homes."

McMahon Homes was a high-end custom homebuilder that served central Texas, and it wasn't a stretch to presume anyone who worked for an outfit like that would side with a landowner in a fight against any arm of government.

A few minutes later, I said. "Kathy Burton was a school teacher in Giddings when she first got out of college. She moved here eighteen years ago. Her husband is a firefighter."

More silence. I researched Kathy Burton further to make sure I wasn't overlooking something before I ruled her out. All I saw was glowing information about her charity work and other efforts for the public good.

Mia said, "Here we go. Keselowski ran his own development company in Houston before he went over to McMahon, and he was once investigated for allegedly bribing a councilman."

"You're kidding."

"Uh-uh. Hold on." She read some more while I waited. "The investigation was ultimately dropped for lack of evidence."

"So he used to give bribes, allegedly, and now maybe he's receiving them."

She continued to look for more information about the case in Houston, but she found little of relevance. Keselowski had eventually sold his real-estate company and moved to Austin nine years ago.

"So we have a prime suspect right off the bat," I said.

I moved on to Ignacia Gonzalez and Mia went to work on Kerri Holt. Fifteen minutes later, we'd found nothing suspicious in the least about either of them.

Scott Easley was next for me, and Mia began to research Marcus Hardy. No sooner had she clicked on his profile page on the city website that she said, "Oh. My. God."

"What?"

She swung her laptop around, saying, "He has a beard here, but picture him without it. Tell me who that is."

I was, quite simply, stunned. I had seen Marcus Hardy two nights earlier. He'd been Kiersten's date at Salty Sow.

Hardy wasn't a former state senator. He was a current city council member.

# 35

"What does this mean?" Mia asked.

"I'm not sure," I said. "But it means something. No way is this a coincidence."

I moved closer to Mia to get a better look at her computer screen.

"There's no question that's the same guy," Mia said. "And now I feel like an idiot for not recognizing him the other night."

"You *did* recognize him," I said.

"I mean for not placing him as a councilman," she said.

"It's the beard," I said. "He looks different. Besides, it was just yesterday we realized the city council has anything to do with all this historical home stuff. We had no reason to make the connection."

She looked at her laptop again. We were both thinking the same thing, but she was the one who finally voiced it. "This woman you've been seeing—Kiersten—has ties to the Dunn family and to this city council member."

"I know."

"Weird."

"I know."

"What's her last name?"

"Stanley."

I watched as Mia did a Google search for two phrases together—"kiersten stanley" and "marcus hardy."

The results were minimal—73 hits, and many of those were repetitive, or Kiersten and Marcus Hardy just happened to be mentioned on the same page for a fundraiser or a ribbon-cutting or that sort of event. None of the hits were particularly informative or enlightening, which wasn't surprising. Not like we expected to find evidence of a conspiracy through a simple Internet search. One time Kiersten had addressed the city council regarding zoning laws, but it had nothing to do with historical homes or the Dunns.

"Try 'kiersten stanley' with 'alex dunn,'" I said.

Mia typed it in and the result was zero hits.

She changed 'alex dunn' to 'max dunn' and tried again.

Nothing.

She searched for 'kiersten stanley' with 'callie dunn' and got several hundred hits. The majority of them—or perhaps all—were related to the fact that Kiersten and Callie were in the Junior League of Austin together. Alicia Potter was also a member.

"Maybe Max Dunn was looking for a realtor and Callie referred him to Kiersten," I said. "And it's not unlikely that a high-profile real estate professional like Kiersten might socialize with a city council member. It could all be completely innocent."

Mia simply looked at me.

"But you don't think that's the case," I said.

"I think, at a minimum, we need to check it out. Don't you?"

"Just to be clear," I said, "what we're talking about is the possibility that Kiersten facilitated a bribe between Alex Dunn and Marcus Hardy."

"Or between Nathan Potter and Marcus Hardy. Probably a good chance she knows Nathan, since they are both in real estate and Kiersten and Alicia are both in the Junior League."

I was quiet for a moment, trying to remember my various conversations with Kiersten since we'd met. Had she ever said anything, even in joking, that would make me think she played it fast and loose with her business ethics? Not that I could recall.

My phone vibrated with an incoming text. It was, of course, from Kiersten.

**Sold that house! Want to help me celebrate tonight?**

"They made an offer and the seller immediately said yes," Kiersten said when we got together that evening. "Of course, it could still fall through, but this buyer is very well qualified, if you know what I mean."

She looked stunning in a clingy red sheath dress with a lace-trimmed V neck that was showing a fair amount of décolletage. I was trying not to get distracted from the reason I was here, but the four-inch heels weren't helping with that.

"Big bucks?" I said.

"Right. And I could tell the house was exactly what they were looking for, so they won't be changing their minds. I love it when a sale just falls into place like that. Makes up for the clients who look at dozens of properties and don't end up buying any of them."

"It all balances out," I said.

"Yep."

We were at a small bar downtown. I'd already forgotten the name of it, but it was trendy as hell, and fairly crowded with attractive young professionals in well-tailored clothes. We had a relatively quiet two-top in a corner, away from any doors or windows. The lighting was subtle and the music was soft, when you could hear it over the occasionally boisterous conversations taking place at larger nearby tables.

I hadn't broached the topic of her date at Salty Sow, and I wasn't going to, obviously. Not now. Was Kiersten going to pretend we hadn't seen each other? Maybe she really hadn't seen me. Or maybe she had been looking at something or someone behind me.

"Well, congratulations," I said, raising my glass of beer.

"Thanks." She raised her wine glass and bumped mine, and we both took a drink. My beer, whatever brand it was, wasn't bad. When

I'd asked the waitress what kind of beer they had, she'd handed me a menu with roughly sixty choices on it. I'd told her to surprise me.

"My work is kind of the same way," I told Kiersten. "Some cases we close in a few hours. Others can take weeks or months. Like this recent one. I can tell you about it now, since it's over and done with."

"Callie told me a little," Kiersten said. "The high points. You found her dad's coin collection for her. Her brother had taken it, and then the pool guy stole it from him."

"That's the theory," I said, "but it took us nearly two weeks to figure that out. I won't bore you with the details, except to say I exhibited all the cunning of Sherlock Holmes and Castle combined."

"I'm sure you did."

"Actually, to be honest, my partner Mia is the one who cracked it."

Here was Kiersten's chance to say, *Was that Mia I saw you with the other night?*

She didn't. Instead, she said, "How come you didn't tell me you were working for Callie's family?"

"Actually, I was working for the insurance company."

"You know what I mean."

"Well, for one, I can't discuss active cases. Plus, I didn't know you were friends with Callie. I just knew you were listing Max's house."

She leaned in closer and put her hand on my knee. "What's the story with Alex and that woman?" She had a gossipy grin on her face. Her perfume was driving me nuts. It reminded me of the things we did in her condo. I realized I very much would enjoy doing them again. I began to rationalize. Kiersten couldn't be involved in a bribery scandal, could she?

"Serenity Sweet?" I said.

"Great name, but what a bizarre way to make a living," Kiersten said. "Not that I'm a prude, as you well know. Whatever floats your boat, right? I just never would've guessed Alex was into that sort of thing."

She was sounding fairly familiar with Alex Dunn. I hadn't noticed that before.

"How old were you when you met Callie? Was it junior high?" I said.

"No, since first grade," she said.

"Really?"

This was my plan, such as it was. Start slow. Learn more about Kiersten's relationship with the Dunns. Then branch out from there.

"Yep. She was very shy and quiet, so I decided she needed a friend."

"Callie was shy?" I said.

"I know, right? Now look at her. The life of the party."

"And a fairly good model for yoga pants."

"Easy, now. But, yeah, she can rock 'em, can't she? She always has men after her. When we go out, it doesn't matter who we're with, the guys are always drawn to Callie. There's something magnetic about her. I'm standing there like chopped liver."

"I know that's not true," I said.

"Come on. If you saw us together at happy hour, which one of us would you hit on?"

"That's easy. I'd try to get both of you back to my place."

"Ha! I bet you would. And we might consider it, since you're such a smooth talker."

I raised an eyebrow at her.

She said, "Tonight, however, you'll have to settle for just me."

What was a guy to do? Yesterday I'd decided I probably wouldn't see her anymore, and here I was about to sleep with her again, while also trying to get more information from her. Was that ethical?

I saw our waitress at another table and signaled for the check.

I am not an old-fashioned guy. If a woman has a strong libido and likes to act on it, I say more power to her. Even better if I am somehow involved in the activities. Obviously, then, I had no complaints when she stripped me down, led me to bed, and climbed on top.

Afterward, at nearly eleven o'clock, we lay side by side in silence for several moments as we regained our breath.

"Ooh," she finally said. "Wow."

"That was nice," I said.

She turned onto her side and placed one hand on my chest. Very briefly, she traced the small, round scar below my left nipple. "What happened here?"

"Long story."

"I've got time."

"It involves international intrigue and small, woodland mammals," I said.

"Let's hear it."

"How about the short version?" I said. "I got shot."

"Ha. Right."

"I know I bullshit a lot," I said, "but not this time."

"Seriously?" she said. "What happened?"

I told her the story as briefly as possible. I had entered a darkened home at night to find an abducted girl. Took a bullet through the ribs. Lost my spleen during emergency surgery. I didn't mention that I'd felt compelled to risk everything for this little girl because my own daughter, Hannah, had also been abducted years earlier, and it had been my fault. I'd left her untended for two short minutes at a public park, but that had been long enough. A detective found her unharmed eight days later, and I hold his name close to my heart every day.

When I was done telling her about the shooting, her voice rose as she said, "I remember that! I can't believe that was you."

"Sometimes I can't believe it either. It seems surreal."

She asked several questions, and I answered them—briefly. Then I said, "Not to change the subject completely, but I made an offer on that house."

"You did? When?"

"Earlier this week."

"And?"

"They passed."

"Oh, crud. How much did you offer?"

I told her.

"That was a little low, but still reasonable. They didn't counter?"

"I had said they shouldn't bother."

"Are you going to go higher?"

Here was a good opening.

"I don't think so. Honestly, I'm a little worried about the way things work with those older homes."

"How so?"

"All that historical landmark stuff. Doesn't the city stop some owners from doing what they want with their houses? Or they try to, like with Callie's house. I read an article about that."

"You're talking about when an owner wants to scrape and rebuild?"

"Yeah. Or even if I buy the house and decide to sell it later. What if there are new rules in place that limit what I can do? That could really lower the selling price, couldn't it?"

"Really, there's not a lot to worry about, especially with that particular house. I checked its background when you asked to see it, and it isn't a candidate for historical zoning. And even if it was, there are only so many things the city can do to stop you. Plus, there are ways to get what you want. You just need to know how to play the game."

*Boom. There it was.*

I did my best to sound naïve, not accusatory. "Like how? What does that mean?"

"It's politics, Roy. There's always some give and take."

"With who?" I said. "The city council? Don't they have the final word on historical zoning?"

Her hand was still on my chest, and she began to rub gentle circles with her fingertips. "Why don't we talk about this later? How does that sound?"

In my own defense, how would it have looked if I'd tried to continue the conversation?


At three in the morning, I woke with a headache and went into the bathroom to find some aspirin. Searched the medicine cabinet and came up empty. I checked the top drawer in the vanity and saw nothing but make-up. Second drawer was for hair and skin care products. Bottom drawer, bingo. First aid. Still, though, no aspirin. I saw some Advil, but I'm not crazy about that stuff. Makes me queasy sometimes.

I saw a little zippered pouch and opened that.

No aspirin there, either.

But I found something that made my headache even worse.

# 36

"You're kidding me. 'There are ways to get what you want. You just need to know how to play the game'? That's what she said?"

"Verbatim. I memorized it."

"Roy. Wow."

It was seven-thirty in the morning and I was driving back to my place. Despite our little celebration, Kiersten had to show a house early this morning, so she'd been up by 5:30 and out the door by seven. I hadn't had a chance to ask her any more questions last night before she fell asleep, and it wasn't like I could say, "Hey, thanks for the incredible sex. Now, let's get back to the subject of historical zoning."

I said to Mia, "But isn't that true even if you're completely legit? You *do* have to know how to play the game."

"True, but come on, Roy. We already wondered if she was involved, and then she says something like that?"

I didn't respond right away.

So Mia added, "I don't mean this to sound harsh, but please don't let your feelings for her cloud your judgment."

Did I have feelings for her? I liked her, sure. We had a good time together. I'd be disappointed if it turned out she made a practice of arranging bribes, but it wouldn't be the end of the world. Just the end of our relationship, which might not have much of a future anyway, considering her dinner date at Salty Sow.

"Roy?" Mia said.

"Feelings?" I said. "You know I'm incapable of genuine intimacy."

I was on Sixth Street, directly in front of the large ad agency, GSD&M, where the famous "Don't mess with Texas" slogan had been coined. Traffic was bad, and somebody nearby blasted his horn at a car cutting in line to turn left.

"Where are you?" Mia asked. "I thought you were calling from your apartment."

Oops. She didn't know where I had spent the night. Well, now she did. She'd figure it out.

"Going out for donuts," I said.

"Right."

"Let's focus on the subject at hand," I said.

"God, Roy. Really? You spent the night with her? Under these circumstances?"

She might've sounded a little jealous. Or maybe just disgusted.

I said, "Right now, we don't know that she *did* anything, Mia. How about if we keep that in mind?"

"Okay. Fair enough."

I'd moved 100 feet in five minutes. Donuts actually sounded pretty good. A reward for suffering through this traffic.

"There's one more thing I need to tell you," I said.

"What?"

"I was looking for an aspirin in the middle of the night and I found something interesting in her bathroom drawer. Keep in mind that Kiersten is close friends with Callie Dunn. They've known each other since grade school, and because of that, she knew Alex Dunn fairly well, too."

"Spill it, already," Mia said.

"I found a hobo nickel."

The resulting pause indicated that Mia had the same response

I'd had last night. She was puzzled and surprised. She said, "What the hell do we make of that?"

"I have no idea. I'm thinking Callie, or maybe Alex, gave her the coin as a gift. That's all I can figure."

"But why does she have it tucked away in her bathroom?"

"And in a small zippered pouch," I said.

"That makes a pretty good hiding place," Mia said.

I finally made it through the traffic light at Lamar.

"Let's let this percolate for a while," I said, "and I'll call you this afternoon."

Truth was, I needed to go home and sleep. I'm sure Mia suspected that, and she could've easily razzed me about it, but she simply said, "Works for me."


I was back on the name Riley. What did it mean?

It *was* a name, right? What else could it be? But who was it?

It was two o'clock, and after two solid hours of sleep, a shower, and some lunch, I was ready to get back at it. I was seated on my couch, laptop in hand, raring to go. But I wasn't sure *where* to go.

Riley.

If I could get into Alex Dunn's Hushmail account, maybe that would be the key. Maybe it would tell me whether Kiersten was involved in bribing a council member.

I typed "Riley" into Google and got 218,000,000 hits. The first one, a Wikipedia entry, told me that Riley could mean anything from a racehorse that won the Kentucky Derby in 1890 to a defunct British car and bicycle manufacturer to a small town in Indiana, Oregon, West Virginia, or Wisconsin.

I tried a search for "riley austin" and got 41,100,000 hits. Oh, much better. Only 41 million to sort through. Austin Riley was a baseball player. B.D. Riley's was an Irish pub and restaurant in downtown Austin.

Then I searched for the phrase "alex dunn" combined with "riley." Got more than 15,000 hits. After I spent 15 minutes reviewing the first several pages, I realized it was all just random unrelated instances of Alex Dunn's name on a page that also contained the name Riley.

This was futile.

There had to be a better approach—not just to figuring out the significance of the name Riley, but to finding out the true nature of Kiersten's relationship with Alex Dunn.

I texted Mia. **Had any brilliant ideas?**

Five minutes passed before I heard back.

**Nope. We getting together?**

I said: **I thought you'd never ask.**

We sat, once again, on Mia's couch.

Occasionally we spoke, and for long stretches we simply sat and thought or surfed the Web.

"I spent a lot of time last night thinking about this bribery angle," Mia said at one point. "If it's off the mark—if there was no bribery—then I have no idea where we'd even go with it next. Anybody who was mad about Callie's McMansion could've done it."

She looked at me, hoping I might have a fresh, creative thought. I shrugged.

Honestly, I'd been slacking off—checking real estate listings for western Travis County. If I wasn't going to buy that house in Tarrytown, then I was going to look for something else. I was done with my apartment. Time to move on.

"Of course, we can't forget that he was poisoned," Mia said. "So I guess it *couldn't* have been just anybody. They had to have had access to his medicine. And to cyanide."

She was covering old ground, but that was common, too. We both did it, on purpose, because there were times when you had to remind yourself of the details of the case so you wouldn't go wandering down a path that was counter to the facts. In this instance, the fact that Dunn was poisoned pointed away from some random angry stranger and more toward someone he knew.

"Killing someone with poison is extremely rare," I said. "So what would motivate somebody to do it that way?"

"Wanting it to look like a natural death," Mia said.

"Exactly. The standard toxicology screen doesn't include

cyanide, and they'd have no reason to suspect it—especially in a sixty-something male with a history of heart disease."

"How do you get your hands on cyanide?" Mia asked.

"I'm not positive about that," I said. "I read an article not long ago about a woman who ordered cyanide online and committed suicide with it."

"Was she here in the States?"

"I don't remember."

Mia started typing on her keyboard, looking for the answer.

I watched her. She was wearing black sweats, a loose baby-blue T-shirt, and very little makeup. Her hair was swept straight back and had gentle waves in it. It got that way when she let it dry naturally instead of using a blow dryer. She didn't like the waves, but I thought they looked good.

"That was in Pennsylvania," Mia said. "She ordered it from a seller in Thailand." She read some more, then said, "Apparently, it's a lot easier to get in other countries." Another pause, then, "Here's an interview with Sanjay Gupta, that TV doctor, where he's talking about how easy it is to get cyanide. It's from twelve years ago, though, so that might have changed."

My phone vibrated with an incoming text and I checked it.

Probably Kiersten. She usually texted me a sweet note after we'd spent a night together.

Nope.

"Heidi has another case for us," I said.

# 37

If Heidi was right—and she usually was—a man named Abel Avilez had reported his $40,000 SUV stolen, but it hadn't been. He had filed the police report five months ago, and his claim had already been paid. The SUV was nowhere to be seen—until a month ago, when it had been driven through a red light and a traffic enforcement camera had snapped two photos, one from the front and one from the rear.

"All of this is in the file I'm sending over shortly," Heidi said on the phone, "but the short version is that a Cadillac SUV just like Avilez's ran a red light and the ticket was mailed to the registered owner—a man named Farmer. This guy Farmer knows it wasn't him or his vehicle, so he goes outside and discovers that his license plates have been stolen and replaced with some license plates from a Mustang. He could've been driving around like that for months. Anyway, I'm also sending you the photos from the traffic camera and it sure looks like Abel Avilez behind the wheel."

Mia said, "So Avilez stole some Mustang plates, put them on

Farmer's SUV, and then put Farmer's plates on his own Cadillac SUV."

"Right. To make matters more complicated, Avilez's wife drives an identical Cadillac SUV. Apparently he liked his so much, they got a second one. When he came up with this stupid scheme, he probably thought having two identical vehicles would keep him out of trouble. He could always say he was in his wife's SUV, as long as they aren't seen at the same time."

"Why are people so stupid, Heidi?" Mia asked. "Why?"

"So we can earn the big bucks?" Heidi said.

"Big bucks?" I said. "I think you might be—"

"Okay, smart-ass," Heidi said. "So we can attempt to remain solvent between paychecks."

"More like it," I said.

"Anyway, the cops confronted Avilez with the photo, but he said it wasn't him. They asked to search the premises and the stolen SUV wasn't there. That's about all they'll do. They don't have much time for something like this."

"So you want us to find the SUV, preferably in a way that would prove Avilez has been a bad little boy."

"Yes, please."

"At this point, he might have it stashed away somewhere for the long term," I said. "Or he decided it was time to abandon it somewhere. Could be a tough find."

"That's why I only hire the best," Heidi said.

"Thanks," I said.

"She has a partner named Roy," Heidi said.

Mia giggled.

"Well done," I said. "Anything else we need to know?"

"I think that's about it. If you have any questions, let me know."

"Will do."

"You kids have fun."

We started with Facebook, because if there's any chance of cracking a case in a matter of mere minutes, Facebook just might be the place to do it. But if Abel Avilez had a Facebook account, we couldn't find it. We found one for his wife, Diana, but her privacy settings were too tight to allow us to see anything. I sent her a friend request from my fake Linda Patterson account, and then we checked their criminal records on various free and paid sites. They were both clean.

Mia began to scan Heidi's electronic file and she said, "He lives in Rollingwood but he reported the SUV stolen from downtown."

"Probably working under the theory that APD would have less time to spend on it than Rollingwood would. I don't blame him. I know the chief in Rollingwood. He gets it done."

I began to check the tax rolls in Travis County and several surrounding counties to see if Avilez owned any real estate in addition to his home. Basic stuff, but APD probably hadn't taken this step. They are simply too overwhelmed with cases, so they have to conduct a triage of sorts to decide which cases get the most attention. For instance, my credit card was stolen once and fraudulent charges were racked up within a few hours. I reported it, and the investigator sounded plenty capable, but she also mentioned that her caseload was currently more than 400. I asked if I would ever hear from her again and she just laughed.

"No other property in Travis County," I said, "although there are a couple of other people named Avilez. Relatives, maybe. If so, the SUV could be stashed at one of their houses."

I gave her those names, and while I checked other tax rolls, she tried to determine if any of these people were related to Abel and Diana. For that, she logged on to a genealogy site. The information on the site wasn't always 100% accurate, and sometimes it was incomplete, but it would be a decent starting point.

However, before she could even start, I found what we were looking for. "Abel Avilez owns 17 acres in Bastrop County."

Mia stopped what she was doing and waited to hear more.

"In a very remote area," I said. "Surrounded by other tracts that are as large or larger."

I scrolled downward on the page.

"It has a small cabin on it—about eight hundred square feet. Based on the appraised value, I'd say it's pretty rustic. The only other improvement is a barn that measures 20 feet by 30 feet."

"A barn," Mia said. "Outstanding."


The only viable option—and I had to talk Mia into it—was to trespass and try to get a look inside the barn. The trick was to accomplish that without getting caught.

Or shot.

I volunteered to do the dirty work, but before I made my move, it was Mia's job to verify Avilez's whereabouts. She would set up outside his place of employment—a bank in south Austin where he was a loan officer—and then tail him when he left for the afternoon.

The odds were slim that Avilez would make a trip to his cabin on a weekday evening, especially since it wasn't hunting season, but why risk it? Mia would keep her eyes on him until I was done. I didn't know how long it would take me to sneak onto his property and check the barn, but I didn't want to feel rushed. It might take just a few minutes, or I might run into unexpected complications.

Of course, there was always the chance that one of Avilez's friends or relatives might be at the cabin, but that could be true at any time, on any day, and there was no real way to avoid that risk. I would simply have to be careful entering the property, and be ready with a line of bullshit to get myself out of there if I ran into trouble. I happened to be pretty good at that.


By four in the afternoon, I was waiting in the parking lot outside a small food mart in the tiny community of Red Rock in southwest Bastrop County. I'd already gone inside the store, bought a cup of coffee, and asked the disinterested cashier if he'd seen a green Honda Civic hanging around, because I was supposed to meet a guy here. He said he hadn't. Now I could hang out for a good while without the clerk wondering what I was doing.

I'd studied Avilez's property on Google Maps, and this was going to be a fairly straightforward operation. His cabin sat on the middle of his 17 acres, and none of his neighbors had any sort of cabin, shed, or outbuilding, within 200 yards. The area was heavily treed, which was a plus. I was wearing a dark green shirt that would help me blend in, but I had opted to forgo camo, because that would make it appear I was there to poach.

Mia texted at 4:37.

**He just left the bank.**

I left the food mart and drove north on Farm Road 20 for a few miles, then turned east on a small county road, then went north again on an even smaller road. This was isolated country. My biggest advantage was also my biggest problem—very few people drove this road. That meant my vehicle would stand out to the locals.

I slowed as I approached the place and saw that the dirt driveway had a chain stretched across it. Good. And no recent tire marks onto the property. Better.

I went past and found a place to turn around. On my return trip, I pulled to the shoulder near some trees close to Avilez's driveway and killed the engine. I couldn't see a single home or building from where the van was parked.

I quickly hopped out and deflated the front passenger tire. Later, I would inflate it with a portable pump.

Mia sent another text: **Update?**

**About to enter. Where is he?**

**Stopped at a neighbor's on Timberline. How's it look?**

**All clear.**

I had spent quite a bit of time at a friend's house in Rollingwood as a kid, and I remembered exactly where Timberline was. In fact, the name of that street evoked a vague memory—something I couldn't quite nail down, like when you're trying to remember a song that won't come to you, or the name of the actress you saw in a movie last month.

I locked the van and looked both ways on the county road. No cars coming. I couldn't even *hear* any traffic from any direction. Nothing but birds and the wind through the trees.

I crossed the road and started up the driveway, ignoring a metal No Trespassing sign nailed to a tree. My story, if I ran into anyone, was that I had a spare tire but no jack. Could I borrow one real quick? I would be very grateful and I'd bring it right back.

As I walked, I kept an eye out for motion-triggered trail cameras mounted on trees. Hunters used those cameras to monitor wild game, but they were also somewhat useful as security devices. I didn't see any. I kept walking as if I had a perfectly legitimate reason for being there.

The driveway was about one hundred and fifty yards long and it curved like a boomerang. Just as I reached the curve, the cabin came into view.

I stopped for a moment and stood still. Saw nothing that worried me.

I took my phone out and texted Mia.

**No vehicles. No people. No recent tracks.**

She sent me a thumbs-up.

Ten seconds later, I was forty yards from the cabin.

"Hello?" I called, but not so loud that any neighbors could hear.

I walked twenty more yards, and now I could see the barn—a metal pole barn—off to my left. No vehicles parked there, either.

"Hello?"

I walked directly to the cabin, which wasn't as rustic as I thought it would be. It was one of those little cedar-sided cabins that are hauled in piece by piece and assembled on site.

I climbed three steps onto the small porch and knocked on the door, which had three small glass panes at eye level. The interior was dark.

I knocked again.

There would be no answer. Nobody was here.

A small sticker on one of the glass panes warned me about a security system, but I recognized it as a bluff sticker you can buy online for two bucks. Better than nothing, I guess, but not a security system. He should at least mount a few dummy cameras.

I stepped down from the porch and headed for the barn.

"Hellllloooo?"

The sun was below the tree line now, but there was still plenty of light.

My phone vibrated.

**Okay?**

**Yes.**

I reached the barn, which had a large, sliding metal door with a padlocked clasp. I walked counter-clockwise around the perimeter of the building. There was a window on the right side that was blocked with a hanging sheet or cloth, and the same thing on the rear side, and again on the left side. Why cover the windows?

I walked back to my van for a pair of bolt cutters and a lock that was identical to the one on the barn door. The same trick I'd used at Leo Pitts's storage locker.

Coming back to the barn, I walked much faster this time. No sense in being discreet now, because I couldn't pretend I was a motorist in need of a jack.

I reached the barn and immediately popped the lock off the clasp.

Slid the big metal door to the left and saw the rear end of a Cadillac SUV.

I took a photo and texted it to Mia.

She wouldn't answer. She knew it would be better not to distract me right now.

I stepped inside, walked to the front of the SUV, and shined my phone's flashlight through the windshield to see the little metal plate bearing the vehicle identification number. It was a match with the missing SUV.

I took a photo of the VIN and texted it to Mia. Then I shot a video of the entire vehicle inside the barn, and I kept it rolling as I stepped outside, closed the barn door, snapped a new lock on, and walked back to the road, careful not to show my van parked on the opposite shoulder.

## 38

Three hours later, I was watching the Texas Rangers, enjoying some pizza and beer, and trying to simply enjoy the sense of accomplishment that comes from a slam-bang case like the one we'd had today. They are rare.

I was honest enough with myself to understand that many of them would be much harder to solve if I wasn't willing to skirt various laws. "Skirt" is a more palatable way of saying "break," as in "break the law."

I broke the law today.

I'd do it again, too, probably fairly soon. Trespassing. Illegally attaching a GPS unit to a subject's car. Even withholding information from the authorities, on occasion. I'd done all of these things.

They worked.

On the other hand, not only did Mia and I serve our clients—the insurance agencies—we often helped the police close their cases.

Like this one.

In this instance, sharing what I'd learned with the police had been tricky.

If Avilez had stashed the SUV on some stranger's property, I could have simply called the cops with an anonymous tip, because the stranger would almost certainly have given permission to search. But since it was on Avilez's property and a search would require a warrant, a tip wouldn't work. The police would need a credible witness for them to attain probable cause, and an anonymous tipster wasn't considered credible.

That's why I'd shot the video.

The video was a way for me to anonymously provide the police with "reasonably trustworthy information, considered as a whole, sufficient to warrant a reasonable person to believe that a particular person has committed, or is committing, an offense." That's how the law is written.

Sure, it would be unclear where the video had come from, or whether the person providing it—me—had broken any laws to shoot it, but the fact that it showed Avilez's allegedly stolen vehicle inside his own barn was indisputable, and that would be grounds for the police to get a warrant.

So when I'd gotten back to my apartment earlier, I stripped the video of any metadata that might connect it to me. Then I emailed it—using techniques to further preserve my anonymity—to an investigator I know at APD. I wasn't sure if he was working the Avilez case, but I knew he'd pass it along to the right people.

The cops would probably search the barn tomorrow, and I was confident the SUV would still be there, because why would Avilez risk moving it? The heat was on, so he'd leave it right where it sat, with no inkling that the cops were about to get a warrant.

APD would know with 99% certainty where the video had come from. They'd know, and Heidi would know, and I'd know that they knew, but that was as far as it would go. The cops wouldn't ask me about it, because they'd know I wouldn't answer any questions. Heidi wouldn't ask me about it, because she wouldn't want confirmation that I'd committed a crime.

Mia and I had talked by phone as I'd driven back to Travis County, and we'd decided to touch base about the Alex Dunn situation in the morning. Frankly, the quick turnaround on the Avilez case highlighted just how much work had been involved with the Dunn case.

Maybe it was time to let it go. We'd found the coins. We'd done our job.

I stuck with the game until the Rangers won 2-1 in the bottom of the tenth, and then I got back online. Earlier, at Mia's, one of the real estate listings I'd seen was a nine-acre tract off Fitzhugh Road, not far from the 57 acres my grandparents had bought in the early 1950s. Despite the massive changes out there in the past few decades, that area still felt like home. And this particular tract had one hundred feet of frontage on Barton Creek. And the price per acre reflected it. It would be an investment, though, right?

I sent a short email to the agent, asking if I could walk the property at my convenience, alone, sometime soon. Wouldn't want to trespass, would we?

# 39

I slept like I'd been drugged and woke at nearly eight o'clock.

No urgent voicemails or texts were waiting for me, but I did have an email from my client telling me that Stacy, the crooked chiropractor, had filed a bogus claim for treatment he hadn't given me. Bam. Another victory for our side.

I took a shower, then made myself some bacon, egg, and cheese breakfast tacos.

I texted Mia at 9:30.

At 9:45, I got a reply from the agent listing the Fitzhugh acreage: **You are welcome to walk the property, or I'd be happy to show it to you anytime! Please let me know if you have any questions! It's a wonderful piece of property with fantastic building sites! And the price is competitive! Thank you for getting in touch! Take care! Clarence.**

I couldn't believe Clarence had failed to put an exclamation point after his name.

I texted Mia again at 10:05.

No reply.

By 10:30, I was starting to get concerned, so I called her. Got voicemail. Said, "This is your partner, Roy Ballard. Please call or text when you get a minute. It's Roy Ballard, by the way. Your partner. R-O-Y. Ballard. Talk to you soon."

At noon, still no response, so I put on some shoes to drive over to her house. That's when I finally heard the tones of "Brick House," her ring tone.

I said, "Hey, there."

"Hey. Sorry."

"About what? Everything okay?"

"Yeah, I'm just…it's been a trying morning."

She sounded unusually tense.

"Yeah?" I said.

"Yeah."

"How so?"

"Long story," she said with an unconvincing laugh. "Let's just not even go there."

"You won't even give me a hint?" I said.

Mia let out a sigh, either because she was exasperated or because she thought I was prying.

"Okay," she said, "but take it easy on me. No judgments."

"That sounds promising," I said.

"No sarcasm, either," Mia said.

"Sorry. I'll be good."

A long pause followed, and I knew—I *knew*—what she was going to say.

"I've been on the phone with Garlen for a couple of hours," she said. "He called from the hospital. He wanted to apologize for everything he's done, and to let me know he's planning to go into treatment."

I hung my head. I didn't want to hear this.

"He's not trying to get back together," Mia said. "He just wanted to know if I forgave him."

I didn't know what to say.

"Roy?"

"What did you tell him?"

"I said I thought treatment of some kind was a good idea," Mia said.

"It'll probably be court-ordered anyway," I said. "But he can say, 'Hey, look at me. I decided to go to rehab. Look at all my progress. Look at my personal growth.'"

Mia didn't say anything, but I could hear her breathing.

"He violated the protective order by calling you," I said.

"I know."

"You should report it."

Silence.

"If you don't report it," I said, "that can make the protective order void. He can say he contacted you and you didn't object."

"I know what it means, Roy."

"I don't want him to hurt you anymore, Mia. You deserve better than that."

"I'm not going to give him the chance. He just wanted to tell me what's going on, and that's it. I'm not taking him back, and I don't plan to talk to him any further."

"What if he keeps calling?" I said.

"Are you under the impression that I can't handle this situation?" she asked.

"No, but I know how a guy like that works. He will manipulate you if he can. He'll say once he's clean and sober, that you and—"

"Okay, Roy. Enough."

"Guys like him don't change."

"Enough. Please stop lecturing me."

"I'm only trying to—"

"Forget it!" she said.

And she hung up on me. She'd never done that before.

I called back, of course, to apologize. She didn't answer. Guess I couldn't blame her.

So I gave it ten minutes, then texted.

**I'm sorry. Not my place to offer advice. I will always support you whatever you do.**

She didn't reply.

* * *

I brooded most of the day—and never heard back from her—so late in the afternoon, I did what most mature adults would do.

I fixed myself a drink.

Just a light bourbon and Coke. That tasted pretty good, so I made another one. A little stronger this time.

I texted Mia again: **I heard your partner is an idiot**.

I had a third drink, and now I was starting to get restless. Maybe I should eat something. Too much booze on an empty stomach. As luck would have it, I received a text from Kiersten: **What r u doing?**

I said: **Drinking bourbon.**

Then I added: **Want some?**

A minute later, she said: **Sure, and some dinner. Come over?**

I hesitated. I'd had enough that I was probably past the legal limit to drive. But there was always a taxi or Uber.

**On my way.**

We did have bourbon, and we fooled around a lot, and at nine-thirty, we had food delivered from an Indian place a few blocks away. I tried not to think about anything, especially Mia, who still hadn't responded to my apologies.

At one point, Kiersten, lying by my side, said, "You're kind of quiet tonight."

"Busy having sex with a beautiful woman," I said.

"Don't let me catch you with her," she said.

I laughed and said no more, but I could feel her looking at me. So I said, "Just a little preoccupied, I guess, but it's all good." Then I told her about the acreage I was considering. Using it as an excuse for my subdued mood.

She asked some questions about the property, and I answered them, and during a lull, she drifted off sometime around midnight.

As hangovers go, this one was about a six on a ten-scale. Not horrible, but my head ached and my mouth was dry. I'm sure my breath was horrible. No problem, because Kiersten was still asleep, what with it being 5:47 a.m. I reached over to the nightstand and grabbed my phone.

Still nothing from Mia.

This was unusual for her. She is typically an extremely forgiving person, an example being her willingness to speak to Garlen on the phone yesterday morning.

I lay quietly and listened to the gentle hiss of the air conditioner through the filter in the return vent. There was surely traffic on the downtown streets below by now, but I couldn't hear any of it.

Mia would forgive me. I knew that. But it left a hollow place in my gut to know she was that upset with me. I felt ashamed for trying to coerce her to behave the way I wanted her to behave. Not only was it overbearing, it was unnecessary. She is one of the strongest people I know. She would not be a victim.

5:51.

Kiersten stirred beside me, but she didn't wake up.

In hindsight, it seemed like a fairly normal morning. Well, not that I routinely wake up beside a beautiful woman who might be involved in a bribery scheme, or that I wake up with a hangover, or even that I wake up hoping I can set things right with my partner, because I screwed up the day before. In all other aspects, though, it was normal.

Until, at 6:02, I had one of those oh-so-rare moments when a memory that had been dancing just out of reach suddenly presents itself.

All I was doing was lying there, and it came to me.

*Timberline.*

Now I knew why that street name had lodged in my mind two days earlier.

The name itself was unimportant.

But it intersected with nine other streets, and now I remembered that one of them was called Riley.

I texted Mia.

**You awake?**

She was an early riser.

**Need your help.**

She often worked out—Krav Maga or jogging—well before sunrise.

**I think I know the meaning of Riley.**

Maybe she was taking a shower or getting a cup of coffee or still sleeping. Or ignoring me.

**Need you to do a search.**

My phone was oftentimes useful, but it wouldn't be ideal for what I needed now.

**Need to know if Dunn ever lived on Riley.**

Finally, she replied.

**Hang on.**

She'd know where to search. The tax rolls wouldn't work. If Alex Dunn ever lived on Riley, it could have been decades ago. Even a general Google search probably wouldn't pan out.

6:14. Still no word from Mia, but I wasn't going to push her. I was just glad we were communicating. If I were searching, I'd check newspaper databases. Kiersten was still sleeping soundly.

At 6:19, Mia sent another message: **He lived on Riley in 1985.**

Yes! Maybe this hunch was going somewhere.

Then: **Found his address in a letter to the editor.**

Great luck that the *Austin American-Statesman* used to put addresses with letters. Nowadays they'd probably get sued for it.

She sent the numbers: **707.**

I said: **Thank you. Stay tuned.**

My theory was that Dunn used the name of his old street as a prompter for his password, which was the numerical address, plus the numeral 2, since the bookmark had been "Riley2." What better way to remember a password without having to write it down anywhere? Most of us could remember all of our different mailing addresses going back to childhood.

That's all it was right now—a theory.

I surfed to the log-in page for Hushmail and entered Alex Dunn's email address, which I already knew. Then I entered 7072 in the passphrase field.

I held my breath and hit return.

*Sorry, we don't recognize that passphrase.*

Well, crap. What a disappointment. I had been convinced my

theory was going to work.

What the hell else could "riley2" mean?

Maybe it was because of my hangover, but it took me a solid minute to figure it out.

I typed again, but this time I entered 707707, operating on the revised theory that "riley2" meant the street address, 707, two times in a row, rather than with a 2 after it.

I hit enter—and without any further complications, I had access to Alex Dunn's secret email account.

📷
# 40

I was too excited to stay in bed, so I slipped quietly out from under the covers, closed the bedroom door behind me, and went into the living room.

As soon as I sat down, I texted Mia: **We're in. It worked.**

I was hoping she'd call me immediately, but my phone didn't ring. Damn, she really *was* pissed at me. Not even a huge potential breakthrough was enough for her to set it aside for the time being.

I would have to worry about that later and focus on the task at hand for now. Like most email accounts, Dunn's Hushmail account had an inbox, plus several other boxes, such as sent mail, drafts, and trash.

The inbox had exactly one email in it—from a person named John Smith, who had a Gmail address that was his name with six numbers after it. Or her name. Couldn't assume it was a man, because this was obviously a fake name with a throwaway email account. The email was dated three days before Dunn's death. The subject field was blank.

I opened it and saw the most recent message from John Smith to Alex Dunn. It was just one word:

*Agreed.*

Below that, Alex Dunn had said:

*You have my word. If they ever tell you I'm talking, they are lying. Now I'm going to delete this email account. You should do the same. No more contact. Agreed?*

Oh, I liked the sound of this. Innocent people don't talk about deleting email accounts and cutting off contact.

In order to read the conversation in chronological order, I started at the bottom and read upward. The long exchange had started more than a year ago.

John Smith: *It's time for the second installment. Meet at the place we discussed?*

Alex Dunn: *Yes. Always the same place. Wednesday at noon. Be discreet.*

John Smith: *Of course I will, but I can't make it until four that afternoon.*

Alex Dunn: *Fine. I'll be there at four.*

Then, a month later...

John Smith: *First of the month again. Same time?*

Alex Dunn: *If you mean four o'clock, that works for me.*

John Smith: *Yes. See you there.*

And another month later...

John Smith: *Third installment. Same time—four?*

Alex Dunn: *Can you do it on Friday instead?*

John Smith: *If we do it in the morning. Anytime works.*

Alex Dunn: *Ten?*

John Smith: *Yes. See you then.*

I was wide awake now, and my hangover was a distant memory. I was looking at pure gold. This was the break Mia and I had been searching for. Of course, there was still work to be done, because I couldn't determine who "John Smith" was based solely on these messages. I'd guess it was Marcus Hardy, but guesses weren't good enough in court.

Both parties had obviously opened throwaway email accounts for the sole purpose of communicating secretly. They exchanged brief messages every month to arrange a meeting when another "installment" was due. Sometimes they had to change the day or time because it was difficult for two busy people to mesh their full schedules.

After their seventh meeting, there was some paranoia.

John Smith: *Did you see that dark sedan when you left?*

Alex Dunn: *The Crown Victoria?*

John Smith: *I'm not a car guy. It was parked in the lot near the volleyball courts. There were only a few other cars out there. It was navy blue.*

Alex Dunn: *I saw it when I first got there. It was empty then and empty when I left. Nothing to worry about.*

John Smith: *I hope not.*

The last part of the conversation occurred the week before Alex Dunn died.

John Smith: *Final installment. Tomorrow at four?*

Alex Dunn: *Yes.*

Then a day later…

Alex Dunn: *I guess we're all done now. Remember, as long as both of us keep our mouths shut, there will never be a problem. Nobody can prove anything.*

John Smith: *I know, and I will never talk. That has to go both ways.*

Alex Dunn: *You have my word. If they ever tell you I'm talking, they are lying. Now I'm going to delete this email account. You should do the same. No more contact. Agreed?*

John Smith: *Agreed.*

And that was it. The end of their communication.

Alex Dunn had never deleted his account. Maybe he simply forgot. Or maybe he wanted to be prepared if this John Smith blamed everything on Dunn at a later date.

My mind doesn't spin often, but it was spinning right now. Did John Smith kill Alex Dunn to make sure the conspiracy was never uncovered? Or was the bribery unrelated to his homicide? What were the odds that three different crimes had occurred—the theft of the coin collection, the bribery, and the homicide? One thing seemed certain: Alex Dunn had bribed John Smith directly, with no middleman.

"Wow, that is an intense look on your face," Kiersten said.

I jumped. She had come out of the bedroom, but I'd been so focused, I hadn't heard her coming.

"Hey," I said.

"Hey. How long have you been up?" Her voice was raspy. She was wearing a robe.

"Maybe thirty minutes."

"You look pretty chipper considering how much bourbon we drank last night," she said.

"I think I just broke the Alex Dunn case," I said. I was so excited, I had to tell her.

She looked confused. "I thought you already figured that out. You found the coins in Callie's pump house."

"I'm talking about the murder," I said.

"Really?"

"Yep."

"You know who killed him?"

"Not yet, but I think I'm on the right track. I found Dunn's secret email account and just started digging into it."

"That's great." She cupped her forehead with both hands.

"You okay?" I said.

"I'm a lightweight," she said. "I don't feel good at all. My head is pounding."

"You want some aspirin? Then some breakfast?"

"How about if we just start with coffee?"

"Sure thing. Where is it?"

"The coffeemaker is already loaded. Just flip the switch."

"How do you want it?"

"I don't care," she said. "Black is fine."

I could tell she really felt lousy. My fault for being a bad influence.

"Be right back," I said.

"I'm going back to bed," she said.

I went into the kitchen and got the coffee going. While I waited, I pulled out my phone again and went back to Alex Dunn's Hushmail account.

I checked the box for trash and saw that it was empty. It probably emptied automatically every week or month, based on Dunn's preferences.

I checked the box for drafts and it was also empty.

I checked the box for sent mail and it had quite a few emails in it, because every time Dunn had replied to John Smith, a new sent mail had been created. I scrolled downward, and downward still, and then I stopped, because I saw something that simply didn't fit.

There was an email from Alex Dunn to Kiersten.

The subject line was simply *I'm sorry.*

I stared at the screen for a long moment. I didn't want to click the link. Whatever I was about to learn was not going to be good, I knew that. What was Alex Dunn sorry about?


What I didn't know at this moment was that Kiersten was in her walk-in closet, opening a fireproof lockbox she used to store important paperwork, along with jewelry and other valuables. But she was nervous and emotional, and she was fumbling with the dials.


I opened the email and began to read the message from Alex Dunn to Kiersten.

*K, quite honestly, I can't understand why you became so angry in Mumbai. All I did was tell you the truth. If I had previously given you the impression that our relationship was anything more than it was, I apologize. That was never my intention and I thought that was clear. After the way things went with Alicia, I decided it was time for me to take some time to—*

"Stop."

I twitched again. Kiersten was standing in the doorway to the kitchen. She was aiming a small handgun at me.

I lowered my phone. I said, "Oh, come on. I wasn't that bad in bed last night."

It wasn't my best line, but I figured it was never smart to say,

"What're you gonna do? Shoot me?"

Kiersten didn't respond, except that she was beginning to cry. The gun was a small, black semi-automatic, probably a .32 or a .380. Not a huge caliber, but deadly nonetheless. What gun wasn't?

"So you and Alex, huh?" I said. "I never saw that coming."

Kiersten still didn't speak. She was working up the nerve to do it. And there was a good chance the neighbors wouldn't even hear the shot.

"Sounds like he jerked you around," I said. "That wasn't cool. I can understand why it made you mad."

"Don't, Roy," she said. "Just don't."

"Don't what?"

She shook her head.

The entryway to the galley kitchen was no more than four feet wide. I was boxed in. Trapped.

"Think this through, Kiersten," I said. "You had a relationship with Alex Dunn, but so what? If you did something to him, they'll never be able to prove it. Why make it worse by doing something stupid now?"

It was a lie. I was guessing Alex Dunn and Kiersten had taken steps to keep their affair a secret. But once the cops started focusing on Kiersten as a suspect, they'd find something. They'd keep digging until they had a case.

"Get yourself a good attorney and you'll be fine," I said.

Kiersten was too smart to buy it. She raised the gun higher and sighted down the barrel, leveling it right at my face.

"How will you get me out of here, Kiersten?" I said. "There are security cameras all over the building. Mia knows where I am right now."

Weak argument. Kiersten had plenty of money. She could be on an international flight in a few hours. She could leave me right where I fell and just take off.

"I'm sorry," she said, beginning to sob now. "I have to."

I stood perfectly still. Perfectly silent. A long moment passed.

Then I dropped straight downward, and before I hit the floor, she pulled the trigger. The shot was even louder than I'd expected in such a small space.

If the bullet hit me, I didn't feel it.

I scrambled to my feet, staying low, and rushed her.

She shrieked and extended the gun again, but before she could shoot a second time, I hit her around the midsection, wrapping her up and driving her backward, and we landed hard on the carpet behind her.

I don't know where the gun went, but she no longer had it.

I grabbed her wrists and held tight, but she wasn't struggling. The fight was gone. She'd given up. It was all over.

# 41

I spoke to her afterwards, of course, but she wouldn't reply. I'm not sure she was able. She seemed to have gone into a catatonia or some sort of shock. She simply sat with a glazed expression on her face, staring forward.

Then I called 911, reported the attempted murder, and made sure to stress that everything was under control and there was no need to enter with guns drawn. A uniformed officer showed first, followed by a pair of detectives, and then we all took a ride to APD headquarters. Forensic technicians would process the condo and gather evidence to build a case against Kiersten.

While I waited in an interview room, I texted Mia.

**Kiersten tried to shoot me about 30 minutes ago. This is not a joke. I think she killed Dunn.**

My phone rang immediately.

"What in the world are you talking about?"

So I gave her the story as quickly as possible, knowing a couple of detectives were going to walk through the door at any minute and

I would have to hang up. I managed to cover the high points in about four minutes.

When I was done, Mia's first remark was, "Roy, I am so glad you're okay."

She was saying that a lot lately.

"Thanks. Me, too."

She said, "Maybe both of us should just give up on dating altogether."

I could only laugh, and then I was suddenly overcome with emotion.

"Mia..." I said.

"What?"

The door to the interview room swung open. "I have to go. I'll call you later."


I told them everything that had happened in Kiersten's condo, in painstaking detail, several times, along with everything else I'd learned that morning about Alex Dunn and John Smith. They grilled me hard for inconsistencies, but that was their job. They couldn't just take my word for the truth.

For all they knew, I'd been threatening or assaulting Kiersten, and she pulled the gun in self-defense. She might even make that very claim, if and when she spoke to them. But the evidence would back me up. It was her gun. They'd find powder residue on her hands. They'd find an unlocked fireproof box in her bedroom, indicating that she had gone in there to retrieve the gun while I was in the kitchen. And the crime scene itself would tell the story. I had been trapped in a small space, with nowhere to go, when she'd fired.

After a couple of hours, they turned me loose, and one of the detectives was even kind enough to give me a ride back to my apartment.

I texted Mia and let her know I was home.

She called and once again I brought her up to speed.

I knew she would have a lot of questions, and she started with, "I agree it seems likely Kiersten killed Alex Dunn, but how are they going to prove it?"

I started to answer, but then I changed my mind and said, "Hey, why don't you drive over here and get me? I need to go somewhere, and I want you to go with me."

"Where?"

I didn't want to talk on the phone. I wanted her near me.

"You'll see," I said.

"It's beautiful, Roy."

We were standing beside Barton Creek. The water ran cool and clear as glass, at least five feet deep and nearly 20 feet wide from bank to bank.

"I didn't know the place would be this heavily wooded," I said. "It's perfect. You can't see or hear any of the neighbors."

"You're serious about buying it?" Mia said.

She was wearing jeans, hiking boots, and a green T-shirt, plus a Longhorn baseball cap. She looked at home in the country. She looked at home *here*, on this particular piece of property.

"Now that I see it," I said, "yeah, I think so."

"Mind if I ask the price?"

I told her.

"Worth every dime," she said, "and you can afford it."

She knew exactly what I made, because we made the same amount. It wasn't a fortune, but it had grown significantly in the past year.

We both stood quietly for several moments and just listened to the burbling of the creek and the cooing of white-winged doves in nearby oak trees.

Then I said, "Here's my theory. Kiersten and Alex Dunn were having an affair while he was married to Alicia. She might've been one of several, based on what Callie and Max said about him. Sounds like he might've given Kiersten the impression they had some sort of future together. But then Alicia asked for a divorce, and suddenly Dunn was free to be with Kiersten—except he didn't want anything more than what they already had. It wouldn't surprise me if the emails between them said something to that effect, but I didn't get a chance to read that far, because, you know, she tried to shoot me in the face."

"The bullet probably would've bounced right off your forehead," Mia said.

"Oh, stop with the sweet talk," I said. "It's tempting to log into Dunn's Hushmail account again and read the rest of the emails, and the only thing stopping me is that the cops specifically told me not to, and I'd likely end up rotting in prison. I like it much better right here."

"Me, too," Mia said.

"After Kiersten showed me the Raleigh house, we went to dinner, and she mentioned that she'd recently had a bad breakup. I think she used the word 'unpleasant.' She was referring to Alex Dunn. I wish I'd figured that out earlier."

"You had no way of knowing that. Why would you even suspect?"

"True, but she also mentioned she'd recently taken a trip to Mumbai, and that's what Alex mentioned in the email. You know what you can buy fairly easily in India?"

"Cyanide," Mia said.

"Exactly. Just walk into a pharmacy and buy it with cash. You don't even have to show an ID. Crazy. I'm guessing Kiersten had been under the impression that Alex was going to marry her someday, but when they were in Mumbai, he told her that wasn't going to happen. First she got angry, and then she got vengeful, and that's when she decided to bring some cyanide home. Maybe she'd already decided to kill him, or maybe it started out as a fantasy that eventually became reality when she worked up the nerve."

"Think the cops might still find traces in Kiersten's condo?"

"Possibly. Depends on how she transported it. They'll also be able to figure out where she and Alex stayed in Mumbai, and then they'll ask the police over there to show Kiersten's picture to shopkeepers in that area. If one of them remembers her buying cyanide, she's done."

"I'll admit, at one point I would've guessed Alicia Potter was the killer," Mia said.

"Hey, me, too."

"Think she killed her sister?" Mia asked.

"I don't think we'll ever know. If Alicia had killed Alex, I would've been more inclined to think she also killed her sister, but now I'm guessing it was really an accident."

Mia said, "You don't think Kiersten arranged the bribe between Dunn and Marcus Hardy, or whoever 'John Smith' is?"

"I really don't think so. The email between Dunn and Smith seemed very clear that they were the only ones in on it. Dunn might've met Marcus Hardy, or whoever John Smith turns out to be—"

"Has to be a council member, whether it was Hardy or one of the others who voted no on Callie's house," Mia said.

"Agreed," I said. "Those emails will tell the tale, and the cops will be able to get a warrant to track John Smith's IP address."

Mia said, "Honestly, I've been wondering why Dunn even bothered with a bribe. Albert Strauss said it takes nine out of ten council members to approve an application for landmark status when the owner is fighting it, and he said that doesn't happen often."

"Yes, but he didn't say it *never* happens. Based on what I know about Alex Dunn, he wasn't the kind to leave anything to chance. He wanted to get at least one council member to vote his way, and he was probably relying on that member to get at least one more member to vote no. We'll just have to wait and see what the cops find out."

Now we turned to face each other.

I smiled at her, but I had butterflies like I'd never had before. My life was about to change. I hoped it was for the better. I hoped I wasn't about to alienate my partner and lose my best friend. I didn't want our relationship to be strained or compromised. But once the words left my mouth, there was no going back. I knew that. And I was moving forward. It was time.

I said, "I apologize about being a jerk."

"You'll have to be more specific," Mia said.

There was no more than two feet of space between us. Her eyes were locked on mine and did not waver.

"I deserve that," I said.

"I forgive you, in case you're wondering," she said.

"Thank you."

"You're welcome."

"The situation with Garlen kind of freaked me out, to be honest," I said. "It made me angry. I'm not talking about the car chase, I'm talking about the way he acted toward you after the break-up."

"I know."

"You mean the world to me, Mia. I want you to know that, in case it isn't obvious. You are the best person I know. So generous and caring in every way. So smart and funny."

"Roy, you don't have to—"

"I need to get this out. Finally. You probably know it's coming. Or maybe you have no idea. And the truth is, I'm nervous. I don't remember ever being this nervous. But here's the thing. I love you, Mia. I've loved you for a very long time. This isn't a passing crush or some silly phase. I really do love you and I've come so close to telling you so many times. I don't want to ruin everything we have right now, but I guess I'm going to have to take that risk. I can't stand it anymore."

What was the expression on her face? A slight smile, or a grimace of pity or embarrassment? Why was she looking at me like that? Was she going to cry?

"Oh, Roy," she said.

"What?" I said. "Tell me."

She placed both hands behind my neck and pulled me close. Then she began to kiss me.

## 42

*News on the hour, every hour.*

*Our top story this morning—*

*A local real estate agent has confessed in the poisoning of software executive Alex Dunn. Kiersten Stanley was arrested early last week after a shooting at her downtown condo involving a local videographer who was investigating the homicide. The videographer was unharmed in the incident.*

*According to a spokesperson with the Travis County Sheriff's Office, Stanley admitted to purchasing the cyanide while on a trip to India with Dunn, and later replacing his heart medication with cyanide-laced capsules.*

*In a related story, City Council member Marcus Hardy has resigned abruptly this morning after accusations that he accepted a bribe from Alex Dunn in connection with the demolition of a historic Tarrytown home.*

*We'll have more coverage of both stories as additional details emerge.*

Want to know when Ben Rehder's
next novel will be released?

Subscribe to his email list.
www.benrehder.com

Have you discovered Ben Rehder's
Blanco County Mysteries?

Turn the page for an excerpt from
BUCK FEVER

# BUCK FEVER

## CHAPTER 1

BY THE TIME Red O'Brien finished his thirteenth beer, he could hardly see through his rifle scope. Worse yet, his partner, Billy Don Craddock, was doing a lousy job with the spotlight.

"Dammit, Billy Don, we ain't hunting raccoons," Red barked. "Get that light out of the trees and shine it out in the pastures where it will do me some good."

Billy Don mumbled something unintelligible, kicked some empty beer cans around on the floorboard of Red's old Ford truck, and then belched loudly from way down deep in his three-hundred-pound frame. That was his standard rebuttal anytime Red got a little short with him. The spotlight, meanwhile, continued to illuminate the canopy of a forty-foot Spanish oak.

Red cussed him again and pulled the rifle back in the window. Every time they went on one of these poaching excursions, Red had no idea how he managed to get a clean shot. After all, poaching white-tailed deer was serious business. It called for stealth and grace, wits and guile. It had been apparent to Red for years that Billy Don came up short in all of these departments.

"Turn that friggin' light off and hand me a beer," Red said.

"Don't know what we're doing out here on a night like this anyhow," Billy Don replied as he dug into the ice chest for two fresh Keystones. "Moon ain't up yet. All the big ones will be bedded down till it rises. Any moron knows that."

Red started to say that Billy Don was an excellent reference for gauging what a moron may or may not know. But he thought better of it, being that Billy Don weighed roughly twice what Red did. Not to mention that Billy Don had quite a quick temper after his first twelve-pack.

"Billy Don, let me ask you something. Someone walked into your bedroom shining a light as bright as the sun in your face, what's the first thing you'd do?"

"Guess I'd wag my pecker at 'em," Billy Don said, smiling. He considered himself quite glib.

"Okay," Red said patiently, "then what's the second thing you'd do?"

"I'd get up and see what the hell's going on."

"Damn right!" Red said triumphantly. "Don't matter if the bucks are bedded down or not. Just roust 'em with that light and we'll get a shot. But remember, we won't find any deer up in the treetops."

Billy Don gave a short snort in reply.

Red popped the top on his new beer, revved the Ford, and started on a slow crawl down the quiet county road. Billy Don grabbed the spotlight and leaned out the window, putting some serious strain on the buttons of his overalls, as he shined the light back over the hood of the Ford to Red's left. They had gone about half a mile when Billy Don stirred.

"Over there!"

Red stomped the brakes, causing his Keystone to spill and run down into his crotch. He didn't even notice. Billy Don was spotlighting an oat field a hundred yards away, where two dozen deer grazed. Among them, one of the largest white-tailed bucks either of them had ever seen. "Fuck me nekkid," Red whispered.

"Jesus, Red! Look at that monster."

Red clumsily stuck the .270 Winchester out the window, banging the door frame and the rearview mirror in the process. The deer didn't even look their way. Red raised the rifle and tried to sight in on the trophy buck, but the deer had other things in mind.

While all the other deer were grazing in place, the buck was loping around the oat field in fits and starts, running in circles. He bounced, he jumped, he spun. Red and Billy Don had never seen such peculiar behavior.

"Somethin's wrong with that deer," Billy Don said, using his keen knowledge of animal behavioral patterns.

"Bastard won't hold still! Keep the light on him!" Red said.

"I've got him. Just shoot. Shoot!"

Red was about to risk a wild shot when the buck finally seemed to calm down. Rather than skipping around, it was now walking fast, with its nose low to the ground. The buck approached a large doe partially obscured behind a small cedar tree and, with little ceremony, began to mount her.

Billy Don giggled, the kind of laugh you'd expect from a schoolgirl, not a flannel-clad six-foot-six cedar-chopper. "Why, I do believe it's true love."

Red sensed his chance, took a deep breath, and squeezed the trigger. The rifle bellowed as orange flame leapt out of the muzzle and licked the night, and then all was quiet.

The buck, and the doe of his affections, crumpled to the ground while the other deer scattered into the brush. Seconds passed. And then, to the chagrin of the drunken poachers, the huge buck climbed to his hooves, snorted twice, and took off. The doe remained on the ground.

"Dammit, Red! You missed."

"No way! It was a lung shot. I bet it went all the way through. Grab your wirecutters."

Knowing that a wounded deer can run several hundred yards or more, both men staggered out of the truck, cut their way through the eight-foot deerproof fence, and proceeded over to the oat field.

Each man had a flashlight and was looking feverishly for traces of blood, when they heard a noise.

"What the hell was that?" Billy Don asked.

"Shhh."

Then another sound. A moaning, from the wounded doe lying on the ground.

Billy Don was spooked. "That's weird, Red. Let's get outta here."

Red shined his light on the wounded animal twenty yards away. "Hold on a second. What the hell's wrong with its hide? It looks all loose and…" He was about to approach the deer when they both heard something they'd never forget.

The doe clearly said, "Help me."

Without saying a word, both men scrambled back toward the fence. For the first time in his life, Billy Don Craddock actually outran somebody.

Seconds later, the man in the crudely tailored deer costume could hear the tires squealing as the truck sped away.

Just as Red and Billy Don were sprinting like boot-clad track stars, a powerful man was in the middle of a phone call. Unfortunately for the man, Roy Swank, it was hard to judge his importance by looking at him. In fact, he looked a lot like your average pond frog. Round, squat body. Large, glassy eyes. Bulbous lips in front of a thick tongue. And, of course, the neck—or rather, the lack of one. It was as if his head sat directly on his sloping shoulders. His voice was his best feature, deep and charismatic.

Roy Swank had relocated to a large ranch southwest of Johnson City, Texas, five years ago, after a successful (although intentionally anonymous) career lobbying legislators in Austin. The locals who knew or cared what a lobbyist was never really figured out what Swank lobbied for. Few people ever had, because Swank was the type of lobbyist who always conducted business in the shadows of a back room, rarely putting anything down on paper. But he and the entities he represented had the kind of resources and resourcefulness that could sway votes or help introduce new legislation. So when the rumors spread about Swank's retirement, the entire state political system took notice—although there were as many people relieved as disappointed.

After lengthy consideration (his past had to be weighed carefully—life in a county full of political enemies might be rather difficult), Swank purchased a ten-thousand-acre ranch one hour west of Austin. Swank was actually planning on semi-retirement; the ranch was a successful cattle operation and he intended to maintain its sizable herd of Red Brangus. He had even kept the former owner on as foreman for a time.

But without the busy schedule of his previous career, Swank became restless. That is, until he rediscovered one of the great passions he enjoyed as a young adult: deer hunting. The hunting bug bit, and it bit hard. He spent the first summer on his new ranch building deer blinds, clearing brush in prime hunting areas, distributing automatic corn and protein feeders, and planting food plots such as oats and rye. It paid off the following season, as Swank harvested a beautiful twelve-point buck with a twenty-two-inch spread that tallied 133 Boone & Crockett points, the scoring standard for judging trophy bucks. Not nearly as large as the world-renowned bucks in South Texas, but a very respectable deer for the Hill Country. Several of his closest associates joined him on the ranch and had comparable success.

Swank, never one to do anything in moderation, decided that his ranch could become one of the most successful hunting operations in Texas. By importing some key breeding stock from South Texas and Mexico, and then following proper game-management techniques, Swank set out to develop a herd of whitetails as large and robust—and with the same jaw-dropping trophy antlers—as their southern brethren.

He had phenomenal success. After all, money was no object, and the laws and restrictions that regulated game importation and relocation melted away under Swank's political clout. After four seasons, not only was his ranch (the Circle S) known throughout the state for trophy deer, he had actually started a lucrative business exporting deer to other ranches around the nation.

Swank was tucked away obliviously in his four-thousand-square-foot ranch house, on the phone to one of his most valued customers, at the same moment Red O'Brien blasted unsuccessfully at a large buck in Swank's remote southern pasture.

"They went out on the trailer today," Swank said in his rich timbre. He was sitting at a large mahogany desk in an immense den. A fire burned in the huge limestone fireplace, despite the warm weather. He cradled the phone with his shoulder as he reached across the desk, grabbed a bottle of expensive scotch and poured himself another glass. "Four of them. But the one you'll be especially interested in is the ten-pointer," Swank said as he went on to describe the "magnificent beast."

Swank grunted a few times, nodding. "Good. Yes, good." Then he hung up. Swank had a habit of never saying good-bye.

By the time he finished his conversation, a man who sounded just like Red O'Brien had already made an anonymous call to 911.

\* \* \* \* \* \* \* \* \*

## ABOUT THE AUTHOR

Ben Rehder lives with his wife near Austin, Texas, where he was born and raised. His novels have made best-of-the-year lists in *Publishers Weekly, Library Journal, Kirkus Reviews*, and *Field & Stream. Buck Fever* was a finalist for the Edgar Award. For more information, visit www.benrehder.com.

## OTHER NOVELS BY BEN REHDER

*Buck Fever*
*Bone Dry*
*Flat Crazy*
*Guilt Trip*
*Gun Shy*
*Holy Moly*
*The Chicken Hanger*
*The Driving Lesson*
*Gone The Next*
*Hog Heaven*
*Get Busy Dying*
*Stag Party*
*Bum Steer*

Printed in Great Britain
by Amazon